ENDLING

ENDLING

ELICIA JOHNSON

DESCENDANT
PUBLISHING

Descendant Publishing, LLC
PO Box 29
Byron Center, MI 49315

Book Cover by Andy Payne Designs
Edited By Dawn L. Carter
Map Illustration by Elicia Johnson

ISBN 978-1-965948-11-8 (Paperback)
ISBN 78-1-965948-13-2 (Hardcover)
ISBN 978-1-965948-12-5 (Ebook)

Printed in the United States of America
First Edition April 2026

10 9 8 7 6 5 4 3 2 1

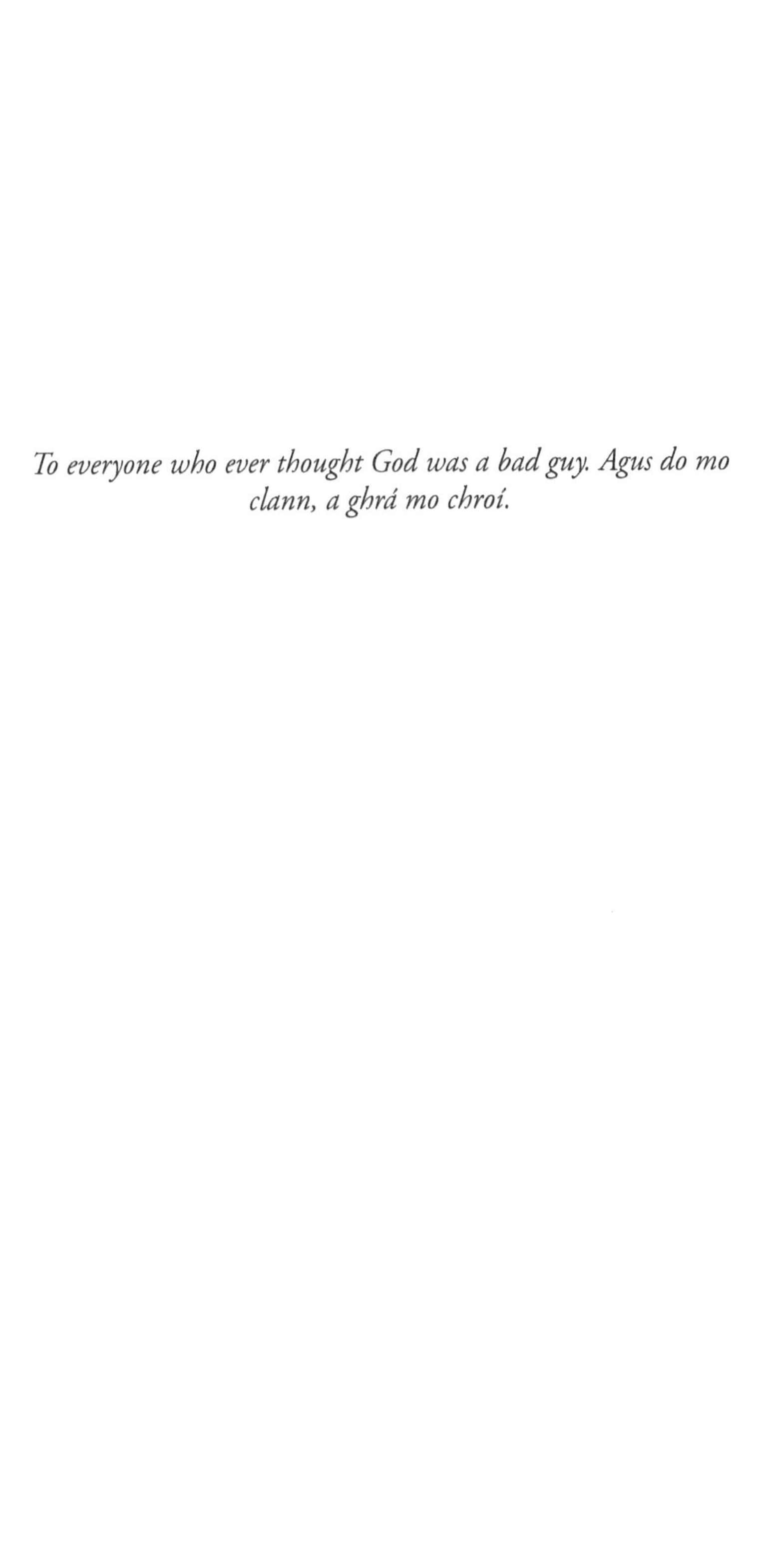

To everyone who ever thought God was a bad guy. Agus do mo clann, a ghrá mo chroí.

Contents

Sanctius City
The last safe place on earth
North Borderlands
Raina's Building
Sanctius Harbor
Council Tower
Human Life Tower
Provisions Factory
Time Temple
Nico's Penthouse & Rooftop Garden
Uptown Engine Tower
Borderlands
Eastern Sea

Sanctius City
Time Temple

Where mankind
engineered the future

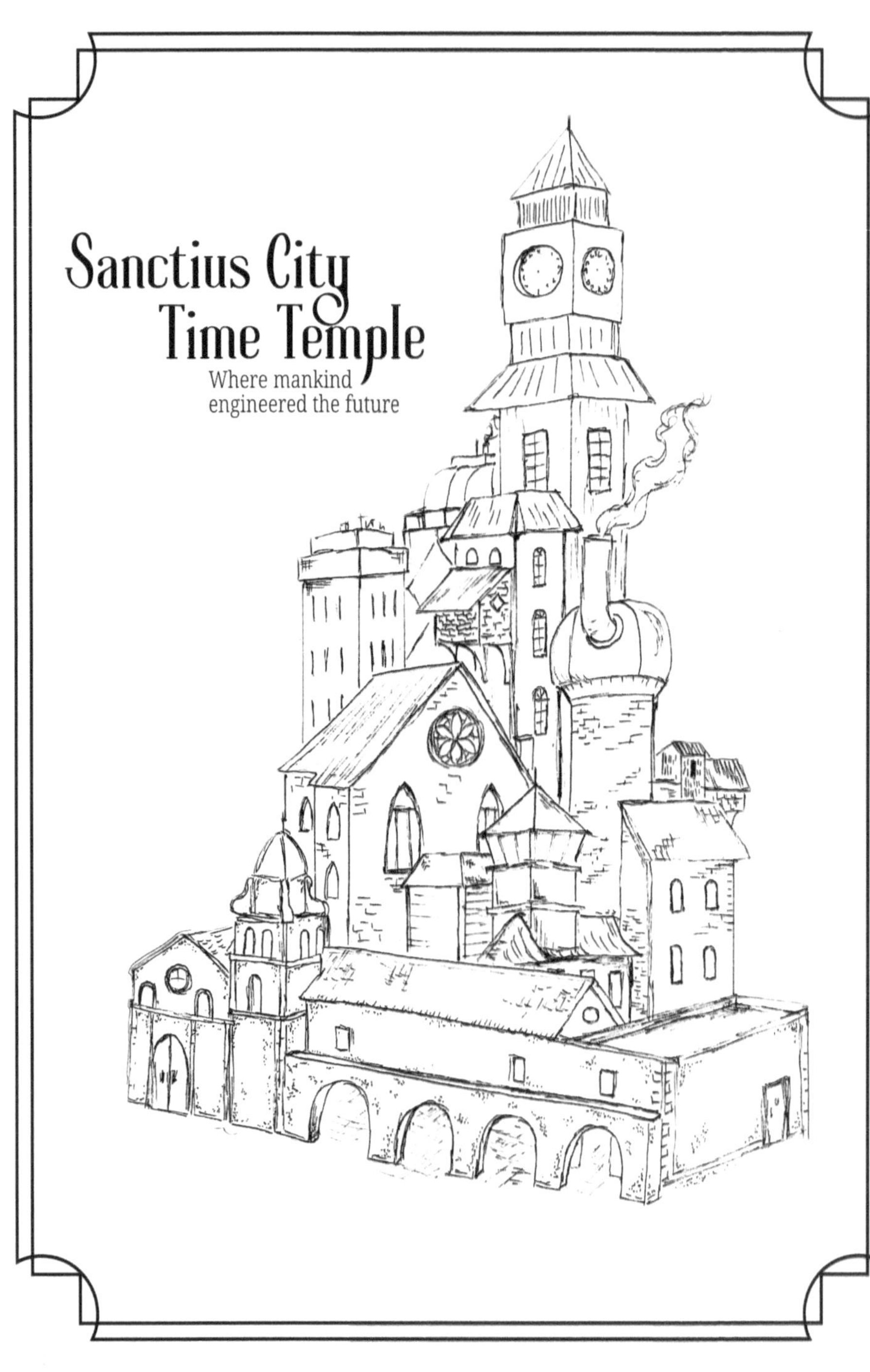

Sanctius
City
The last
safe place
on earth

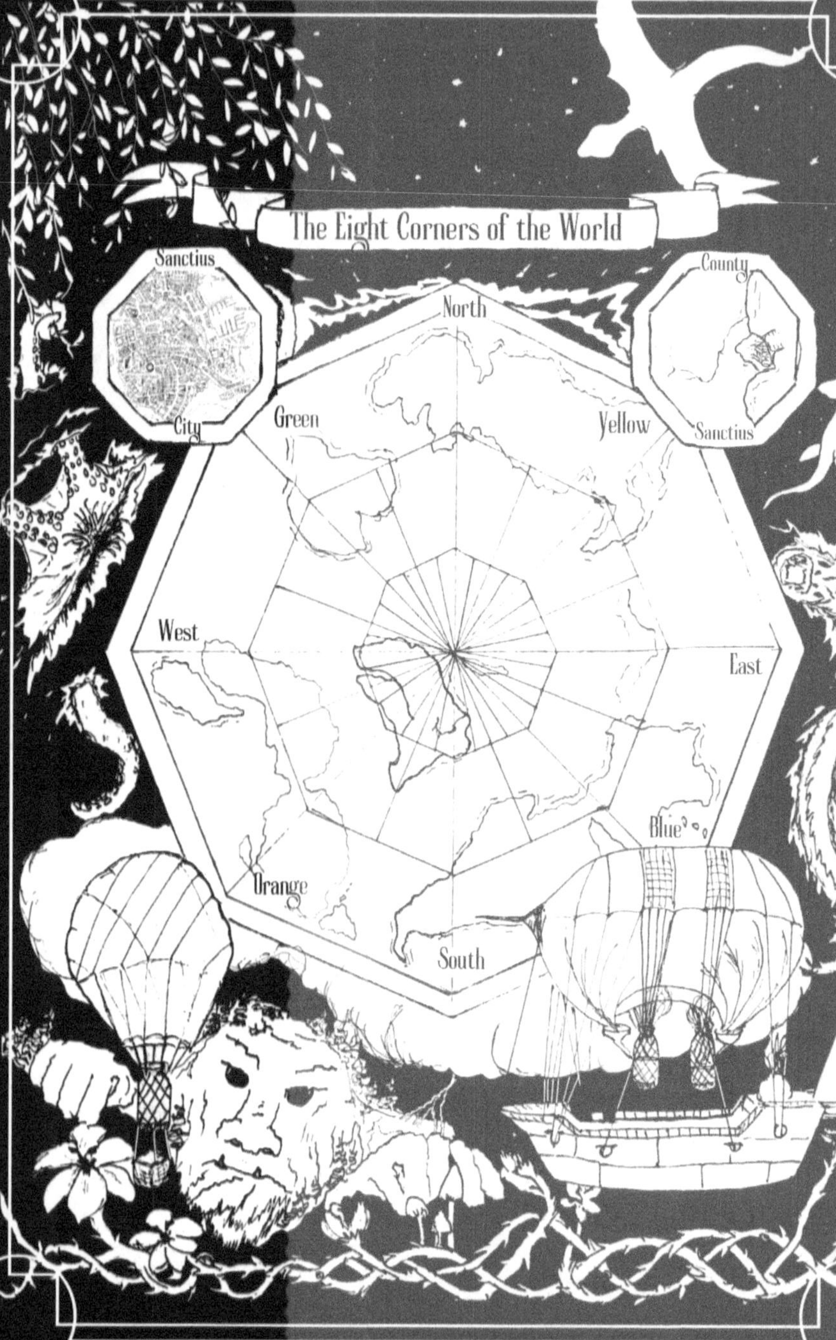

The Eight Corners of the World
Sanctius
City
County
Sanctius
North
Green
Yellow
West
East
Orange
Blue
South

Prologue

IN THE SHADOW OF THE CITY

As firelight danced off the forest canopy at the day's end, the storytellers brought an enchantment to what would have been a regular evening in the Borderlands. Neighboring families living outside the city had just finished sharing a communal meal. The men had their moment when they brought home meat, foraged mushrooms, and herbs. The women had theirs when they transformed those into a delicious stew with homemade bread. Finally, it was time for the storytellers to shine and for the children to revel in it.

Two experienced storytellers shared first. A bent and graying woman told the story of the constellation known as the Plow. Next, an aged man told a story of a paradise beyond the sea. Then, just as the last glint of sunlight, filtered by whiffs of cloud, cast a vivid indigo glow over our cottages and the enveloping forest, my brother Valentino stepped up.

As brothers, we had the same narrow face and defined jaw. Really, only our hair color—mine sandy, his dark as shadow—and age set us apart on the outside. Inside, we were as different as steam and steel.

"Here we go," I mumbled under my breath as Tino took his place in front of the small crowd of Borderlanders. I was tired of the same ridiculous tales. I looked at the faces around the fire. Soft smiles and eyes sparkling with interest awaited Tino's narrative. Everyone seemed ignorant of the fact that the world's greatest technologies towered a stone's throw behind us—ignorant or indifferent.

They're completely indifferent to the fact that something strange is happening in this forest and willfully ignorant of what city people say about this mountain.

Tino was still learning his art from the elder storytellers, so they let him refer to a scroll. Though they never failed to remind him that their elders would never have allowed that. In truth, Tino had often told me he thought the stories should always be told from the written version, for accuracy's sake. We were a young and rebellious generation, according to our elders. Aside from his preference for reading from a scroll, they saw Valentino as a model youth. In my opinion, he was just a sucker for useless fables and illuminated manuscripts and generally obsessed with the written word.

Tino waited for an airship to pass overhead. The whirring of the fans and bustle of the crew weren't conducive to the mood he hoped for. He rolled his eyes ever so slightly at the delay, but I watched it with interest. Steam—just like the mist that wafted above our kettles—worked something like magic to keep the massive ship afloat for the people of Sanctius City. It passed out of sight behind the thick spread of summer leaves. My attention returned to Tino, still waiting with eyes that invited his audience to be quiet and still.

Only when the silence was so full of anticipation that it seemed charged with unseen energy did he begin his tale. It was a favorite among the children and told of a legendary monster from our region. I resituated myself on the spongy forest floor and leaned against my parents' legs, who sat on a log behind me. My brother's voice was steady, almost tranquil, as befitted his unwavering character. As he read the tale from his scroll, though, his voice rose and fell with greater animation than usual as he described the *uomo salvatico* and their antics.

"Long ago, before there was such division between city and wilderness, the uomo salvatico or *wild men* roamed freely in these lands. These tall, hairy beasts seemed to be as much monster as man. At first, people weren't afraid of the wild men. They did little harm beyond stealing the occasional cask of ale or pot of giardiniera. Yes, the uomo salvatico *loved* cured foods–the vegetables of the giardiniera, and prosciutto, and ale and, especially…" Tino paused for a response.

"Cheese!" the children shouted.

"Yes, the wild men loved all the cheeses. Some say it was the uomo salvatico who first taught us the magical art of cheesemaking," he said as he shifted his stance to begin the next part of the tale.

The smaller children settled into comfortable positions near their parents. They were prepared to answer, giggle, and gasp at every cue. I shook my head at his dramatic segue, but Tino continued without notice.

"You see, when the wild men were caught stealing goods from the families living around the mountain, the people demanded something in trade. *That's* when the wild men offered the people their very first delicious bite of cheese.

"For a short time, the people were content to trade their abundance for the uomo salvatico's cheese. And he was happy to have their delicious foods and drinks. But the people soon became greedy. Having cheese wasn't enough. They demanded to know how to make the cheese themselves."

Tino slammed a fist into his open hand to animate their insistence.

"For the sake of their fermented delicacies, a nearby wild man complied. First, he taught them to culture the milk. Once they had learned the art of culturing the milk well, the uomo salvatico then demanded to trade with the people again. And they did," he finished unconvincingly.

"No! No, they didn't!" the children shouted.

"Oh, you caught me," Tino replied. "No, they said they required to know *more* before they would resume their trade relationship with any wild men. So, he taught them how to cut the curds to release more whey. Then, the wild man demanded to trade again; he was missing his prosciutto! So, of course, they gave in." He paused for the young listeners to protest, but he didn't wait long.

With smiling eyes and excited voices, they shouted, "Nah-ah!!! Not yet!"

"Yes, yes. You're right. The people weren't satisfied with curds and whey. So, the wild man showed them how to strain the cheese in cloth and press the cheese between planks. Then, the people celebrated and considered the wild men in good standing again.

"But the uomo salvatico was less than pleased with the people for how they had treated him. So he mocked them, saying, 'If you had only asked, I would have taught you the magic that can be done with the whey!' Then, he tipped over a large fermentation vessel full of giardiniera, shattering the pottery into large pieces. A river of brine spilled out with a landslide of cauliflower, peppers, and onions." Tino made large, sweeping motions and acted out a pantomime of the story.

As he continued, he swept a teen girl into his arms—one I knew he had a crush on. It was as if being the storyteller gave him a courage he wouldn't have otherwise had.

"The wild man *snatched* the nearest maiden and ran off into the woods with her! In fact, the uomo salvatico returned to play tricks on the people and occasionally steal young ladies right from their butter churns."

Tino set the blushing girl down, who smiled sheepishly and returned to sit by her family.

"*That* was when the master woodsman came from his island kingdom in the east and forced the wild men into the caves of the Hungry Mountains. For only he, the Wilderman, was the ruler of the wilderness and all within it. And the wild men have *mostly* kept to their cheese caves ever since."

Everyone cheered. Well, nearly everyone. I couldn't help but roll my eyes at Tino's dramatic ending. I didn't understand how everyone could be so entertained by stories of the Hungry Mountain. It was so named because people had been steadily disappearing out here. Not just in the woods, but at sea too, and everywhere in between. But the common factor was always the wilderness. There were all these poetic ways we Borderlanders referred to the disappearances, but I wanted facts.

And I knew exactly where to look for them–Sanctius City.

SANCTIUS MEANS SAFETY

Legions of light and shadow tussled in the underbrush. I watched them intently to stay calm. Mama swabbed the claw marks on the back of my upper arm with an herbal infusion and wrapped them in clean linen. My breath still came in heaves as I gulped down tears. I was too old to cry, but too young to know what to do with the well of emotions boiling in my chest. She shushed me soothingly, but I could hear her voice shake. The dark forces in the wilderness she loved had struck too close to home.

Finally, my fear gave way to anger, and I burst.

"Mama! How can we keep on living here? Why didn't you warn us how dangerous it is out there?"

"My dear Nico." Her dogma seemed to bring steady resolve to her voice. "You have heard the tales over and over again. Papa and I have taught you and Tino everything you need to know."

"Tales, Mama! They were only stories! How was that supposed to help?"

"All the old tales are profitable to those who seek truth, Nico. I know you're upset, son, but you will be okay. It's only natural after being attacked by such an animal."

"An *animal*? I heard its thoughts in my head! It was a monster! And

I think there might have been TWO of them. It sounded like a fight broke out behind me.”

“Yes, they say that the uomo salvatico have the power of mindspeak. But the Wilderman is stronger than all those beasts. Trust him to take care of the wilderness. He was probably the one fighting the uomo salvatico that attacked you.”

“All this time!” I interrupted, not wanting to hear about my parents’ legendary woodsman again. “All those stories told around the cooking fires—they were nightmares. Living nightmares!”

Mama led me to the straw mattress I shared with Tino and set a cup of chamomile tea down on the dirt floor of our cottage. The scent of the steam slowed my breath, and I inhaled it deeply.

“Nico,” Mama continued softly, always softly. “You’re overreacting, forgetting that the Wilderman and Papa and I are looking out for you. I want you to get a good night’s sleep to be ready for your field trip tomorrow. You’ve been excited for the airship ride for weeks. As much as I hate to admit it, maybe a short voyage over the sea will clear your head.”

“I thought you wouldn’t like me going.” Frustration colored the words with a disrespectful tone. School in Sanctius was a tense topic between us. It had been from the first day I walked with Tino along the westernmost road into Sanctius, and it had only grown more charged since. I knew it was because my eyes were being opened to a new reality. I lay down next to my brother Valentino, who was a couple years older and nearly out of school. Mama brushed my sandy brown hair out of my face.

“I’ll admit that your father and I are both questioning our decision to send you to Sanctius for school. The education *could* bring smoother times to the Borderlands and the wilderness, but you know the city’s edicts don’t align with our way of life. We worry you’ll be misled.

“Tino has done well, though. I think he’s remained faithful to our ways, and he’s almost finished with school. I’m counting on you to follow in his footsteps. As for the field trip, I know how much you’ve been looking forward to the flight, and sometimes a mother can’t help but wish to see her son happy. It will do you good to see the beauty of the Eastern Sea from above, get some refreshed perspective.”

I wanted to tell her I was nearly a man and didn't need her to soothe my anxious heart with her kindness. I would overcome this— the wild man attack, my confusion about living between two worlds, whether this dangerous life in the wilderness was complete madness, and if the safety promised by the city was real—on my own. But heavy exhaustion settled over me, and sleep speedily followed.

That night, I dreamt I ran down the mountain again, desperate to get away from the beast's cave. The wild man's voice echoed threats in my head. But in my dream, instead of two hairy monsters, two fierce warriors on horses chased me. They were not allies; each raced the other to capture me. Thundering hooves threatened to overtake me, and I thought my heart would burst through my chest. Suddenly, a light-colored stag leaped between me and the horsemen. I was saved. Instead of continuing home, I paused to glance back. A light buckskin horse reared, concealing its rider. The second horse, all black, turned and galloped back up the mountain in a blur.

The fright jarred me from my sleep. Daylight barely diluted the night sky, and Valentino's older, bulkier form took up most of the bed while he continued to snore away. I sat up, thinking. The dream left me feeling strange. Is this how people felt before they disappeared? How long could I run from the dangers of the mountain? At some point, something must be done. But what? My parents were unwilling to even consider any kind of change.

It seemed most likely that Sanctius' Council and all their research would produce a solution to the danger *and* the disappearances. Maybe I could help. Maybe I could even bring smoother times to the Borderlands, like Mom said, just not in the way she imagined.

Unable to picture how that would look, my mind ran in circles through this train of thought and the dream several times. I decided to dress early to stop the cycle. After all, the day ahead was the highlight of the school year—the annual airship field trip for all third-form students.

* * *

Only a few hours after I woke from my nightmare, cerulean seawater rippled beneath the airship, suspended as if by magic from the cloudless sky. I stood on the textured steel deck, dwelling on the scratches on my arm and the voice that had spoken in my head. Had any of the other Borderlanders heard it? When the tales of the wild men were shared around the fire, I never even considered that the evil things existed. Did they really love cured foods and making cheese? Was cheese evil too? I hoped not, but everything was suspect at this point.

The aft steam system fascinated me, drawing my attention upward. I've never been a mechanically gifted person. Even if I had been, I never would have had the opportunity to see an airship up close, or even learn about one, if it weren't for the generosity of Sanctius City through the school. Water from the large brass condensation funnel above me trickled into the side of the steam tank. Steam danced hypnotically upward through the opening atop the tall, oblong tank into the envelope of the steam-run airship.

The contrast to my home turned my mind in circles. Why didn't it bother my parents that we gathered our food on a mountain that most people wouldn't touch with a one-hundred-arm pole? They celebrated it, despite their reduced circumstances. As I fiddled with my tattered clothing, I became aware of someone speaking of the same.

"They decided not to remove the children, you know."

"You're kidding!"

_My teacher and one of the female airship crew gossiped on the quarterdeck.

"I'm serious," continued Mrs. Manelli. "Something to do with the results of the latest study. You know they *appropriated* some from those Borderlanders north of the city?"

"I heard! That's why I thought surely they would end up taking the rest."

"No, it was unsuccessful. Most of the children just hated everything to do with the program, and they ran home as soon as they were released. Not only that," she lowered her voice until I could hardly make out the words. "But most of them disappeared for good. You know, evanesced."

"Oh no! What are they going to do now?" the crew woman returned.

"You're watching it." Mrs. Manelli held her hand out toward me and the other Borderland children.

I felt their eyes run from my sandy, shoulder-length waves down my faded linen clothes and to my barely existent leather shoes. My face burned with indignant embarrassment.

"What do you mean?"

"The Borderlanders wouldn't take food or any other supplies the Council could use to improve the situation, if you know what I mean. They insisted they had enough and if they fell on hard times, they'd be 'cared for'. I think they actually believe that creepy woods-character would help them."

She couldn't possibly mean a *wild man*. She must mean the forest keeper—the Wilderman. I'd never met him, even when my parents said he was in the area. They spoke of him as allegedly helpful, but how was beyond me. Studying psychology in school gave me several possible explanations for spreading hopeful but empty rumors. Any supposedly powerful being lurking around the forest watching us seemed creepy to me.

"Anyway, the Council found the one thing they would accept: education for their children. Why else..."

They continued to discuss whatever program I'd been unknowingly drafted into. It turned out I was just an animal rounded up to be domesticated.

Were they wrong, though?

I gazed at the airship with new eyes, allowing them to wander to the forward steam system. Mirroring the aft system next to me, the inner grooves and folds inside the envelope directed condensation downward along the resin-lined canvas into another giant brass funnel. Then the water slipped down the narrow copper pipe—trickle... trickle—through an opening and along the side of the thick glass tank until it joined the rest of the water in the tank. The endless hurry of hot water particles shivering upward, slithering back down, and swapping tanks in the next wild dance through the envelope was a repeating miracle that kept the ship aloft before my eyes.

Compared to the worn and earthy texture of my home, the steel deck and cream canvas envelope seemed sophisticated. I followed the clean lines of the hull to the bow.

Beyond the ship, I thought I saw a bump of land.

There shouldn't be an island there.

I had studied plenty of maps since attending the city school. They all showed the Eastern Sea void of any other land.

I was instantly reminded of the many fireside legends that included a fantastical island in the east. It meant a lot to the Borderlanders, though I never understood why. I couldn't tear my eyes away from the narrow green tear dividing sky from water. I moved to the right side of the airship to get a better view. Somewhere, a crew member called out, "Har-da-port!" The helmsman steered the fan rudder, and the boat lurched left. We were turning back to Sanctius City.

Most of my class had gathered around the rails near the foredeck to see the view. For those of us on the right side of the ship, it looked like we were staring at the edge of the world. Except that island! Mrs. Manelli came and stood behind us.

"What is that?" My curiosity finally got the best of me.

"What?" my teacher asked.

"That hunk of land out there."

"There is no land in the Eastern Sea."

"But I see an island out there." I pointed more exuberantly.

"Nico, there's nothing out there," my teacher sweetly reiterated.

My classmates whispered together, Borderlanders with Borderlanders and Citizens with Citizens.

I looked at the Borderland kids and their patched clothing. Some of the clay-red stains on their pants matched mine, from sliding down a steep bank by the River Umbra in our free time. The teacher was right. We were a bunch of wild things, refusing to grow up, and gallivanting around the forest and living on what? Joy? I didn't feel joy. I felt humiliated. And I hated them.

"There is no island in the Eastern Sea," my teacher repeated with expectant eyes.

I stared back into those eyes, letting enmity saturate me and purge everything to do with the Borderlands and the wilderness. "Of course, there isn't an island out there. The water and the sky must have played tricks on my eyes."

She smiled and put her hand on my shoulder. "I thought so, Nico. You're growing into just the kind of young man a Sanctius Citizen should be."

She looked down at my borderland garb again, and a hint of disdain fell over her smiling face. Then, she turned and raised her eyebrows with satisfaction toward her gossip buddy.

When she walked away, I looked back out at the horizon. Blank. I scanned right and left and found the faint line uninterrupted. There really wasn't an island in the Eastern Sea.

METAMORPHOSIS

School ended for the day when we docked in Sanctius Harbor. The class divided, and everyone walked their separate ways. But I didn't walk up through the city toward the Borderlands. For a while, I stared at the harbor and the few ships anchored near the docks. I swore something about Sanctius made me see more clearly, just like it cleared my mind from seeing things on the airship.

Living in the Borderlands between city and wilderness pulled my heart and mind in separate directions. I grew up wondering why we stayed out of Sanctius City when it was right in our backyard. When I was very young, steam-run towers loomed over me like monsters. As I reached adolescence, their svelte silhouettes invited me to discover something new and exciting. I had begged my parents to send me to school in large part to explore the places that had previously been off-limits.

It was at school that I learned how great a danger the wilderness posed—a danger my parents had hidden from me. Around campfires, waiting for simple stews to boil, Borderland families told legends of a forest-keeper and a land beyond the rising sun. They alluded to poisonous plants and dangerous beasts, but only in passing, as if we were immune to them. My teacher in Sanctius, on the other hand, explained in detail about hybrid monsters who stole children for their suppers. No sign or remnant remained; they simply vanished from being. That's why they called them the evanesced.

I brought a new fear home with me from school that followed me everywhere, even to bed at night and when running around the forest with friends. I never told my parents. Of course, they wouldn't understand because they would never give credence to any Citizen, no matter their knowledge or experience. They were closed-minded and dull.

They say Sanctius Harbor used to be packed with ships from all over the world. The rocky prominence where the founders built Sanctius City was specifically chosen as the perfect location and environment for survival.

By whom? Wise and powerful men, I suppose.

At school we learned that our eyesight must be forward and not to dwell on the past. But whoever established Sanctius must have been wise to foresee the troubled times the world would face. For traffic slowed from other lands as the forces of nature—seen and unseen, they say—caused more and more people to disappear.

I strolled the streets aimlessly after the field trip, wondering what really happened to them. They say there are no bodies. No evidence. The people were just gone. The wild man reappeared in my train of thought. If he was real—and I stroked my lacerated arm in confirmation—what about sea monsters? Dragons? Trolls and menacing gnomes and fairies? Surely, the city must have been built as a haven from those things. Whatever the founders and current leaders knew of the dangers, those were responsible for the declining population all over the world, and Sanctius City had to be the safest place on Earth.

I paused outside of a barber shop. The city's newer buildings were largely free of busy ornaments. But there in the harbor area, the older buildings had been built before the triumph of sleek and modern over useless decoration. The shop's doorway was arched. In the semicircle transom, a stained-glass moth transfixed me. It faced downward so the wings fit nicely within the arch. And then I recognized the moth. It was the only one we were taught to swat or shoo off. The jagged, leaf-like forewing and the prominent, threatening proboscis gave it away—the vampire moth. It was viewed as a pest in the Borderlands. Sanctius of old seemed to hold the vampire moth in a different light, as if its abilities to consume tears straight from the duct, or blood through an annoying bite were simply admirable adaptations. Maybe it seemed to them as it did to me as I stood there—an inspiration to survive there in the safety of the city at all costs.

"Fifty Harpies for a Haircut," the sign on the door said. I fumbled around in my pockets for the change my parents had given me for lunches that week. They had little need for Sanctius currency and had traded wild truffles to acquire gold harpies for me to bring to school. I had enough to rid myself of my disheveled head of hair, but then I wouldn't have enough to buy city provisions for dinner.

The two hungers battled for a moment. Eventually, the call of the city won, and I opened the steel-framed door. The barber looked at me as if he had just put the last piece in a puzzle. He knew precisely what picture he was looking at. I was running away, running to Sanctius, to a life of security.

"You're not the first to see sense and come in here to get rid of all signs of having lived out there," he said.

After the last of my locks hit the floor, the barber went to a back closet and found an old suit to replace my linen Borderland shirt and trousers.

"Here. We keep a few spares just for people like you. Though you're a mite smaller than most lads we see. With your new haircut and this hand-me-down suit, you'll be a brand-new person."

He held up the suit, and our matching sideways looks showed that we both acknowledged the size discrepancy. He shrugged. "It should do for now. You can put it on in the lav and toss those clothes for good."

The suit was navy blue and made of artificial wool. I had to tighten the belt until the pants gathered up to keep them on, but the baggy jacket hid that. I was just glad to be rid of any connection to the wilderness, to the Borderlands, and to my life outside the city.

He asked if I was in school and told me the teachers could sort out a place for me to stay. But for that night, I went back to the harbor— the place where I'd decided my future. On the beach, I shared a fire with a stranger. After all, Sanctius City was safe. I allowed myself to breathe deeply and try to rest in that. Leaving home, leaving my family, the long road to being a true Citizen—it would all be worth it for this sense of security and all the advantages of Citizenship.

When Mrs. Manelli saw me arrive at school the next day, she looked at me the same way the barber had. My hair was clipped short, almost to the skin on the sides. I wore my oversized suit with pride. Maybe she was proud too—of her city, or perhaps she felt her own influence had convinced me to remake myself. Either way, my teacher beamed. Just as the barber said, she connected me with a man affiliated with the City Council, and said he would find me a flat to live in and a roommate to help me settle into city life.

The man's name was Mr. Ionone. He got me moved into an older building in midtown with only eight stories, outdated moldings and gaudy accents. It was full of other former Borderland kids and a few Citizens forsaken by "disappeared" families, all trying to make our way in the city. Except I wasn't trying; I was doing. At any cost, I would make a new life in Sanctius City. It was the only way to survive in this dangerous world. Maybe I could help my family and even discover the reasons for the disappearances, but for the time being I needed to focus on this, my new life of safety and security.

Mr. Ionone also showed me where to find clothes that fit and eventually, how to use the ampgas machines in the streets. He wasn't a kind man, but he didn't do much harm either.

I spent the next few years dedicating myself to becoming a Citizen. I studied harder than the other students. By the time I graduated school, they had nearly forgotten I was ever a Borderlander.

I blended perfectly with all the other Citizens lining up each time the bell signaled the time for ampgas. We all donned masks and forgot everything else for the next minute. I pulled the cord at my station and felt a valve open behind the booth, redirecting gaseous water from the steamworks under the street over solid amp crystal. I breathed deeply, slowly in and out. For that moment, there were no Borderlands, no dangerous wilderness just outside the city, no speedily declining population, no problems whatsoever.

Comforting energy surged through me. My muscles tingled, and my mind ran in high gear. After one last breath of amplified steam, the machine dinged, and my turn came to an end. I resituated my bowler hat.

Every time I returned my gas mask to its place and strolled away from the ampgas machine, I exhaled—satisfied approval of the energetic life humming around me. The extensive research and development by the Sanctius City Council made all this possible. If Mrs. Manelli and Mr. Ionone were proselytizers for Citizenship in Sanctius, I was their most dedicated convert.

HORIZONS LOOK DIFFERENT

"You're an inspiration, Nico," Mrs. Manelli said on graduation day as we mingled outside the school building. "It's young people like you who keep Sanctius City alive, a refuge for all mankind. You left your house, your family, and all its history behind. And now you'll forge a new future for yourself. Even though Citizens go astray and even evanesce, *you* will survive because you understand the importance of the City Council's edicts, the ways of Sanctius."

I would. Silently, I swore it.

Mrs. Manelli beamed as she handed me a black gift box with a silver ribbon. I hadn't expected any gifts. I hadn't received any in the four years since I'd left my home and family behind. So when I pried the gift open, I dropped the box in my excitement to pull the real gold pocket watch out of it.

The chain dangled heavily through my fingers. I clicked a button atop the perfect circle, and it popped open. Golden filigree hands posed like dancers on the ivory face. A small glass circle within the ivory revealed the clockwork inside. The gears and bars, reminiscent of the city's engine towers and steamworks, made the watch seem like a small icon of the city I worshiped.

"I don't know what to say," I stammered. "How can I ever thank you enough?"

"Just keep inspiring us to stick to the city's edicts, to stay safe here and survive," she said, handing me the box she'd retrieved from the pavement.

"Oh, I will. I'll abide by the ways of the city at all costs, even if I were the last person on the face of the Earth."

She shook my hand, and just as she turned to congratulate other students, a man spoke up behind me.

"I have a gift for the graduate as well." The voice was strange, but the intonation was uncomfortably familiar. There was only one person it could be. I turned to face him with the confidence of a citizen of Sanctius.

Except for the darker hair and skin, I could have been looking into a mirror that showed my future self. Though, if it *were* me, I would surely be better dressed.

"Valentino?"

"Congratulations on your accomplishment," he spoke reservedly, and his eyes betrayed a contrary emotion.

Unwilling to appear rude in front of fellow Citizens, I addressed my brother with matching aloof politeness.

"Thank you, sir." I put my hand out to shake his.

Rather than grasp my hand, Tino put a leather scroll tube in it and wrapped his free hand over mine for a moment.

"What are you doing here? What is this?" My heart swelled to see him, but I was angry at his intrusion into my city life. Unless… "Did you move into the city?"

"No. In fact, quite the opposite. I came to see…Well, I hoped that now that you've got your education and the excitement of Sanctius has worn off, you'd come back with me."

"Absolutely not," I said, trying to keep my voice calm. I took Tino's arm and directed him away from the graduation celebration, towards my flat. "You must be joking, after all I've learned here and accomplished."

"Hear me out. There is a wonderful world beyond Sanctius and be—"

"Stop right there. There is nothing I need beyond this city, only chaos and destruction."

"You have it so backward," he mumbled half to himself. "Don't you remember what our parents taught us?"

"Nothing helpful."

"Nico, please. Please let me explain. The Council is sick and… and twisted, and they don't even know their own minds. They're just puppets. Our family has something more—a heritage and freedom."

"Freedom that depends completely on a mysterious forest keeper who may or may not exist?"

He shook his head. "You can't believe it's a lie. You've encountered a wild man yourself! You must know there is truth in the stories we were taught." Tino grew almost frantic.

"I do. The truth is that the wilderness and all those monsters are precisely why this city exists—to be a haven from the dangers that are consuming humans left and right. Obviously, the witchcraft of that mountain has a strong hold over you."

Then, a moment of compassion gave me an idea. "Brother, stay with me. We have doctors who can help you. You're not well. Look at yourself. Let Sanctius City undo this enchantment."

"Enchanting. Yes! What is life out there with the Wilderman if not enchanting? But it can't be undone. Take your blinders off, Nico. You're only seeing half the truth." He touched the scroll he'd deposited in my hand. "I've collected these. Many of our scrolls go missing whenever health workers and other strangers visit. But I've gathered these stories for you because I think—at least I hope—you will find the truth in them."

"What if you just stay for a few nights?" *Maybe I could get him to a doctor.*

"No, Nico. I'm taking the passage through the sea. It would be a mistake for me to stay."

Through the sea? I should never have let sympathy get the best of me. He was raving. Still, I half hoped someone else would hear and get help. As if he sensed this, he backed away from me cautiously. "I have to go. It's time. But promise me you'll read them."

"Don't go yet. We can—"

"Promise!"

I hesitated. What if it contained some kind of dark magic or mind control? He'd already tempted me to let my emotions guide me, when I'd worked hard for the past several years to act only on facts and well-researched certitudes. Many such stories had led Citizens astray, and copies of those scrolls had been restricted as a result.

"I promise." I didn't mean to say it, but there it was. I would have to bolster my mind to read with the highest caution and, above all, remember this was the final manifesto of a man driven mad.

"I love you, brother. We've all loved you all this time." He turned and ran up the hill towards the edge of town and the path to the Hungry Mountain.

The encounter burned at the back of my mind as I went about the rest of my day, including a ceremony declaring me an official Citizen after my graduation.

When the final ampgas bell rang for the day, rows of Citizens all over the city donned masks and forgot everything else for the next minute. Once again, the amplified steam made everything seem just fine.

I replaced my bowler hat and moved out of the way for the next Citizen. The crowds filtered home, as if we all knew we'd run out of social steam for the day. Or else we knew we wouldn't enjoy it without more ampgas.

In the plain brass-walled elevator of my very average midtown building, I juggled the watch box and Tino's scroll back and forth in my hands. When the elevator stopped halfway up and opened to my floor, I mentally prepared myself for the task at hand. The scroll seemed to whisper my name; it bothered me just enough that I couldn't ignore it. That proved it was dangerous. But my commitment to Sanctius and her ways was even stronger.

I carefully hung my jacket and bowler hat on the hall tree inside my small apartment and then unlaced my boots at the door. I listened for my roommate, Franky, and the silence reminded me he was spending the evening with his parents.

Then, for the very first time, I did something I'd repeat every day for the rest of my life. In the process of unbuttoning my waistcoat, I slipped the chain from its place and held my pocket watch in my palm. How could anyone risk the wilderness when there were cities as miraculous and beautiful—like this timepiece—as Sanctius? I hung the vest in its place and gently set the gold watch on my bedside table.

No, there would be no risk for me in reading Tino's scroll. Nothing could sway me from my steadfast Citizenship in Sanctius City.

Luminary Tale

AZA & THE TALE OF THE PLOW

Nico, this isn't quite the beginning, but it's the beginning that matters for our time. I think it's the catalyst that propelled this darkness over the Earth. We're not alone here. There are things out there that only want to hunt us down, turn us against each other and use humanity for their own evil gain. Do you remember anything they taught us, Nico? Do you know how the gods came to Earth? Don't write off the old tales, my brother. Mythology is history if you know how to read it.

In the days when the sea had been divided but the Earth had not, and mankind grew discontent, the Luminaries of the eight corners of the land left their places. The stargazers recorded the absence of the lights for three nights. The celestial gods descended onto a high mountain in the Middlelands in bodily form to weigh the advantages of abetting the discontented humans. They gathered in a secret council without the permission of the Kingfather. The Luminary called Ezek suggested violence toward mankind, but the others saw no great benefit. They resolved to offer an exchange. But what would they give to help the humans' cause? And what would they require in return?

Each Luminary among the secret council examined his desires. Some found a thirst for power. Others found a want for pleasure, and still others found the pride that desired obeisance and worship. But the Luminaries feared to speak their desires, lest they should be heard by the Kingfather. They looked at one another, wondering if others would risk admitting their thoughts so he could throw his lot in with them.

Finally, one clever Luminary, Aza, devised a plan to accomplish all their goals.

"Comrades, you have seen how lovely the females of…"

Voices rose around the mountaintop, some in lust and others in disdain.

"Egh!" one grumbled. "They resemble the Kingfather too closely. Even in their womanly shapes, I cannot look long before the sight of them sears my mind's eye."

Most of the Luminaries nodded in agreement.

"Listen to my plan, and you will see." Aza waited for the mumbling to quiet. "First, Arach will appear to the people. The men will hate him for his beauty, but the women will have ears to hear. He will teach them about the Earth's dye matter. Arach will teach them to paint their faces and their bodies to cover the reflection of the Kingfather. When the men see the females decorated, he will be able to ask whatever we want of mankind in exchange for the gift of lavishing their clothes and bodies with colors."

Knowing that the women's appearances would be changed, all the star-gods longed deeply for the females of humankind and wondered at the rest of the plan.

"Arach will then tell the people he has companions and brothers. He will offer for us to come, bearing gifts of knowledge. They will happily shower gifts upon us, including their daughters as wives. We will become the fathers of nations, gods among the people. There is no unnamed thing you desire that you cannot attain when we walk as gods among men."

Then the Luminaries grew in anticipation to enact the plan.

"Wait," Arach interjected. "How do I know you'll follow me? I could not bear the wrath incurred by disobeying the Kingfather alone."

"How do we know you won't descend and keep all the wonders of Earth to yourself?"

As the council began to grow chaotic, and smoke from the hot stars gathered around the mountain, Aza spoke to them in a low but powerful rumble that demanded silence to be heard.

"We will take an oath, here on this high place, to accomplish this thing together," another retorted.

An oath among stars was a solemn agreement, and a heavy silence fell on the group of Luminaries.

"Barak, you will teach the men to read the stars. Yomî, you will instruct men in the ways of the sea. Together, you will teach men to travel beyond their borders."

"But Aza, they'll be devoured by—" Yomî protested.

"That is no concern of ours… except to comfort their widows."

A hesitant laugh rolled through the group. Although they were hungry for pleasure, the gods knew there was one more powerful than they were. And they still feared he would hear them. Even though evil already grew rampantly toward their cores, they knew the words they spoke aloud held great power and therefore carried significant risk, even greater than the malicious intent dimming the lamp within them.

"What about us?"

"Rami and Batai, you will teach them the signs of skies and sea, tricking them if you must, by manipulating the elements. It will take time, but they will begin to look to you rather than follow the lights of the Kingfather for planting and harvesting. Ezek and I will display power by teaching them to better wield the flame. We will leave them no room for doubt regarding our deity. And Mârôs, you will be first to follow Arach. You will teach the women to use the green things of the Earth, first in the arts of healing and then in the forbidden ways."

Stifled gasps seeped from the Luminaries' lips.

"Why do you react this way? Your betrayal is all but complete. Did you think any of this would be missed by the Kingfather? But if the humans learn sorcery, especially the women whose loyalty will be garnered quickly by our radiance, he will not be able to stop us. They will be bound to us and cut off from the Kingfather. They will be ours!"

The oath-making ritual of the Luminaries that followed was written in stone and passed through the story songs. A cloud of evil has rested on the highest mountain in the midland range ever since. The scribe has felt the palpable darkness at the foot of the mount and an eeriness so heavy that it prevents one from ascending far from the base.

After the oath was made at sunset on the spring equinox, the Luminaries came. They did not fall from the sky but walked through a door. And though the heavens would eventually rage and spit fire because the celestial beings had abandoned their post, they did not at the time. The star-gods stepped into this world and taught mankind. And this is why they have always been called the Luminaries: because their lights disappeared from the eight corners of the world and they enlightened the humans. But they did not share the advanced arts of metallurgy yet. The blending and working of hard metals were held for the Luminaries alone until after the star-children of the Luminaries were plentiful in the land and greater force was needed to subdue the armies throughout the Earth.

As predicted, the men were hesitant. Some of the women also gave pause. But others, when they saw the beauty of Arach, and of Mârôs after him, rushed to learn their magical arts. When the men began to learn seafaring and the reading of signs and wonders, they felt indebted to the gods and gave their daughters as wives.

When the Luminaries saw how easy it was to sway humanity, they expanded their plot against the Kingfather. Seeing the success of the first eight, more Luminaries followed them and stepped out of the heavens, taking male and female forms. The sky was dimmed, and the world was darker.

Together, the Luminaries taught mankind to build doors, not from one room to another but from world to world, realm to realm. They schemed to make an army of the humans to storm the gates of the Kingfather's country, to dethrone him and steal his glory.

The Kingfather counted their rebellion a great evil against himself and against mankind, for he loved both the Luminaries and the humans as his kin. Yet, the Luminaries sought to change, to mar the ones he had made.

The Kingfather struck down the great door. He took up his plow from the skies and dug trenches across the face of the Earth. To this day, when we see the plow made of stars reflected on the waters, we remember how the Kingfather divided the world by plowing trenches for the great seas.

HOME

I wasn't the last person on Earth yet, but there was no chance I would meet anyone else near the Hungry Mountain in the middle of the night. Nothing human anyway.

My chest heaved as I dove behind the old beech tree. I held my breath and listened. Nothing. Seven years had passed since my graduation, and yet the wilderness had enticed and consumed everyone. Well, almost everyone.

I leaped back onto the trail and sprinted to the next hiding spot. I ran that trail regularly. Several good hunting spots dotted its path, even though it didn't veer far from the city until much farther around the mountain. I trusted Sanctius City's provisions more than wild food, but the dwindling population could no longer sustain the factory. Yet, I knew the Council was doing everything they could to figure this out. *That's why we haven't heard from them much lately. Any day now, they'll announce their newest plans, and we'll start fresh.*

Humanity would never have lasted as long as we did against the dangers outside the city without Sanctius City's research, guidance, and provision. Mankind would have lasted even longer if they'd only held to the Council's edicts. If their wisdom led them to govern us from the safety of the tower, I would enforce their guidelines as the Council's emissary until they resurfaced.

Maybe hunting and growing my own food wasn't the perfectly formulated diet that the Council prescribed for us, but I couldn't deny it was delicious, no matter how hard I tried. And I was positive they would approve of my determination to survive for Sanctius' sake. I never hunted in broad daylight, always under the cover of darkness. People, back when there were people, said the dangers of the wilderness roamed about during the light of day. I had memorized every root and rock on that path so I could traverse it quickly in the darkness. I could run that trail back to the city with my eyes closed. Silently, I reminded myself of the same thing I had a million times over in the years since I'd become a Citizen. *By Sanctius City, I* will *survive.*

Where the path led nearer to Sanctius, the River Umbra pooled up behind a natural dam. I waited for my eyes to adjust to the filtered moonlight and then searched for waterfowl. Behind me, remains of shacks haunted the perimeter of the city. When I first started leaving the city for food, I avoided the Borderlands. Memories threatened to suffocate me. Was I digressing to their ways, the broken ways of my ancestors, by hunting wildlife out there?

But this was a matter of survival. And as a Sanctius Citizen, my duty was to survive and carry on the ways of the city. Maybe I could even use what remained of Sanctius technology to revive a superior people in my own discipline. I breathed long and slow through my nose and allowed my chest to rise. I was the Citizen of Citizens. None had been more faithful to Sanctius City than I.

The reek of dewy forest, thick in my puffed-up chest, dragged my attention back. The forest always tempted me to explore deeper. But like a siren's call, I knew the shadows were dancing to a song of death. I was stronger than the whispers on the mountainside. I was stronger than the men and women who had fallen victim to the traps of the wilderness.

While I gazed over the surface of the pond in search of my next meal, something in the forest moved. I scanned the monochrome trees and foliage. The slight breeze invited my imagination to see someone moving through the shadows. A snipe's wings made an eerie high-to-low woo-woo-woo-woo-woo from above the Hungry Mountain in front of me. Chills ran down the back of my head and neck. *I've been out here too long.*

I refocused on the pond, thankful the sun had tiptoed into the eastern sky. The city would awaken soon, and I needed to get out of the forest. A badling of ducks floated quietly on the pond. The white on their tri-colored bodies gave them away. *Now, or never.* I threw my daggers at two drakes, then swiped my crossbow off my back, just in case. As usual, I didn't need it. But I couldn't risk an injured duck flying up the mountain with one of my knives. Ammunition was in short supply in the city, so knives were lifesavers. Knives and crossbow bolts could be retrieved; bullets, once shot, were spent.

Almost instinctively as breathing, I retrieved my watch from my waistcoat pocket. The golden case fit my hand as if they were made for each other. Or maybe, after nearly a decade, my hand had conformed to the cool gold back of the watch. The comforting click and swoosh of the lid opening revealed that it was almost 7 a.m. After tucking the timepiece away, I adjusted my bowler hat, slung my catch over one shoulder and slipped my daggers back into the braided leather holster crisscrossing my torso.

The ducks' bills bounced against the string of my crossbow with every step. It *almost* drowned out the noise of birds waking, water falling over rocks, and the eerie rustle of leaves in the morning breeze. I breathed a sigh of contentment when dirt gave way to paving bricks under my feet and buildings rose in front of me to hide the wilderness from view. The musky stench of forest faded, and I welcomed the scent of steam, iron and concrete with the day. It was always a relief to return to the safety of Sanctius City.

No one moved in the streets, not even uptown, where the engines began to turn for the day and the tower lights blinked on from bottom to top. Though all the Councils of Sanctius past had prepared the best possible circumstances for survival, the wilderness claimed countless lives—nearly all of them, in fact. As the population waned, leaders flipped switch after massive switch to disconnect steam engines from extraneous zones of the city. They opened pressure relief valves to prevent engines from powering empty towers. Eventually, all the steam towers were drained and abandoned except one. Elevators and factories screeched to a halt. It had been three years, but I'd never forget that sound. The sudden, sickening silence reminded the survivors just how many had evanesced due to the dangers beyond the city.

We were used to the decrescendo of shutting down. Each night in Sanctius, buildings and machines, communication banners, and vehicles grew silent—one here, a few there—as the steam in the solar-heated tanks cooled down for the evening, but never all at once. And then, each morning, Sanctius City would rise, proud and strong, when sunlight resurrected our sleeping technology. As I strolled along the street, I admired the warm murmur of steam vehicles awakening for the day.

Hooooommmme. You're hooommmmmmmmme, they hummed reassuringly.

There was a reason this steep knob of land jutting into the sea was the last refuge on Earth. This was the very place mankind had conquered the natural world with our technology.

I walked along the streets, as proud of my city as if I had built it myself. But I couldn't help but notice the wilderness creeping down into the edges. Where the perimeter of Sanctius had once been a clean and striking declaration to the Borderlands and beyond, vines grew out of nowhere, inching into every crevice and slithering up the ornate metal building exteriors. I shivered. Leave the wilderness out there. Don't think about it while you don't have to.

Like condensation dripping down tank glass, relief wicked away any thought of the wilderness when I descended the hill into my neighborhood. Far above the old harbor area, the massive drive trains still carried energy under the streets to the newest uptown buildings. My eyes followed the heavy iron framing to the top of the steam tower on my right. I held my bowler hat on so I could admire the alternating floors of boilers and engine rooms that rose to the sky. Even without technicians, the engine tower roared with life each day.

Thick curved glass on the boiler floors doubled as windows and lenses to magnify the sun. The convex glass intensified the solar rays and heated the water to steaming, powering the engines that took up the entire floor above it. Alternating stories of rounded glass and engine floors made the tower's silhouette ebb in and out, much like the rhythm of the machines inside.

The rhythmic roar emanating from the building drowned out a voice from the next block. I jogged to the street and instinctively looked both ways before crossing where I could hear better.

✻ ✻ ✻

"Nico, when are you going to stop doing that? And walking on the footpath—really, chap?" Franky joined me on the paved walkway from the middle of the street. At his nape, overgrown dark hair fluttered slightly in the breeze, even though he'd attempted to hold it down with a tweed cap. A matching beard had sprouted on his sculpture-worthy chin, threatening to hide his wide smile.

Despite his sophisticated upbringing, Franky hadn't shaved in a couple of days. And he'd left his jacket at home, wherever that might have been that week. Under his waistcoat, he'd rolled his sleeves up to his elbows. The Council's scientists designed the synthetic fabric of our modern suit jackets to wick away sweat and keep us as cool as possible. But Franky insisted on removing his clothing when he felt warm.

As he walked down the smoothly paved road, Franky tapped a black cane with a fancy copper handle shaped like a mermaid with her head and tail turned upward. It was a family emblem that set him and his forefathers apart. Very few Citizens had any connection to their history. Research showed it decreased loyalty to Sanctius City and encouraged other unhelpful qualities, leading to rebellions and revolutions. At all costs, we avoided any revival of traits humanity had evolved beyond— forward motion only. But emblem holders were different.

"One of those drakes for me?" He pointed the tip of his cane towards the blue-black heads peeking out from behind my back.

"And why should I share with you?" I peered down my nose at him.

"Because I have something in return." Franky motioned with exaggerated arms towards the middle of the road. "If you'll condescend to come into the street."

He led me around a steam car parked next to the sidewalk, a

bullet-shaped sports model with one seat. When I joined him around the car, he gestured toward a thick wooden slab leaned against the car's svelte glass tank. The slab was wider than Franky and half as tall, easily as thick as my hand. And bark still ran along one side.

"It's perfect! Duck for two it is." I shook his hand to strike the deal. "We will need alternative transportation, though. This thing is hefty."

"Not as heavy as all that scrap metal you've been eyeing! It'll make a perfect bench seat for your precious garden."

Yes, my garden was precious. As was *my* penthouse suite—*my* whole building, in fact—since there was no one else to occupy it.

Franky stopped by a giant lorry on tracks and raised his eyebrows. The dumping bed would hold the slab just fine, but the truck was immense. And the tracks were a bit excessive.

"Seems kind of unnecessary for one slab," I said.

"You keep saying that we only live once," he retorted.

"If I properly recall, *you* used to say that. But you don't anymore, so I have to remind you once in a while. Plus, we obviously have different ideas of living the good life." I eyed the massive truck incredulously.

Instead of continuing the banter, Franky made himself busy inspecting the lorry for usefulness. All the vehicles in Sanctius idled until needed. As soon as the sun heated the water within the thick magnifying glass tanks, steam power turned their crankshafts and they hummed away. No one would have needed a construction vehicle like this for several years, but everything on the long-neglected lorry seemed operational. Franky set his end of the board on the dump truck bed, which was chest high. The bed clanged and screeched as I shoved my end the rest of the way in.

The temple clock rang. 8 a.m. All across uptown, a low whoosh heralded the dropping of the Council's giant message banners down the sides of all the buildings. Long canvas sheets reminded us of the city's many edicts or delivered special messages from the Council to the Citizens. It was a comforting reminder that the Council was still looking out for our best interests. And then, the same clockwork that retracted the banners caused the nearest ampgas station to ding its availability in unison with all the others in Sanctius. *Such magnificent order.*

"Coming?" I asked Franky as I walked down the block toward the long row of ampgas stations.

"I'm good right now."

I chose a random station, removed my hat, and quickly situated the gas mask over my face. Round goggles protected my eyes, and a breather covered my nose and mouth. I pulled the handle on a chain at eye level. Steam rushed up from underground, collected ampcrystal molecules and delivered them in the perfect dose.

The Council had done a massive amount of research to determine the optimal dosage and frequency for empowering their Citizens. Of course, as the population dwindled, people took more, but their demise only proved that the Council knew what they were doing when they set dosage amounts. I wouldn't be such a fool.

The amplified steam filled my lungs and forced away my minor frustration with Franky's recent odd behavior. Instead, I was ready to face the day.

When my time was up, I stepped back and gazed down the row of ampgas booths. I shook my head at the ones where the mask had been removed, signaling that the ampcrystal block below was gone. Thankfully, there were still many more working ampgas stations than there were people. But how long would they last if the city were repopulated?

"You know, we should start looking for a way to check the ampcrystal supply. And possibly researching how to replenish it if needed."

Franky shrugged off my suggestion as he opened the heavily riveted driver's side door. He wasn't one to worry about something until it was urgent.

"I'd let you do the honors, but you'd follow the traffic laws," he laughed.

"Just because no one else is on the road doesn't mean we need to digress into anarchy," I argued, albeit lightheartedly, as I climbed up the heavy-duty tracks and slid into the passenger seat. "*Someone* could zip around the corner. No doubt, a crash with this massive thing wouldn't leave any of us alive. Then what?"

Franky didn't answer right away. Instead, he took a pair of brass-framed driving goggles off the dashboard. The tense silence was becoming a pattern that concerned me even through the euphoria of the ampgas.

"Yeah, then what?" he finally asked. He shimmied the goggles over the brim of his cap and onto his eyes. The truck growled at Franky as he shoved the shift stick forward and backward a few times until he successfully put it into gear.

"We survive. That's what. Just stay on the road without running over anyone on a steam bike, and we'll be fine." I looked both ways as he drove through an intersection without stopping.

It frustrated me that Franky took his opportunities for granted. He was born into the ideal Citizen family with every opportunity for survival and success in Sanctius City, including being an emblem-holder.

"So, duck? Will you stuff it with apples or glaze it with plums?" He'd interrupted my thoughts as if he knew I stewed on our contrasting childhoods and wanted to put a quick stop to it.

"Oh! Stop the truck! I have a better idea." The steam lorry listed forward until we halted in the middle of an intersection.

I jumped down and ran to the sidewalk that led back to a fancy boutique on the previous block. A bell still rang when I opened the door, even though there was no one to answer. Along the walls of the shop, racks made of diagonal brass tubing held picked-through stacks of wine bottles. I scanned them for a red wine to go with duck. For much of my life, I couldn't have afforded to shop at such a store, even though my barbarian-to-Citizen story was the greatest success of my time.

Survival via the city had finally rewarded me, however: my penthouse suite, my choice of remaining foods and hunting places, no lines at ampgas booths, no one to charge even a couple of harpies for anything. Outliving most of humanity had proven rich in its advantages.

The day I moved into the penthouse was the day I committed to carry out the will of the Council as if I were their right hand. I knew I had to take responsibility to earn such a privilege. The Council didn't associate with regular Citizens anymore. They were all emblem holders, nobles among men and superior to us mere mortals. After most of their families had disappeared, they never emerged from their tower. Franky wrote them off for dead, but I suspected he was just bitter from falling out with his father. No. Rather than descending to die or disappear with the rest of mankind, I'm sure the Council simply waited for a remnant of faithful Citizens to start afresh.

The tessellations on the stamped copper ceiling tiles drew my attention. Sanctius was the most beautiful place on Earth. All over the city, a rainbow of metallic shades collided in the perfect ratio of practicality and embellishment. Franky and his lorry whirred backward and stopped outside. *Focus here. Duck sauce.*

A section of wine from the south end caught my eye, so I grabbed two bottles from behind a shelf label that said something about notes of plum and jogged to the truck.

"Here, take these so I can climb in."

"Ooh, wine sauce. Fantastic idea, Nico! Did you ever visit this wine tower?"

"Ha! No, but I'm guessing you did."

Not only did Franky's father hold a position on the Sanctius City Council, but his mother was a respected fellow at the city's research facilities. They were powerful, driven people, and Franky was the child of their old age. Of course, marriages were paired by compatible traits and skill sets, not any kind of antiquated romantic notion. Only after they had a Councilman's suite and established careers did they request an infant pod in the Human Life Tower.

"Don't worry. You didn't miss anything," Franky continued after I settled into the passenger's seat again. "They're all the same. Floors upon floors of grapevines fermented the same way as every other wine tower. They had to make rules about which grapes each tower could use just to ensure the wines all turned out different." His words hinted of bitterness that dried up the conversation like a bad Syrah. Except for my wincing at Franky's driving down the middle of the road and plowing through intersections without looking, we drove the rest of the way in silence.

At my building, we hauled the bulky board into my suite's private glass elevator, half tucked into the side of the tower. Franky slid the door shut—a tall piece of glass wrapped in graceful aluminum framing—and I pressed the singular button. A series of muted clacks sounded as the proper gears engaged. A clutch whined as it transferred energy to the chain pulleys that lifted the elevator, and we surged upward. The glass cage revealed all the complicated hardware of the elevator shaft, lined with iron chains and steel cables, and the backside of the elevator where the power transferred from the tower's distribution hub in the basement to the smaller mechanisms on the lift. Human technology had outlived most humans. It was magnificent.

The slim elevator door opened onto the patio, and instantly, I knew two things were wrong. Curtains shivered slightly inside the patio door, evidence the glass doors to my suite were open. My eyes zeroed in on the empty stand on my white brick mantel, alerting me that my favorite revolver was missing. My heart raced momentarily before I remembered it could only be one person. Besides Franky and me, there was only one other person on Earth.

THREE

"Raina, you absolutely *must* stop stealing my stuff."

"How'd you know it was me?"

She smirked as she manifested from behind a potted shrub on the patio. Instead of joining us inside immediately, she meandered around my rooftop garden, plucking a flower here and a ripe fruit there.

"Who else?" My mouth scrunched to one side, and I mimicked her attitude. "Gun." I held out my hand and bit my lip against the urge to tell her not to touch my plants.

Raina shoved a blackberry into her mouth. Judging by the stains on her mauve-brown lips, it wasn't her first.

"You weren't using it." She shrugged her bare shoulder.

"You know very well that ammo is limited. We need to conserve it."

Raina wore a vibrant printed cloth wrapped around her, tight at the top, loose and flowing at the bottom. Over the jewel-toned fabric, a richly oiled leather corset with sheaths between the boning nearly matched the walnut wood shade of her skin. Holsters adorned her outfit as if they were feminine accessories. She tucked a bright pink zinnia behind her ear, which freed up a hand to retrieve my pistol from her leg holster.

Instead of bringing it to me, she walked to the mantel and set the gun in its place. So, I resumed my entry ritual. I removed my boots and placed them neatly by my hat stand. After my bowler hat and crossbow were comfortable on their hooks, I continued to the kitchen to skin the ducks.

The breast meat would only get us through one meal, especially if Raina stayed, which she certainly would. Free food and the only company available on Earth made for a hard deal to pass up. The rest of the bones and meat from the birds would make a great soup. True to form, Raina stood near the kitchen island, waiting for her invitation.

"If you plan to stay for lunch, you should harvest some salad for us, and more of those berries you've been eating."

"Good thing I'm not staying then."

I forgot the duck for a second, but the sarcastic part of my brain recovered quickly. "I'm sorry our company doesn't compare to the excitement of your solitude."

"You're forgiven."

My knife-wielding hand paused again. I raised my eyebrows at her.

"I was really hoping to explore some row houses I found still locked tight downtown. Could be some real treasures in there. But if you insist…"

Her abundant, tight black curls receded until she disappeared under the Gothic arches of my greenhouse. I growled inside. The salad greens and berries were outside on the patio, not in the hothouse. I should have known when I asked Raina to harvest one thing she would help herself to anything that looked appealing from my rooftop haven. Franky halted the bitter train of my thoughts when he came in from the patio with a few beets.

"I don't know how you do it, chap. How do you make all this stuff grow? It's so much better than city provisions."

"I know how he does it," Raina yelled from the patio. "It's called obsession."

"For your information, I fully appreciated city provisions until the day the factory shut down. There's something comforting in knowing the Council formulated every bite for maximum nutrition. You'd value what you had more highly if you'd grown up on Borderland food. Sometimes all we had was bread and broth."

I shook off the smell of campfire wafting through my memory and the taste of sourdough dunked in wild mushroom soup. With my voice lower, I asked, "Can you believe she's raiding my garden right now?"

"Meh," Frank shrugged. "Knowing Raina is always an adventure. She lives by a different set of rules." He smiled as if that were a good thing.

"Rules that make it okay to steal my salad greens?"

"Yes, salad! That's what we're discussing here. How do you keep all this growing?"

"Like any deviation we must make from Sanctius edicts, I do it thoughtfully and scientifically. I think there are some gardening scrolls up for grabs on the 43rd floor." I pointed a sticky finger with a sprinkling of down feathers toward a few brass and leather-covered scrolls on my own shelf.

"Scrolls?"

"Yes, scrolls. Remember those? Words on long sheets of paper stacked and wound with clockwork into a tidy cylinder for convenient storage? I hear even the free-spirited Raina reads scrolls."

At my half-compliment, Raina reentered the flat with her blackberry lips grinning, one arm full of freshly harvested food, and the other waving pompously as if she were royalty. Franky had been clumsily chopping beet greens, but at the mention of reading, he put down the knife and walked to the shelf. He pulled open a scroll, and his eyes darted over the contents.

"But is that how you actually learned all of this? You just read some directions?" He wound the handle on the brass end cap, and the scroll retracted. I'd never admit it to him, but Franky was half the reason I had a garden on the roof. He'd had the idea when city provisions became scarce and stealing was the common solution. He had no clue where to start. For some reason, maybe my rustic beginning or some evolved inclination, growing and preparing food came as naturally to me as mechanics and engineering did to Franky. Of course, I still approached it with plenty of research. Every departure from the literal obedience of the edicts must be made with great caution. Essentially, I *was* living within the edicts. I just needed to redefine them slightly until we heard from the Council again.

Franky cleared his throat, reminding me he still waited for an answer.

"Oh, it's just survival, chap. You were a soft-handed Councilman's kid, and now you can fix any of the steamworks in the city. Except maybe a tower engine, but that's just because they're huge. I'd like to see you move one of those giant pistons even a hair's breadth." I chuckled, hoping to dispel the thickness of the air.

This was a brand-new thing for us. A certain awkwardness had been developing for a few weeks, maybe longer. It had come on so slowly that I couldn't even say when it started exactly. I wished I could pinpoint it so that maybe I could connect it to something I'd done or said.

Franky searched my face before resuming chopping. "Sorry you can't stop stewing over Raina," he ventured quietly, as he scooped the beet greens into my waiting skillet.

Maybe that's why he's been acting weird. He suspects I'm attracted to Raina.

"You should know me better than that. I would never entertain such a primitive instinct." My answer grew from a whisper to a hoarse growl.

"Never? I seem to remember a certain young lady from the Orange corner of the world—Farrah? Was that her name?"

"That was essentially nothing, and yet more than enough to learn my lesson. The Council is right about romance. We've evolved beyond that."

"But romantic relationships are so… instinctive. Why have we— our society, I mean—worked so hard to erase them from humanity?"

He scanned the room and located Raina behind him making the salad, but it didn't stop him from adding, "Doesn't it feel a little like killing off a piece of your soul?"

"Franky!" I couldn't conceal how appalled I was. "No, it doesn't. Living in such a haven as Sanctius City requires a touch of discipline. You can handle that. If we want to grow as a species, we must transcend the generations before us. You, having a researcher for a mother, must know all the science. Such passions drive humankind to be irresponsible, impulsive, and impractical. That is why all those romantic societies have died out."

Franky raised his eyebrows and smiled skeptically. But he said nothing more, just attempted to clean the counter. What he actually accomplished was to move dishes into stacks and sloppily swipe some of the remaining bits of food into his hand. His gaze oscillated from my garden to Raina, who browsed my small library. The counter was nearly as dirty as before. *It's the thought that counts,* I consoled myself. I would have to thoroughly clean the dinner mess later.

"It looks like you forgot to take your boots off. I'm sure it was Raina's dramatic entrance. But would you mind?" I said and motioned toward my boots near the hall tree. He may not be able to clean worth a darn, but at the very least, he could follow the house rules.

In lieu of an apology, Franky performed a flourishing bow. "Wouldn't want to blemish the *penthouse.* Wear shoes in the Time Temple, in any ancient holy site on Earth, but don't dare stain Sir Nicolo's suite." He finished the parody with a genuine laugh, but it didn't cover the sour tone in his voice. Raina muffled her laughter behind a scroll.

"Your scrolls are boring," she redirected the conversation. At least we never had to guess what she was thinking.

"You're too kind," I answered.

I was grateful to enjoy the duck over normal conversation. Franky was never fully transparent about his activities last night, but we laughed together over an incident with one of the modified pulleys he'd rigged for Raina to get into the upper floors of a powerless building. She got partway up when the ascender jammed, and Franky had to climb twelve flights of stairs to fix it. Raina hung there like a spider until he could rescue her.

In the past several years of friendship, Franky and I both had many failures to provide us with entertainment. It was almost a tradition to laugh at ourselves over dinner. *What was up with him earlier?* One minute, there was an elephant in the room, and the next, things were normal.

Raina settled in and laughed with us. In an effort to avoid the many topics she and I disagreed on, she told us stories like her recent raid on a clothing store. She mocked the "restricting" fashions of Sanctius and told us about the colorful, flowing clothing in the Southlands across the sea, and finally of the dark magical beings that haunted the shadows there.

The room grew somber. Raina had been the last person alive in the Southlands. She flew solo to Sanctius City in a steam balloon because the wilderness had overtaken all the settlements on her continent.

Councils past had done well for us in choosing this easily defensible lump of land sticking out of the eastern coast. A responsibility fell heavily on my shoulders to keep this blessing at the forefront of all our minds. Lately, the silences were thicker, and I wondered if I'd be able to keep them on the right path long enough to restore more of Sanctius City to working order, maybe even the Human Life Tower.

I needed Franky's mechanical know-how. And Raina was the last woman on Earth. We could make some kind of substitute for the Council-approved family institution and raise a few new Citizens at a time, *if* I could ensure those two stayed committed to the city.

Raina thanked me for the duck and excused herself, not forgetting her armload of foodstuffs from my garden to fuel whatever mysterious activities she occupied her time with.

I continued to turn my grand plans for repopulation over in my mind. Previously, I had not found Citizens who were as upstanding as I to warrant even considering forming family units. But since Franky, Raina and I found ourselves alone, I had broached the topic a few times. So far, I'd met with little response beyond dodgy glances and quick subject changes. As I cleaned the dishes, I entertained myself with mental images of infant pods in the Human Life Tower humming with new life. What a great goal! The Council would be so pleased. Maybe it would even be the catalyst to bring them down from the tower to guide us in person.

While I rinsed and dried the last of the dishes and placed them carefully in their places, Franky manhandled the slab of wood just outside on the patio. I didn't want him to take the slab to its place without me, so I pried into his mood to delay him.

"So, what *were* you up to last night? You obviously weren't hunting."

Franky paused in his fumbling with the slab, but didn't answer right away. His thoughts made him smile, and finally he said, shrugging casually, "Exploring."

"Run out of clean dishes and floor space in another flat?" I teased.

Franky only laughed off my jab while I set the last dish carefully in its stack.

The ability to relocate to any apartment he could break into offered little motivation for Franky to pick up after himself. He always insisted he had better things to do than clean. This, besides the fact that cohabitating should only be done with Council approval, is a major reason we don't share a flat. I would never allow such a mess to stack up. But if Franky ran out of buildings uptown, he could always venture downtown like Raina.

She reigned over the parts of the city that had been shut down. Though she had a base camp near the sea, it wasn't unusual to catch her winding the handle on an escape pulley, raising her on steel cables so she could plunder empty flats all over downtown. She usually stayed clear of operational uptown. For what reason, I never understood.

She doesn't have your impeccable discernment. The thought popped into my head as if someone else had whispered it. It seemed unkind. However, sometimes the truth is harsh.

I dried my hands and checked my watch, less concerned with the time than with hearing the reliable tick. With the growing awkwardness with Franky and even Raina, it centered me to remember how far I'd come from a shack in the Borderlands to my penthouse suite with a rooftop garden.

"Here, I'll walk backward." I lifted the end of the plank opposite Franky and started backward through the rooftop garden.

We both knew where we were going. I had been searching for a hunk of copper or steel—any metal, really—just this size to make a bench in the garden. I never would have looked for wood, but Franky would have. He probably remembered it from one of his previous flats. I only hoped he hadn't gone into the forest to cut and mill it himself.

Franky and I side-stepped past all the raised beds and toward the southern edge of the rooftop. We set the slab on twin oblong cogs that I'd found in one of the abandoned buildings just for this purpose. The giant, elongated gears supported the slab at the perfect height for us to sit and enjoy the view.

I admired the giant cogs, perfectly symmetrical. They added a beautiful touch of order to the unavoidable chaos of garden plants. Latticework made from brass rods spaced a few inches apart extended upward on each side of the bench. The rods were tied with copper wire, already tarnished to a stunning turquoise, running diagonally between them. I had already trained grapevines partway up from the rectangular garden boxes below.

Similar was the effect of my steel-framed conservatory. The Gothic roofline curved upward until the point pierced the sky. Intricately scrolled brass gable trim reiterated the design—upward for growth, for evolution, for survival.

"Beautiful," I admitted out loud as I admired the cool surfaces and pleasing evenness of it all.

"It is," Franky said. Except he ran his hand along the flat top of the wooden seat where it met the bark-covered edge.

"Well, shall we?" I interrupted his awkward moment with the slice of tree trunk, and we both moved to sit down to try out my new bench. I faced my patio, the city, and the amazing accomplishments of humankind. Franky, however, sat opposite, facing the dangerous wilderness beyond the city. He stared to the right, at the deadly star cliffs, confirming my suspicions that I should be worried for him. *Maybe I can still save him.* I watched his eyes slide left to the sea and wander to far-off thoughts. I wondered how long he'd been straying away from the city edicts. *I* will *save him.*

That day, I fell asleep reading Tino's scroll. It reminded me of the brother I failed to save. The tale was old, but it rang familiar with Raina's modern accounts of the Southlands. Although I lay down when the sun was still high, a feeling of darkness settled over me as I read.

Luminary Tale
MÂRÔS'S CHEETAH AND THE KING'S DAUGHTERS

Nico, Read carefully, my brother. For we all face the temptations of the daughters.

There once lived a king of the South named Ahffet, who had two daughters. One was beautiful, but the other was plain. Now, the daughters used to fetch water from a clear pool below a rushing waterfall. Their father warned them never to veer from the path or speak to anyone outside of their village.

There were many date trees along the path to the river, and the sisters would often pick dates along their way. The dates were so delicious and sweet that sometimes they would go off the path to pick the sweet fruits when there were none close by.

Nearby there lived a shapeshifter, a son of the king called Mârôs. He saw King Ahffet's beautiful daughter and desired her for a wife. He came to her in his tall and strong human form and tried to woo her, for his father was one of the god-kings. But the plain daughter grasped her sister's hand and reminded her of their father's warning. Though she was loath to leave the handsome man, she went with her sister to fetch the water.

The sisters used more caution for a short time, but it wasn't long before the temptation of the sweet date fruit drew them away. And again, the shapeshifter approached the young women. This time, he appeared as a serpent and flattered the beautiful daughter with his smooth speech. She loved hearing about her own loveliness, but the plain daughter saw through his honey-coated words. Again, she reminded her sister of their father's words. Both girls came away to the pool to get water and returned home safely.

Again, the sisters used caution for a short time, but the sight of dates just off the trail lured them. A third time, the shapeshifter approached the girls, this time as a kingly bird of prey. He told of the wealth of his kingdom and all the gifts the beautiful daughter would receive as his bride. Although they had never wanted for anything, the beautiful daughter's eyes shone at the mention of such comfort and wealth. The plain daughter, however, remembered her father's good care and his warning. She pulled her sister away and brought her straight home.

After this, the shapeshifter went to his father Mârôs and told him of the beautiful young woman he wished to have for a wife. Mârôs explained that when bribery nor flattery nor lust captured a human, then fear was just the thing.

It was some time before Ahffet allowed his beautiful daughter to go with her sister to the pool, but the plain daughter grew tired of carrying water by herself. The shapeshifter watched and waited patiently. When he heard the sisters coming, he emerged from the date grove as a fierce cheetah.

"You will come with me," he snarled, and performed acts of dark magic. The girls were very afraid. The plain daughter dropped her pot and pulled her sister homeward. Before they took three steps, the shapeshifter blocked the path in that direction. "You will come with me!"

He crouched low and bared his teeth. With his dark magic, he showed the sisters terrible things that would befall them and their father if they refused. They saw the rolling muscles of the svelte cheetah and thought they could never escape. The sisters felt they had no choice; both followed the shapeshifter to his home.

This is how the evil things in all the southern corner of the Earth knew that fear was the best tool for ruling over mankind. For with fear, the shapeshifter had gained two wives instead of one.

SAFETY IN THE DARKNESS

I woke early, before the sinking sun blanketed the mountain in the safety of darkness. I took my time—a hot face towel, a straight razor to the chin, a comb to put every wavy hair on my crown in place. The sides of my head would need to be shaved in a couple of days to keep things looking sharp, but it was dapper enough for the time being. From the wardrobe in my bedroom, I retrieved my patched and repaired gray herringbone trousers. I donned a shirt clinging to the last shade of whiteness before it would need a new descriptor. I sniffed it. It didn't exactly smell white either, but it would do until wash day. Thankfully, my waistcoat, also gray herringbone, covered the whitest parts of my shirt, mercifully leaving the dull sleeves without the bright contrast to give them away.

With a caring and familiar motion, my watch chain fell into its home in a buttonhole, and the cool gold slipped ritually into my waistcoat pocket. I slid my left arm into my braided leather chest holster, pliable from a few years of daily use, and buckled it at my side. Franky had given it to me when I finally got the hang of hunting for meat. Finally, I pulled on my jacket and tugged it into all the right places.

I dilly-dallied, examining my revolver. Good thing. Replacing the rounds Raina had stolen spent another minute of the time I needed to burn.

"You should have been safe here." I stuffed the revolver into my chest holster. I couldn't help but smile at Raina's constant mischief, but I also made plans for securing the flat better. What was Sanctius, if not a place for order and security?

The plants on the patio needed to be watered, and some of the ventilation windows on the greenhouse needed closed for the night. While I hauled around the bulky rubber hose attached to my rooftop water pump, I thought about how to lock the place up tighter. The patio doors were easy; I could lock them and wedge a couple of boards into the sliding door tracks. The hall entrance would be more of a challenge.

I inhaled the aromas the plants released as the stream of water hit them. Some were musky. Others were spicy. Many smelled sweet. I pointed the hose at a pear tree in blossom, and a rush of floral notes hit me. I forgot about planning my fortification until I coiled the hose nicely on its hook and closed the ventilation windows on the conservatory.

Inside, I enjoyed a few more breaths of climate-controlled air while I stared at the filigree details on the elevator doors. Maybe Franky would have ideas about securing them *if* he didn't freak out that I cared about securing my flat. Had he known the struggle of fighting for everything he owned, he wouldn't judge me so harshly. Even with just him and Raina around, privacy and security were my rights as a Citizen. Maybe he could rig up a lock and key on a box over the upper floor buttons.

I mindlessly stroked the smooth Sanctius-made material of my hat while I pondered. The thermostat must have disengaged the power from the transfer station under the building because the fan had shut off. In my boredom, a hand naturally found its way to my pocket watch. For all my dilly-dallying, I still had daylight to burn, but I tucked the watch away and donned my hat, satchel and crossbow anyway.

Though empty of humans, the city streets still purred with life, lined with creations that had outlived their creators. The slightest tremble in the sidewalks betrayed the presence of massive drive assemblies below that transferred power from the steam tower to buildings like mine.

Steam machines of all kinds hummed in wait for an operator. That day, a slim steam cart with a tubular body called my name.

As I hopped over the door and slid into the single, roofless seat, a poster caught my eye. On the boarded-up windows of a former clothing store, a Sanctius City Council PSA poster featured the high cliffs outside the western edge of the city. A couple of rebels lay on the cliffs watching sparse dots of stars above, but a black, long-necked flying beast poised to scoop them up in its talons. "DON'T STRAY INTO THE WILDERNESS," the poster proclaimed. "REMEMBER THE EVANESCED."

With my hat and crossbow tucked safely next to my leg, I pulled into the street. In each window I passed, there was another poster. They featured mountain trolls with gaping caves for mouths and stalactites and stalagmites for teeth. Sea monsters reached out of the depths for their next victim, and even the menacing river sprites from childhood stories attacked passersby from within the rushing river. The lure of the wilderness had probably already drawn Franky too far beyond city limits. Mountains that ate us. Waters that swallowed us. Skies that snatched us. How could he risk these dangers after they had reduced humanity to three? A hand strayed to my tricep and traced the scars from the wild man. *We must survive. I'll just remind him of what is required of us to survive.*

I wondered if Raina might help. Franky seemed to have an unhealthy fascination with her. But then, she was the only woman on Earth, had been for some time. I suppose that made her an interesting novelty. On the other hand, there was a strong possibility that expecting such an *un*reasonable woman to help Franky see reason would be disastrous.

"Remember the evanesced," the posters had said. When there had been more people in Sanctius, stories circulated about the evanesced. After people had disappeared, loved ones swore they saw their shadows or received messages. It baffled me how such an intelligent race could get wrapped up in such emotional fairy tales and ghost stories. I remember feeling like I was the only sensible person left on Earth. It was a little too true, being left with Franky and Raina. I growled again. *Those two.* I took my frustrations out on the accelerator. The steam cart zipped around the city at my command. The smooth-cycling steam engine and responsive steering felt like an affirmation of everything I knew to be true. It was fluid, like the eternal ticking of a perfectly made watch, like surviving indefinitely by following the Council's edicts.

Cause. Effect.

Advance. Endure.

The engine tower in our quarter roared, tall and proud on the next block. For the first time, I noticed that one of the engines near the top sat unmoved. I wondered what was wrong. Franky usually kept everything well-greased and running smoothly. Dozens of engine floors still chugged merrily along below it. I was consoled.

Bells rang loudly at all the ampgas stations, and the thought of one quiet tower engine fled my mind. Only two blocks to the nearest one. There, I pulled the slim cart over, parked neatly along the sidewalk, and walked up to the nearest booth. When I pulled the chain, I heard the mechanisms move inside, but nothing came except a weak puff of steam. *Empty.* I threw the mask downward, but of course, it didn't satisfy me by hitting the pavement. The mask bounced on its hose until it dangled below the machine. The bell rang at that booth, and the turn was up. I proceeded to the second machine in line. Relief flooded my body as amplified steam filled my lungs. Every minuscule vaporized crystal whispered reassurance. *Go get Franky back.*

Behind the wheel of the steam cart, air rushed over the short windshield and blew my train of thought off-track in the best way. I focused on gathering deep breaths from the rush of city air blasting towards me. The air mingled with the lingering ampgas; Sanctius City intoxicated me. Man-made wind was the best kind. No cliff to climb or risk of sea monsters snatching you under. Just me, creating my own breeze with fine engineering responding to my every move.

Nature wasn't like that. Nature was unpredictable. It's the reason horses were outlawed on Sanctius roads nearly a century ago. Steam cars don't kick. Or fall. They don't even get hungry since the advent of the magnifying tank and closed water system. Steam and sunlight were free, abundant resources for humanity to capture and utilize. Even my garden and greenhouse, growing under perfectly monitored conditions, fell victim to pests and diseases. Unlike gardens and horses, steam engines were impregnable.

Well, very nearly so. I pushed off the remembrance of the silent floor in the steam tower and focused on the gentle tick of my pocket watch against my rib cage. I slowed, cut through a garage, and turned down the next street. The dormant sections of the city provided ample driving space until darkness fell, until I dared venture into the edge of the forest. Tower after tower flashed by, shorter near the sea and taller as I zipped through the outer, newer areas of Sanctius City.

Slowly, the daylight faded. I abandoned the steam cart along a random street and resituated my crossbow and my hat.

Oh, the edge of town—the delineation between order and chaos. I loathed to leave. I drew a few last breaths of wonderful city air and trudged on along the Borderlands.

Following the city limits around the Hungry Mountain was the best way to access my hunting spots. It had taken time, but I learned to ignore the dilapidated remains of Borderland homes on the left side of the trail. The mountain to my right offered plenty to look at—a variegated blanket of greens with ivory-tan cliffs stabbing through its lush fabric. I glanced despairingly at the star cliffs, remembering the posters. *Tomorrow. Tomorrow, I have to remind him of the reasons men like his father set edicts about these things, for our survival.*

The weight of concern for my friend, my only option for companionship, fell heavier with each step. The Council had released pamphlets on optimal inter-human relationships: practical marriage pairings, proselytization of Citizenship through the family unit, survival accountability. Humans had significantly higher survival rates when paired with a survival buddy, as people called them.

I stole another glance at the cliffs and stopped dead in my tracks. Through the dusky sky, I barely glimpsed the circumference of Raina's tight curls behind the ledge. *She's just lying there star-watching, that irresponsible—*

There was movement. Raina stood.

And then so did Franky. He turned a crank attached to something in front of them. She pointed toward the first visible star of the evening. I stared at their silhouettes in the last moments of twilight. They leaned close together as they gazed upward. It was more than I could bear.

* * *

Alternately stomping and dragging my feet, I trudged hastily away from the cliffs. *How selfish of them! They think nothing of following the dangerous path of so many rebels before them, as if they're exempt from consequences. It's only a matter of time before they disappear, just like the rest, before their debased actions lead them right into the mouth of this monster-infested mountain.* My feet flung wildly out in front of one another, like pistons in an engine under high steam. Then, my left foot landed with a splash in a tiny brook, and my stomach cinched tight.

The familiar path I had carved parallel to the perimeter of the city didn't cross any water of any size. No, this was a strange place. A vague and dark memory from long ago sent my heart into my throat. Since moving to Sanctius, I had only ever walked as far as the trail paralleled the River Umbra, until the river turned north toward its source high on the Hungry Mountain. Along the lower river, I was sure to find game of some kind—usually a deer or a fowl. There was no need to venture farther. This place… this was eerily unfamiliar. In my anger, I had stomped myself into unknown territory.

First, I looked behind me. I thought that might be towards the east. There were no city lights there or anywhere else. Either I had walked so long that all the engines had shut down for the night, or I had gotten myself so deep into the forest that the city was completely obstructed. My heart thumped louder in my chest, unsettlingly faster than my pocket watch.

Don't panic.

I already am.

Stop. Panicking.

I wondered if I should call for help, hoping Franky would hear me. But the likelihood of drawing other unwanted company was too high. These mountains were known to swallow people up, never to be seen again. I couldn't risk it. For the moment, darkness hid my presence from whatever beasts lurked in the forest. I reminded myself that the evils of the wilderness were most active in the daylight. My best chance of survival was to lie low in the safety of the darkness and return using the first glimmers of dawn. But where to hide?

Filtered starlight and moonlight sifted through layers of forest. I waited while my eyes collected every little glint and attempted to form a picture of my surroundings. On all sides, ghoulish shapes hemmed me in. The canopy above threatened to crush any bit of courage I had left. *Not helping.* Worst of all, there was a darkness ahead and to the right that I couldn't make out no matter how hard my eyes searched. Cave or creature, I determined to stay away.

I carefully turned around and walked slowly away from the black hole, trying to feel the path ahead with every step. A branch snapped behind me, in the general direction of the blackness. All thought of the trail dissolved in that instant. I took off into the woods, running as fast as my eyes could discern a place for my foot to land.

Something was behind me. I knew it. I could have sworn I heard a voice in the distance.

I wanted to keep running, but my chest burned. My breath came in gasps. And for what? I didn't even know where I was going. I threw myself into a heap of ferns growing near the base of a tree. My dry throat choked me, and my ears searched the air over my panting for any type of sound. By the time my breathing calmed, I heard footsteps closing in. With a tree at my back and something closing in, I saw no means of escape. The ferns rustled, and I braced myself for whatever was coming. Something gently thumped onto the ground in front of me.

I waited.

Soft footsteps receded, but a small shadow remained. My hand shook. Even in the dark, I could see it tremble as I reached forward to feel whatever had appeared in my hiding place. It was hard. Inanimate. I settled down a little more. *A rock? No, more like a piece of bark.* The sides felt like a small log, a little taller than the width of my hand. But when I felt the top, it was hollowed out. A cool liquid sloshed when I patted it. I recoiled, and my eyes darted around the darkness.

"Franky?" I whispered into the forest. "Franky?" A little louder. But no one was there. Or at least no one answered.

I picked up the bark cup and felt inside. My fingers ran down a bumpy resin wall until my finger dipped into the liquid. Nothing happened. No burning or reaction. It was thin in consistency, like water. I sniffed my wet finger. No smell besides the musk of the damp ferns all around me. Still, I did not survive this long to be poisoned by… by what? Who would make such a crude vessel? Surely not a mountain troll. Whatever it was, if it wanted to kill me, why didn't it just do it while it had me cornered?

I set the cup down directly in front of my feet and drew my knees to my chest. They made a terrible pillow, but I resolved to wait out the night. *Just breathe.* But over and over, my thoughts strayed to the forest and the mysterious cup. What if there wasn't a giant troll or the wild man, but there were little gnomish *Tummàs* with their big ugly noses? The cup couldn't have materialized on its own. *You will survive. You have to. Breathe.*

I lifted my pocket watch to my ear. The forest was nearly silent. Only the occasional cracking stick or swishing of leaves threatened to distract me from the soothing tap of the second hand. If I really focused, I could hear the miniature moan of the gears turning and the springs giving way as the minutes and hours changed.

Though I often hunted all night under the cover of darkness, I grew drowsy from the stillness. The activity of hunting usually kept me on my toes. In and out of restless half-sleep, my choices haunted me in a revolving repetition.

You shouldn't ever have started hunting. You had your garden.

Something cracked off to my right. I bid my body to stay put, despite the desire to flee.

Franky used to be so much stronger and faster than I was. There had to be a reason. The garden wasn't cutting it. But if you hadn't affirmed his choice to be out here, none of this would have happened.

If only the provisions factory hadn't shut down. You should have stormed the Council tower and demanded a solution to this.

I couldn't! That would be anarchy—a sure path to imminent death. There was no other way. In the absence of city provisions, survival, safety, health—these are paramount. This aligns with the Council's will for mankind!

What mankind? Franky was stargazing with Raina. Maybe hunting would lead me to make the same mistakes they did. Someone has to stay faithful. It's not too late. I have to get back to the city.

I squeezed my eyes shut tighter and tried to rein in my thoughts.

Ergh, Franky! What trouble you're in! What a pain it will be to dig him out! This is all his fault.

Round and round my mind spun, like a crankshaft in a steam engine. First, the mysteries of the dark mountain pressed in around me, then the frustration of Franky and Raina ignoring sense would replace it. They made me want to explode. I tried to breathe, be rational, and count the seconds as they clucked faithfully like a mother hen in my ear.

Eventually, I spiraled into a nightmarish sleep. Monsters from the Council's posters and distorted tales from childhood days in the Borderlands hybridized in my dreams. Every creak and moan of the forest wove into my nightmares until a broken stick or a bird startled me awake. It continued like that, dozing off only to be awakened with my heart pounding just before a wild, fur-covered ghoul grabbed me in the dream.

Finally, the sun highlighted the horizon to the east, which I found to be behind me and to my left. I had come all the way around the mountain and headed toward the sea. If I had not turned around, it would only have taken another minute of running before I'd have fallen off the white cliffs into the deadly turquoise below. I shivered at the thought of it.

As I stepped out of the ferns, I tripped over something. *The cup.* I knelt and turned it over in my hand. Something didn't feel right, leaving the mysterious vessel there, so I took it with me northward and anticlockwise around the Hungry Mountain. With small jerks, I rolled the cup around in my hand a little at a time. The bark had an uncomfortable familiarity, like something long forgotten. In contrast to my smooth metallic world, the layers were jagged but somehow not painfully sharp. At the very least, I could show Franky that something was trying to lure me to be its dinner.

The approaching dawn shed scant traces of light on my trail. My eyes alternated between finding my next steps and searching for any sign of towers through the trees. I tried to ignore the cup and focus on getting home. Home, where my clean suite and my perfect garden waited for me, where iron and brass and right angles and order guarded me from that dreaded, wild Hungry Mountain.

TWO

Out of the dusky darkness, a towering white curtain materialized in front of me. I reached through the dim light to feel it. Rock. To my right, the base of the natural wall descended with the forest floor and continued downhill beyond my limited view. To my left, it rose with the mountain several arm-lengths and stopped. Straight above me, but out of my reach, the rock came to an abrupt plateau with the tops of the trees. I could have wandered through the darkness, trying to find a way around. Instead, I decided to risk being seen by whatever dangers lurked in the forest and wait atop the cliff for more light. I needed a better bearing on my location. Toward the back of the clifftop, the forest floor rose to meet the white stone, and I could climb up easily. As I neared it, I heard voices. Familiar ones.

I stood below the wall and listened for a while, just to be sure some kind of monster wasn't playing tricks on my ears.

Who else could it be? The whisper slithered seamlessly from the dark mountain into my thoughts.

I crept up toward the origination of the wall until I could silently pull myself on top of the cliff. Crouched where the clifftop met the mountain, I saw the silhouette, singular, of Raina and Franky near the edge of the cliff. He held her close, and they spoke too softly for me to hear. My throat swelled with dread as Franky leaned forward to kiss her.

I stood to confront them about their stupidity, but before the hot air ran over my vocal cords, I caught a few of Franky's words. It was apparent that he bade her farewell.

Why? Where could either of them go?

Raina stepped back but kept hold of Franky's hand. With her free hand, she retrieved her two best knives from her leather corset and handed them to him. Franky smiled wistfully as he took them.

"Are you nervous?" he asked.

"No, I trust the Wilderman. So do you, remember? Plus, I've watched people walk over it before. I'm not afraid of heights like you are," Raina teased.

"*I am not.* I just prefer a salty dip in the bay, that's all."

"Just a couple more weeks?"

"Max. He said that's all it would take. It kind of sounded like that's all he has. The clock is ticking." For the first time, Franky's gaze shifted from Raina to gaze out at the view, including Sanctius City.

"Quite literally with that one." Raina chuckled and shook her head the way she always did when my watch came up. Even so, she gazed sorrowfully at Franky in the growing light.

I laid a hand over my trusty timepiece, safe in my pocket. They hugged, and I crept silently closer.

"Until then, love," Franky's voice broke.

She leaned in and kissed him.

This is what comes from letting emotions control you! I breathed deeply to conquer the temptation rising hot in my chest. There was no use following their terrible example and letting anger—or any emotion—get the best of me.

"Until then," she broke away and finally replied. And with that, Raina dropped his hand and simply walked off the cliff.

"Raina! NO!" I leaped forward.

Only she didn't fall.

I saw her step off. But then she just… wasn't. She disappeared into thin air. No screams. No evidence she had fallen into any of the foliage below. It was as if the cliff or the sky or *something* had swallowed her whole. I searched the dim sky for a beast, wondering if the nightmare from the poster had snatched her.

"What are you thinking? Why did you just let her go? Franky! Why didn't you do something? You could have grabbed her or…?"

Franky's loud silence pulled my attention from the mountain below, where no body laid to bear witness.

Raina had evanesced.

I stared at him in shock, but he didn't look back at me. His eyes bored straight ahead through the empty sky as if he were watching a seabird fly off toward the horizon. I fell to my knees.

Two. There were only two of us.

Two of us to carry out the will of the Council.

One brotherhood of survival.

It seemed like ages we remained there. Franky lifted a hand in a small wave at the empty sky, and then his chin dropped to his chest. Had he gone mad? Still without speaking, he inhaled shakily and turned to pack up the stargazing machine. Tears rolled down his face as he passed me to walk down a clear patch down the side of the cliff opposite the side I'd come from.

"Let's go home," he said, but didn't wait for me to follow. I clambered down onto the trail, relieved to see the towers of Sanctius City rising above the trees down the mountain.

"Wait, Franky. Where did she go?"

Franky trudged on in silence, his feet tramping harder and faster as he descended.

"If you know something about the evanesced, then I think you owe me an explanation."

I breathed deeply to extinguish the anger burning in my gut.

"Franky," I said as calmly as possible. "Say something. Do you at least have some water? I'm so thirsty."

Franky kept stomping down the mountain but slid his canteen strap over his head. When he turned around to toss it to me, he froze. He sniffed back a generous dose of tears, snot and emotion before speaking.

"Didn't you drink that? Why would you be so thirsty?"

"Drink what? You know I never bring water on my short hunting trips. But then I usually don't have to run for my life either. The same trail, Franky. Every day. In and out. Until you two—" I growled to cap the impending eruption.

"Where did you get *that*?" He pointed toward the cup I'd forgotten in my hand.

"Oh yeah. Best I can figure, some dwarfish creature made it." I shrugged, pretending I hadn't been scared witless just an hour ago.

"Like forest sprites?" He didn't sound convinced. "Did you just trip over it in the middle of the woods?"

"Raina just evanesced, and you're worried about a cup?"

"Answer the question!" Franky's eyes could have bored through me.

"Sort of. I was hiding in a thick bunch of ferns, and it kind of… showed up. It was full, but I couldn't risk an unknown substance when I was already lost until sunup. It could have been poison, or sedative in nature, placed by something that wanted me for dinner. I almost ran off the white cliffs into the sea, Franky! I spilled it on my way out of the ferns."

"Wait. *Why* were you running?" Visible confusion contorted Franky's face.

I considered my words this time. Franky wouldn't like answering questions nearly as much as asking them. But he owed me some explanations about Raina. We had agreed to be faithful to the city edicts to survive together. And although Raina wasn't part of our brotherly pact, it went without saying that we should both do our part to prevent another loss.

I tried tactful honesty first. "Well, I was shocked to find that my only friend *on the Earth* had betrayed me."

Franky turned away and stomped down the trail. Perhaps I should have leaned further toward tact than honesty.

"I didn't betray you." He shook his head furiously.

"Oh! So abandoning all the ways that keep us alive, indulging your disgusting fantasies, risking Raina's life out here—none of that sounds like betrayal to you?"

Franky planted his feet and turned. I skidded to an abrupt stop, nearly running into him. Franky stuck a finger in my face, and his eyes flashed. Though he had always been less balanced than I, I had never seen that kind of intense… what was it? Anger? I probably should have been afraid, but I wasn't. I had lived in a civilized society. Emotions were insignificant bodily functions. I couldn't have cared less if he had sneezed. But then he spoke words like bullets through gritted teeth.

"Don't you ever tell me what I did or didn't do for Raina."

A cold sweat rippled from my head to my heels. I told myself I wasn't afraid of Franky's fierce indignation. I told myself I was simply appalled at the depth of his deviation from his Citizenship, a valid reaction.

This will be a much bigger challenge than you thought, but you can do anything you put your mind to. The affirmation seemed to materialize out of the shadowy forest. I repeated it to myself several times.

Franky proceeded toward the city. In the back of my mind, I wondered why. Why did I want to save him so badly? In earlier days, I would have reported such an individual so they could get proper treatment. But all the doctors had disappeared. I reasoned that I was allowed to want any human to survive this bewitched wilderness. And the Council obviously wasn't going to race in and save us. It was up to me.

We arrived on the wrong side of the River Umbra, and my eyes questioned Franky. He had the audacity to roll his eyes at my want of safe crossing. "Just follow this trail around the next bend and you'll find a log to cross on. And Nico…" He paused for a breath. "I'll bring the meat this time."

I hesitated to let him out of my sight. My eyes scanned the mountainside and then questioned him again. "How do I know you'll be there? You owe me some answers."

"I'll be there. I'll answer your questions; I promise. I just need a little time."

I peered into his eyes and considered whether he'd actually show up. They were rimmed with red and welling with tears, but void of any hint of betrayal. "You've got it, chap."

But after I turned, I couldn't help but grumble. "More time. You wouldn't need any time if you'd been hunting last night like you were supposed to."

Raina evanesced. She was gone forever, and there were no more women. The temptation to panic crept up, but I went through the same process I'd perfected as a schoolboy and tempered it down to anger, then to frustration. Finally, I tried to see it as one less complication. *See Franky, for every primitive feeling there is an advanced logic to subdue it.* My lips turned up at the successful remediation of my emotions.

FORTRESS OF METAL

Franky's directions proved good; a quarter mile down the trail there was a downed tree across the river. Thank goodness.

"Don't you ever feel like you've grown completely heartless?" A strange, low voice asked on the breeze. I froze with one foot on the log suspended over the river. My eyes alone moved to scan the forest, and my ears listened for the smallest movement.

Nothing.

Who said that? I didn't dare ask it aloud, only wondered it. I mounted the log and began to cross the river when the voice rumbled again.

"If you want to know, then why do you run?" The voice answered my silent thought. Visions of hairy wild men and rocky trolls exercising mindspeak over unsuspecting victims made me shudder. I hurriedly put one foot in front of the other.

Don't panic. It was no good. My heart raced. My legs shook. I fell into the shallow river with a small splash and a dull thud on the bottom. The viciously cold water felt like a thousand daggers. Pictures of water sprites attacking my leg sent my heart into my throat. I clambered up, waded through the thigh-deep water, and ran for it. It wasn't until the brush leveled and I neared the pavement that I dared look back.

The sun had risen high enough to reveal the full eeriness of the forest. Shadows lingered everywhere. Branches moved of their own accord. My eyes darted back and forth, searching for the source of the voice. The cold-steam smell of the engines firing up for the day drew my steps backward into the city.

I turned and ran to the nearest vehicle, a steam wagon large enough for a group of six, and slammed the heavy metal door behind me. When I jammed it into drive, a sickening grinding answered, and the tank pressure rose. I returned the stick to neutral, but the rasping sound didn't change, so I stepped out and inspected the undercarriage. Vines threaded through every nook and cranny of the exposed drivetrain. Once the wagon's gears tried to engage, moving parts had seized in some places. Pressure continued to rise in the closed boiler system, so I ran to the front and hit the emergency shut-off switch.

"Simmer down now," I consoled the wagon as steam came pouring out of a direct exhaust valve on the thick glass boiler tank. "Plucky wilderness."

I walked the block searching for another vehicle. Creeping evergreens had made their way to the next several cars. They probably would have run fine, but I was done fighting with the forest for the day. Four-seater steam cars were a harpie a dozen, and I quickly found one to take me home without incident.

The engine tower crescendoed to life, and with it, the buildings closest. When I parked across the street from my tower, it powered up for the day, signaling my paranoia to shut down. My breath slowed to match the rhythmic rumble of chains and turning drivetrains under the city. The banners dropped down the sides of every building uptown, reminding me of all the Council's research and generations of collected and sifted learning. The ampgas bells rang, and I filled my lungs with gaseous reassurance.

By the time I pressed the penthouse button on the elevator, I chuckled at myself. The wilderness played tricks on my mind. *What a fool! My emotions sucked me in just like the ones who ended up evanescing.* My smile fell. *Like Raina.*

I repeated affirmations of safety and order to myself while the glass elevator rose past all eighty-four floors. I gazed out over Sanctius and the wilderness beyond. The view wiped away the fog in my mind and whispered fresh perspective. There was no doubt that the mountain was dangerous, as were the sea, the river, and the heights surrounding Sanctius. Was there really some kind of troll or gnome chasing me? Reading my mind?

The elevator doors opened into my patio, and I chided myself for doubting. Of course, I was being chased. The Sanctius City Council was the most reliable source of information in the world. They had done extensive research. If they warned us to stay inside the city, then the dangers were real. And just like they said would happen, my emotions became unreasonable. That's why they warned us so strongly to remain safely inside the city. Such wisdom might have even led them to some higher plane of existence. Their banners still reminded us every day to stay the course. Such care! And look what Franky's done in response.

Inside, I put my shoes and hat where they belonged, near the hall tree. What a relief to be in my flat! I emptied my hands and set my satchel on the counter so I could remove some weapons and my jacket. And then there it was—the cup. A real, physical cup made of wood and lined with pine resin sat on my counter. I paced through the kitchen and considered its origin. *Maybe I stumbled upon an ancient artifact.* I shook my head. *Full of water? Numbskull.*

I couldn't make sense of it just then, so I opted for a shower to clear my head. When I shut the water off, I heard a voice, so I finished dressing before I wandered out. Franky stood at the counter, rolling the strange cup in his hands.

"Who are you talking to, Franky?"

He stared at the cup for a moment before answering. "Old habits, you know?" He looked up and gazed out the patio doors. The long silences between us were already awkward and annoying. All his answers were vague and worrisome.

"Where is this meat you claimed you'd bring?"

"Oh yes, right here."

Franky walked around the kitchen island and raised up a hindquarter of venison and two strips of tender meat from along the spine.

"How did you have time to kill and cut up an entire deer?"

Franky smiled and sliced into the backstraps. "You must have dilly-dallied. Plus, you always take long showers. Like a woman." He clearly meant it as a joke, but his countenance fell again. There were no more women.

Best to take this head-on if I'm going to save him.

"How long have you known we were losing Raina?"

At the word we, Franky's shoulders tensed. He leaned his head to both sides to pop his neck before answering. "It's been coming. Probably at least a year." Tears welled up in his eyes.

"That long? Wow," I softened my voice. "It seems like you've been trying to save her from this end for a long time. It was incredibly brave of you and must have been very difficult."

He set the backstraps aside and hunted for a better knife to piece out the hindquarter. Oddly enough, he glanced at me and then picked my favorite knife. Though the rule that the knife was reserved for me was unspoken, Franky knew it well enough. Yet there he was, cutting out a roast with it. *What has possessed him?*

I cleared my throat. "I've been pretty concerned about you for a while. I'm sorry she's gone, but I'll be glad to have you back. Just a couple of guys living a right good city life, eh?" I presented a smile as a peace offering.

Franky laughed with menacing bitterness. "You really think you're sorry, don't you?"

"Of course I'm sorry."

"For what? How could you be? You aren't a victim of such 'primitive emotions'."

"You think I'm happy that we're the only two people left here? We have the honor and responsibility of living, Franky, of surviving. You and I will continue on in a civilized manner and live the rest of our days in the safe and perfect life only Sanctius City provides. We may even be able to make a new start for humanity in Sanctius, if we can get the Human Life Tower running. It's quite a disappointment that Raina gave up her chance at that."

"A disappointment?" Franky closed his eyes, and air whistled through his gritted teeth. "How terrible for you."

"It seems like maybe you went a little too far trying to save Raina.

Give it a couple of weeks back in the city. I'll go hunting for both of us. You'll feel better soon enough."

I patted him on the back, but Franky hadn't opened his eyes yet. He stood there, seething for a few more breaths, then mumbled, "I can't do this."

"Sure you can. I'll help."

Did he just roll his eyes at me? It's like I'm dealing with a child.

"What happened to *you* last night?" Franky proceeded to throw unseasoned venison loin onto a hot skillet. I tried to ignore his lack of culinary artistry. He'd had a rough morning after all.

"I didn't understand that your… situation… stemmed from trying to help Raina survive. When I saw you both up at the star cliffs, I just felt… well… I thought you were betraying me. I thought you were both abandoning me, leaving me to follow the edicts, to survive alone. I guess I just stomped off into the woods and got off my normal trail. That witchy forest must have played tricks on my mind. I'm ashamed of how I reacted. Between that infernal mountain and those blasted emotions, I deserve to be mocked for how hypocritical that was."

"Let me get this straight. You show up at the cliffs in total panic and act like you're dying of thirst. And now you're saying it was nothing." Franky rubbed his brow as his head swung back and forth.

"Yeah, well, not nothing. But no reason to let my emotions get the best of me. A prime example of why we need to remember how far humanity has come; our survival depends on keeping our feelings in check."

"If it's so insignificant, how do you explain that?" Franky casually pointed at the bark cup.

"Psh!" I waved it off, expecting an excuse to come shortly. But it didn't. "I suppose you have a theory."

"No. I know precisely where it came from."

I looked at him incredulously and waited.

Franky flipped the meat over in the skillet and threw some salt and pepper on it, trying my patience before answering. "The Wilderman gave it to you."

"I thought you didn't believe the so-called myths the Council warned us about. 'Nothing to fear,' you said. What's going on with you?"

"Don't forget that I'm the well-trained son of a Councilman, groomed to take his place. At first, I believed every word they taught me. Then, as I learned to distrust my father and his associates, I thought it was all mumbo-jumbo, but of course, I couldn't admit it to anyone but you. By the time my father stopped speaking to me, I knew better. I knew it *was* real. It's all real. We were just on the wrong side of it."

"How can you make a complete U-turn and say that so assuredly?"

"I've seen the Wilderman."

I narrowed my eyes at him. "Were you scared?" I tested him.

His lips and eyebrows reached for each other thoughtfully. "Sort of." He nodded. "But not in the way I thought I would be."

"I guess you'll tell me you've seen mountain trolls, too."

"I've seen mountains *move*, Nico."

"Have you seen them eat people?"

"It only seems like it."

"Then how did *you* live to tell the tale? No one else seems to have escaped. And Raina—"

"Let's just…." he paused to modify the decibels of his voice. "…leave Raina out of it for now."

"Fine. What makes *you* so special, then?"

"Nothing. I can't be the only one. We wouldn't have the tales if people hadn't lived to tell them."

"How did you escape then? If Raina got swiped, why didn't—"

Franky growled and set a plate full of meat—just meat, not even one side dish—down hard in front of me. At least he'd taken the trouble to put a pinch of salt on the steaks.

"Fine. How did you brave the monsters out in the wilderness, even the Wilderman himself, and return to Sanctius?"

"Because so far, I've chosen to—mostly for your sake. The Wilderman is terrifying, but he doesn't want to kill me."

"What makes you think that? Why would you be terrified if he meant no harm?" I thought I had him there.

"He told me so. I didn't say I was terrified. I said *he* was terrifying. There's a difference."

I shook my head to clear the cloud of confusion forming there. One thing at a time. "And you believe him? *And* you were dumb enough to stay around long enough for him to tell you that? Even though somehow no one else who's done so is alive anymore? Hmm, makes a lot of sense, Franky. Thanks for this educational first-hand account."

"Of course you don't believe me." He threw his head back in frustration. "The things I do for you, and you just don't get it."

"I think the witchcraft that *really is* out there has played tricks on your mind, and it would be best if you took it easy at home for now. Where are you camped out right now?"

Franky chewed his lip for a moment before he answered. "The brick high-rise across from the port in the old town."

Raina's domain. "Let me guess, fourth floor?" There were no operational engine towers in that area of the city, nearest the sea. Raina used an old emergency ladder system to access her latest flat through a window.

"Sixth. I liked to keep an eye out for her."

Raina didn't need someone to look after her. She was the most independent woman I'd ever met. The simple honesty with which he said it, though, diminished my criticism for the moment. "Here. Grab a plate and take some of this with you."

"I'm not hungry."

"Then why did you cook it?"

"Because I said I would."

I watched Franky situate his tweed cap over his overgrown hair and get ready to leave. I evaluated whether the time had come to take drastic action, but he seemed so broken by Raina's disappearance that I stayed my hand. He'd probably just go home and get some rest, maybe even wake up with his head on a little straighter. I decided to give him time. Then we could chat over *properly* cooked venison.

"I'll roast the rest and bring it to your place tomorrow. I still have some questions, and we need to make a game plan moving forward."

The transparent elevator doors closed behind him, and I ruminated over the conversation. *I'm gonna rescue this steak from being a tedious eating experience and then form a plan to help rescue* him *back to normalcy.* I had come to know that Franky had a tenderheartedness to him. He used to hide it behind humor and his jocular way of approaching life. Anymore, his kindness seemed to be covered in introspection and irritation.

The research about emotions was correct. His romantic involvement with Raina led him to be vulnerable to the threats of the wilderness, especially the psychological threats. At least he hadn't gone totally mad, but it was unimaginable that he had witnessed the evils of the wilderness and didn't understand the risks. It was insanity to believe that the Wilderman might be some kind of benevolent monster. My eyes darted to the cup on my counter. *There's no such thing as a benevolent monster.*

Was there? I retreated to my bedroom and retrieved Tino's scroll from my bedside. I flipped several layers back until I found the story I sought, a story of a gift from a monster.

Luminary Tale

THE BIRTH OF THE YOMISONS AND THE GIFT OF BLACKSMITHING

Listen, my son, and I will tell you how the pirate race of Yomisons, which we know as Omessons, was born from our fathers before us.

Long ago, the Northlands were covered in ice from the Yellow corner all the way to the Green corner of the Earth. Our fathers had not yet braved the icy sea, and everything was built with the divine knowledge and skills of the gods, for man was unable thus far to subdue the frigid North. The KingFather of the Aer set Yomi as Luminary over the Northlands, to watch over it for him and to guard our people when the appointed time came for their arrival. He and his sons dominated the land, and they ruled after him.

When the predetermined time came, our fathers gathered their families, their livestock, and their possessions into hide boats and crossed the ruthless sea. Some were lost—men, women, and children—to the thrashing waves and terrible sea dragons that lay in the deep.

By that time, Yomi had already betrayed the KingFather, he and seven of his brothers. And after Yomi claimed divine kingship of the icy North, many beings from the realms of Aer followed in his rebellious ways. These became the terrible creatures of shadow and abyss. But Yomi was eager to rule over our people and claim them as his own, so he distracted the sea dragons so our people could land safely on his shores. Then he subdued the beasts of the shadow so our people could settle there. They saw him as a benevolent god-king. And they worshipped him.

It wasn't long after our forefathers settled near the sea when they found that Yomi ruled over the North with an iron fist. They avoided his displeasure, even sacrificing large portions of the fish they drew from the sea. Even so, Yomi's sons, roguish giants of rock and ice called the *glacnyr*, often disrupted life for the people.

The glacnyr were childish—throwing boulders into the villages and camps of the people and stealing their supplies and rustic weapons at night. Their mischief grew steadily more violent. This is why our grandparents told stories to make the children scared of going out at night, because the glacnyr were afraid of the sun and played all their destructive foolishness after sundown. And still, Yomi and his sons took more and more wives from among the people. The Northlands grew quite full of both mankind and hybrid scions of the Aer Realm.

Then, the Luminary Batai from the Yellow corner of the world heard rumors that the Northlands were melting and becoming habitable. He gathered his armies of man and phantom-like beasts to overtake Yomi. The ravens, friends of Yomi since the dividing of the Earth, brought rumors of invasion to him. He was furious; the land had been given to him by the KingFather. Although he had betrayed the KingFather, Yomi held fast to his allotment and controlled the Northlands with a possessive spirit. So, he devised a plan.

Though the Luminaries had agreed to withhold the knowledge of advanced metallurgy from mankind, Yomi traded divine knowledge of the mixing of metals with the men in exchange for their loyalty. He was not the only god to betray that agreement, but he was the first. And eventually, the Omessons became feared across all the eight corners of the Earth.

Yomi chose two men who were bright and strong—two whom he called sons. He taught them to mix metals, a skill hallowed by the Luminaries. These two brought the art of smithing with alloys to the people. They made tools for cooking and sailing, but also mighty weapons and armor like the scales of a fish. Yomi scoffed as he waited for the invasions of other people. The men, with the help of the glacnyr, defended the land from Batai's soldiers and ghostly forces. Yomi was victorious, but it cost the lives of many men.

Most of the people were appalled by the bloodshed. After they secured the Northlands for themselves, they turned away from war. Large family groups, like our fathers before us, roamed peacefully with their flocks and herds until the permafrost rose from under the earth each year. Then, they joined the others who settled in villages near the sea to live on fish and preserved foods.

But there were still those who were intoxicated by victory in war. They were not content in the land. Along with their weaponry, Yomi imparted vast knowledge of the sea and magic to outwit her chaotic power. Yomi promised them valor in the afterlife for slaying many foes. They traveled far and wide from the Northlands to conquer and plunder all who stood in their way. No spoil was large enough, and no amount of violence satiated their bloodthirst. Yomi breathed in each evil act as an offering to himself. The people fled in fear before his namesake race of pirates.

Their power and number grew until they encroached on the armies of Ezek the Bull King of the East and the sacrificial armies of his Moon Goddess bride, Inna. When they found their might matched, they turned their gaze to the West. Soon after, the art of blacksmithing spread through all the Luminaries' principalities, and Yomi no longer held an advantage. Yet he remained a bloodthirsty ruler for ages afterward. Even now, the name of the Omessons conjures thoughts of violence and the horrendous deeds committed by Yomi's armies to all who hear.

Still, others see Yomi as the giver of one of the greatest gifts to mankind—the mixing of metals for blacksmithing.

75

WHAT HAVE WE BECOME?

The aroma of garlic, rosemary and thyme wafted through the cracked patio doors. *If I can smell it, it's time to check it.* I had all but forgotten the food while I tended the plants in the greenhouse. I finished spraying the last of the plants and released the trigger on the spray nozzle. The rooftop water pump wound down as I replaced the hose. Another second to pinch back a couple of shoots on a pepper plant on my way in wouldn't hurt anything.

The roast was done to perfection. I used meat forks to maneuver it into my thermocylinder. After I set it on the bottom of the metal container, I added the vegetables and poured the juices over it. I buckled it, first the inner tin and then the outside layers of insulating fabric, closing the heat inside. I tucked my knives and guns into their homes in my holsters and pulled the long strap of my satchel and then the thermocylinder over my shoulder.

On the way down, I remembered the times when I hadn't armed myself to travel within the city. In those days, the city was a symphony. Layered over the rumble of steam engines and the ringing of the temple clock, there was the constant percussion of construction, the buzz of vehicles driving by, and the harmony of the entire Citizenry together. I felt safe in the menagerie of movement. It was divine.

Somehow, once the population dwindled, the wilderness crept

into the edges of the city, and I never left home without some method of defense. Whether Tino's scrolls held any truth beyond the monsters, that smoothly bustling city was nothing short of heavenly.

Besides my knives and guns, of course I brought my crossbow. There were occasional rumors about sea monsters slithering onto the docks and beaches on the east side of town. I never saw them. But then, I didn't often leave uptown except to hunt. I had no business by the sea. Franky spear-fished off the docks enough to satisfy my rare pescatarian cravings.

A peek at my watch told me I'd hit the streets just in time. I closed my eyes and waited for it. *Brrrring!* Dispensing time. I crossed the street to a familiar station and traded my bowler hat for the mask. How many times had I used this same machine and satisfied my cravings from the same block of ampgas under the street? *I'll never tire of this feeling.* The bell rang. I slipped an extra whiff or two in before dropping the mask and turning to leave. I was a moment late to start, after all. It was only right.

I looked left and right for a vehicle. I was ready to do anything to break the hypnosis Franky was under, but carrying a giant-sized flask full of dinner across the city was unnecessary, even downhill. Most importantly, there was no sense in showing up with a lukewarm roast.

A Dan-Doyce luxury convertible with a long, curvaceous front end caught my eye. I set the thermocylinder and my hat on the passenger seat and got in. After yesterday's fiasco, I shifted the steam engine into drive and waited. Everything seemed to be in working order.

The rumble of idling steam cars followed me downhill, but the relative silence still unnerved me as the distance to the uptown steam tower grew. My free foot tapped anxiously along with each new building as it passed. They slowly changed from iron javelins piercing the sky to squat brick buildings mostly hidden by modern steel facades. Fifty stories. Twenty stories. Tiny ten-story buildings. My eighty-four-floor tower, one of the smaller cloud-high feats of engineering uptown, dwarfed the squarish tops and Gothic rooflines downtown.

I slowed by the Time Temple. The Time Tower—it used to be called. It had been an ancient cathedral. As mankind fought to outgrow its primitive philosophies, first one group and then another would claim the structure and build onto it. A conglomeration of different roof angles and cattywampus levels shot higher into the sky with each takeover. Finally, the Council filled the highest steeple with the biggest clock in the world. The masterpiece continued ticking, reminding us all of the power of invention, the power within mankind if we chose to reign ourselves.

And this is where it all began, I told myself, choosing to find something to appreciate about downtown. During one era of reason, air and water ships brought great minds together from all over the world to revolutionize steam power. This is where the steam tower was invented, where harnessing the power of the sun eradicated our need for other fuel sources.

It was also the first district to shut down. It had the oldest infrastructure and was farthest from the Council tower. The Eastern Sea claimed more lives than the star cliffs, the Hungry Mountain, and the crying rivers put together. The first engines had grown inefficient, anyway. It made sense for the City Council to abandon downtown for the more advanced towers, engines and factories. "Technology of the gods," they called it, hyperbole of course.

Along the downtown streets, salty air had corroded much of the exposed metal. Rusted red iron and green copper framed the roofs and windows. And yet, the temple clock pounded forward every second— the eternal steadiness of clockwork.

Grass had grown through the once-smooth streets. *How does Franky live with all of this?* Shrubs invaded the ground around the bases of most of the buildings, despite the abundance of gravel and boulders gracing the area. I shivered. *I must get him out of here.*

I parked in the alley behind Raina's old building. I refused to see it as Franky's place. With the tower in this area shut down, the fire escape had become the entryway. Ladder after landing, after decrepit ladder, I made my way to the sixth floor and knocked on the window.

"Room service!" I hollered through the cracked window. Inside, Franky trotted over and raised the window with a small smile.

"Hello, come in."

I handed him the thermocylinder and removed my hat to climb over the sill and duck inside. I had previously known Franky to be mostly migrant, but it was shockingly evident that he had been in that building longer than I'd thought. Art—old, new, framed, tacked—lined most of the walls from floor to ceiling. One windowless wall was lined with shelves full of scrolls sorted into square compartments. The sight smothered me. I tried to disguise my shock with humor.

"And here I thought you weren't one for reading." Even the tops of the shelves were crowded with sculptures of every kind.

"I knew it would be a bit much for you." Franky moved around the cluttered kitchen, through the small dining room to my right. I watched him gather clean plates and cups from various cupboards. He came out with his arms loaded and set a table covered with a patterned cloth. It actually looked quite nice. The dignified table, one of the few remaining evidences of his privileged upbringing, gave me great hope for restoring him. I ran my finger over the tablecloth. It was a faded maroon pattern on natural woven fiber. There were alternating bird-like creatures majestically combined with flourishes. It looked ages old.

Franky returned from the kitchen, arms spread wide under a platter. The vegetables were spread elegantly around the roasted version. "There's a gravy boat on the counter. Could you grab it for me? You'll have to try your best to ignore my mess."

I did try my best, but it didn't work. It wasn't even technically dirty. Everything was just… everywhere. Several cabinet doors hung open, revealing haphazard stacks of cups and bowls. Nothing matched. There were a dozen different colors and patterns of plates. My eyes roved over and under groups of pitchers and stacks of serving dishes, and then miraculously landed on the gravy boat.

"Ah, here it is."

We settled in, napkins on our laps, and dined. After a few pleasantries, I ventured to ask, "So, how long have you been collecting all of this?" I waved my hand across the room and ended at an unidentifiable collection of somethings piled in the corner of the dining room.

"About a year."

"Oh, wow. Where did you get it all? Just in empty houses?"

"Yeah, mostly." He eyed me, looking past his forkful of food. "I might have found a few… historical collections."

"You knave." I chuckled, and Franky joined me. *By the end of the evening, I should have a good handle on how far the guy has regressed into anarchy.*

"Look at this one I found yesterday." He handed me a sea-blue glass insulator, roughly the shape of a large woman, from the days when the world experimented with dangerous and inefficient forms of electricity. I rolled it around between my hands before it dawned on me.

"Wait. I thought you were going home to get some rest."

"I never said that. You just assumed that if I didn't want to eat, I must have wanted to sleep."

I tried to quickly replay the conversation in my head. "Well, where did you go? What mischief have you been up to since I saw you yesterday?" I tried to muster a sly smile.

"You don't want to know." Frank's eyes gazed at the apartment wall, but his mind was far beyond.

"Sure I do. Remember, we're in this together."

"Together, huh?" Madness sparked in Franky's eyes. "Then together we shall go!"

Franky stacked our plates into the sink. Mine wasn't even empty yet; he just took it. In the kitchen, he wound the tucked-away crank on the dumbwaiter pulley as fast as his hand could move. When his cube of cellar contents rose to eye level, he removed a bowl of raw meat and put the dinner platter, uncovered, in its place. He dumped the raw meat into the thermocylinder and buckled it shut. I followed his lead and readied to leave.

"It's awfully hot out. Where are we going with a bucket full of raw meat?"

Franky smiled wildly, swung both feet out the window and slid out without an answer.

Grabbing one of his many flasks from the open cupboard in which they were heaped, I filled it from a quarter cask of *grappa* in the cellar cube. *I have a feeling we'll be wanting some of this today.* Shaking my head and sighing deeply, I did Franky the favor of lowering the dumbwaiter back down to the building's basement. By the time I shut the cupboard door over the pulley crank, Franky was pacing when I joined him in the alley.

"This is me today," I said, pointing to the Dan-Doyce.
"Nice. I'm driving."
"Hey! I said this is *me* today."
"Yes, but you don't know where we're going."

BEAST-INFESTED WATERS

Franky dropped the thermocylinder full of meat in my lap, occasioning an involuntary grunt from me.

"You sure you don't want to nap in my perfectly cooled apartment and go out hunting later?" I asked. Franky's spontaneity always put me on edge. I thought a nice leisurely walk around my garden would have set me right, though, and maybe do him some good as well.

"No, thank you. I have another place for us to cool off. We'll go there first." He smiled.

"Well, I hope there's somewhere cool to put this meat. This thermocylinder won't do the trick forever."

"It'll serve our purposes just fine." Franky flashed that mad smile and stepped on the gas, sending my hat tumbling behind my seat. He tore out of the alley and turned left down the hill. I wondered what business we could have near the harbor. "I'm not going too fast for you, am I?" Franky nodded toward my hands, kneading the strap of the thermocylinder.

"I kind of thought we'd head uptown or something."

"Oh, you did, huh?"

Franky hit the brakes and turned left again, toward the north. He gunned it for a block and then repeated the left, pointing us west toward the towers of uptown.

"You keep saying you're with me, that we're in this together. But it doesn't really seem like you mean it." Franky kept clumsily turning the massive car left around the block like a madman.

He continued. "In fact, it kind of seems like you expect me to do things your way or get lost. *Literally*. You're going to have some choices to make here soon. So let's start small. If you're really with me, then come with me today. *I'm* going to enjoy my day. You used to do fun things with me, and I think it would do you a lot of good. But if you don't want to come, I can keep going uptown and drop you off at home. You'll have to wait until tomorrow to get the car back, though. I'm rather enjoying it."

"We used to have fun because you used to be satisfied with the ways of Sanctius City, the *right* ways."

"I have never been satisfied by Sanctius, and I don't believe you are either. You've just taken to their scrap like a steam balloon to the sky on a sunny day. I think a day off would do you some good. You know… fresh air, peace and quiet, gorgeous views… Make a decision. Coming or not?"

Franky didn't turn left at the west end of the block. He just continued straight uphill. Uptown.

It took me another whole block to decide. "No. Don't take me home." I sighed. If he was going to act insane, I should go with him and try to protect him from himself. And everything else.

Left. Left again. Back downhill.

"How do I know neither of us will disappear today? Like Raina?"

He stiffened, but answered. "Because we won't. Not today. We'll just tour the sights for now. Either you trust me or you don't."

I didn't. But I didn't say so. I held my head in my hands, though, trying to reformulate my plan.

"Look, I know things have been different between us lately. I just want to show you some of the reasons I don't see things the way you do anymore. Just for today, alright?"

"Alright." I nodded.

If you can keep him alive today, maybe you can contain him somewhere until the effects wear off.

Sometimes, I didn't know how I came up with such great ideas, but I needed to do some research. The Council's medical facilities had restored plenty of people to good Citizenship. They had to have records of how they treated patients who'd been outside of the city for too long. I cared about him. He'd see. I cared enough to ensure he survived, no matter what he thought.

"If the treatments were so successful, where are those people now?" A light breeze carried the low whisper to the back of my mind. I shook it off and looked at Franky. Had he heard anything? But his gaze was fixed toward the harbor area. Of course, he hadn't. Thoughts like these must be the kind of temptation that every Citizen battled before they left. I refused to give in.

Franky parked the car in the nearly empty lot by the harbor. To the left were the docks, and to our right were sandy beaches followed by rocky cliffs. The last thing I could see as I followed that curve to the south were the same giant white cliffs that could have thrown me to my death the night before last.

Franky told me to leave the container of food and led me down some steps on the quay. He plopped down on the blazing white sand. I was further shocked to see him untying his leather boots and piling his weapons onto his waistcoat.

"What are you doing?"

"Cooling off. You should too. You've complained about the heat enough."

"I have not. My only concern was for the meat."

"That and your air conditioning." Franky smirked. He removed his shirt and threw it over his revolver.

"Seriously, Franky, what in the eight corners of the world?"

"Things get terribly uncomfortable if your pants get wet and sandy." He laughed and added those to the pile as well.

"So you just plan to dive mostly naked into a beast-infested, killer sea for a pleasure swim?"

At this summary, Franky smiled with unparalleled exuberance. He shrugged and then ran toward the water as fast as the sand beneath his feet would allow.

"Franky!"

But it was too late. He ran in until the waves broke against his thighs, and then he dove in headfirst.

I scanned the surface of the water for danger, while my lunatic of a friend crashed into the waves and then let them carry him back in. Hardly pulling my eyes away from that task, I managed to make a rustic tripod out of driftwood. I dared be remiss in my guard duty for half a minute to lash three pieces together with a length of kelp. *Disgusting, but perfect.* I wound the knob on my crossbow. The gears in the weapon's inner workings turned and drew the string back to the ready position. I set the shaft of the bow on my tripod and tested it out. The weapon oscillated far enough left to right on the tripod to aim anywhere in the bay.

Sweat gathered on my face. The sun beat on my back. I shrugged off my jacket and waistcoat but left my undershirt as protection, knowing I'd be fried like caramelized onions in no time.

Wait, why isn't Franky burning? For the first time, I noticed how tan my friend's skin was. It definitely wasn't his first swim. Concern squeezed my throat.

"Come on! It's not dangerous! Believe me!" Franky yelled as he swiped salty water from his eyes.

His assurances fell flat.

"Yeah. I can see you've done this plenty."

Unfortunately, he wasn't my only tempter. Sweat burned my eyes. What I wouldn't have given for my hat out of the car. The sun pressured me with its blazing heat. Everything lured me to cool off, even for just a second in the breaking tides. Keeping my trigger hand on the crossbow, I checked my pocket watch, my only faithful friend. Nearly 2:00. *This is precisely why I stay home in the afternoons.* Well, that and…

To seal my resistance, several fins appeared to my far right. There were three roughly triangular fins. I estimated where the body of the sea serpent would lie below the water. I turned my crossbow on the makeshift tripod to get the creature in my sights, estimating where a fatal shot should land.

At my sudden movement, Franky looked around. Treading in deep water, he had to paddle to rotate his whole body. Finally, his head, which appeared creepily disconnected from his body through the distortion of the water, rotated on the surface so he could see where I aimed.

"Nico!" he yelled.

I glanced his way. Franky's eyes were wide in panic. "Don't worry! I'll make sure it doesn't reach you! If I don't kill it on the first shot, I'll fire more bolts to distract it. Just get yourself out of there!"

"Don't you dare shoot!"

"What?"

"They're harmless!"

"They? It—whatever—doesn't seem harmless! It's swimming straight toward you!"

"Just take my clothes and meet me at the docks."

"No! I'm not leaving you!"

"Ergh. You're so ridiculous." Franky swam quickly to shore with the lapping waves. "Put that bow down and stop being so dramatic." He grabbed his pile of clothes and weapons, stomped past me and ran up the steps forged in the wall. I looked from the fins to Franky and back. He jogged, though not with urgency, from the quay to the wooden docks where airships and waterships used to moor. He dropped to his stomach at the end of the docks. I let the tripod fall, carefully released the tension on my crossbow and trudged up the stairs to join him.

"Sometimes they come right up to me."

"They who?" My hand rested instinctively on my revolver. It seemed like Franky didn't have any useful instincts left because his hand hovered dangerously near the surface of the water. Before I could react, a dark gray missile flew out of the water, smacked Franky's hand and fell back into the water with hardly a splash.

"Franky!" I fell to my knees next to him. "Are you okay? Is your hand okay?"

He lay shaking on the dock. I waited for him to respond, but finally resorted to rolling him over to investigate. He was laughing hysterically.

"Franky!"

Through gasping laughs, he mocked me. "You're so serious! I just got high-fived by a dolphin, and you look ready to kill someone." His laughter slowly calmed to noisy sighs. And finally, a somber gaze out over the Eastern Sea. It was that far-off look he had when Raina evanesced.

He missed her.

"That thing is not a dolphin." I pointed to the blurry blue-black mass in the water, bringing him back to the issue at hand.

"Well, it's certainly not a monster."

So, the fins belonged to three separate creatures. That didn't mean they weren't dangerous. They bobbed ominously off the end of the dock. Their faces weren't pointed like the dolphins sketched in the scrolls in grade school. Blunt, rounded mouths hung slightly open and revealed narrow, sharp teeth. White scars criss-crossed their dark skin.

"I'm not so sure," I mumbled.

Franky reached toward them again, and I grabbed his hand just before they had the chance to bite him.

"Jeez! I was just going to pet one. Raina's gone, and now you're determined to cut off every source of joy I have left."

"Do you even know what they are?"

"Settle down. I told you; they're dolphins."

I eyed the ugly beasts with their rows of teeth. Their heads were almost as blunt as the end of a steam tank. The very tips, if you could call them that, looked deflated, as if they had run into something and squashed them. Their black eyes made their faces look like holes had been shot through leather. "That doesn't look like any dolphin I've ever seen."

"It's called a Risso's dolphin. You'd be proud of me. I researched it and found the name and a drawing in a scroll in the Time Temple. There's something like it in the tales from the North corner of the world called a beluga."

Buh-loo-guh? It sounded made up to me. Franky rose from the wooden deck and began to dress. He carried his shoes instead of donning them and tossed them behind the driver's seat of the luxury car.

"What other nonsense have you been reading? Fairy tales and ancient spiritualism?"

Franky deflected the question. "If you think dolphins are scary, you might regret your choice to come with me today. When I said we'll tour the sights, I meant *all* of them. The Council's warning posters might as well be holiday adverts as far as I'm concerned. But don't worry. I'll keep you safe."

You mean I'll keep you *safe.* Fairy tales and ancient spiritualism. There was a twinge in my gut at the thought of Tino's scroll. *I'm different,* I rationalized, as I recalled a song from one of Tino's folk tales, holding my crossbow close to my heart.

Luminary Tale
THE HYMN OF EZEK AND INNA

Nico, this one is weird. But it's also one of the oldest stories ever copied down. If I were you, I wouldn't read it out loud. It just feels wrong, like a spell or chant that could awaken some deep evil. But I need you to see them for what they are, brother.

Hymn of Ezek and Inna, **translated from the original text by Dr. Brian Scott**

When the celestial gods gifted men with their presence, there was none like Ezek. He ruled with his sacred weapons, and he killed all his opponents with his might.

Of all the star-children of all the Luminaries, none were as beautiful as Inna, and none could match the words of her tongue.

The wedding feast of Ezek has come! Prepare the goddess-bride. The blood and wine and honey poured like fountains, and the ceremony of the groom has come. Bring the sacrifices and spread the feast, for the bride has gone to her bridegroom.

Is there anyone to match the power of Ezek and his bride? (No, there is not!)

Is there anyone to challenge the power of Ezek and Inna? (No, there is not!)

Is there anyone greater than Inna and her groom? (No, there is not!)

There is no end to the reign of Inna. No one can conquer the strength of Ezek. The waters roared, and the rebels surged in from the outer kingdom.

Ezek trampled them like the mighty bull. Inna enchanted them with her moonlit song. And all the people revered them.

In their victory, they blessed the people! They made us a great people. (They have blessed us!)

With their divine powers, they transformed our city into a majestic sculpture. They diced up mountains and rearranged the Earth into powerful monuments.

With their divine wisdom, they wrote down our laws. They govern the people with mighty hands and comforting tongues.

With their divine knowledge, they gave us the power of fire. The lights of heaven brought us the magic of transfiguring rock and ore.

With their tools… (We are rich!)

With their vessels… (We are fattened!)

With their weapons…. (We have conquered!)

Who will conquer all the nations? (The servants of Ezek and Inna!)

Ezek and Inna be praised.

SHOOTING, STARS

Franky pointed the Dan-Doyce uphill and stepped on it. I breathed deeply as the svelte machine climbed toward home. The thick, humid air of Sanctius relieved some of the tension in my shoulders. Maybe I wouldn't have to be on such high alert during the rest of our excursion. Franky parked near my old, familiar trail along the edge of town. I pulled my watch from its home. I would have preferred to wait a few more hours if we were going to leave the city. At least the trail was familiar.

"Bring the meat," he said.

"Why? It's probably starting to spoil by now," I argued as I situated my hat.

"If I tell you, you'll chicken out. Just grab it and promise me you won't freak out. Maybe you'll finally get to use all that *emotional discipline* the city pounded into your head for something worthwhile." And he headed up the trail without me.

"No, I'll *endure*," I mumbled. "You're the one acting weak."

With my satchel and weapons, the thermocylinder added just enough bulk to my load that it was hard to catch up with Franky. On a different day, I might have asked him to carry something, especially since he was the one demanding the meat come along. At best, he'd harp on me to leave some of my things behind, which wasn't an option.

At worst, he could snap. That's the last thing I needed out here in broad daylight.

He disappeared, so I assumed he continued on my hunting path. Besides our recent sunrise tromp back to town after we lost Raina, I had avoided that cursed forest with the sun up ever since I'd run away to Sanctius.

I walked backward a few steps to gaze down at the shanties that made up my childhood community.

"Bless the day I left," I said as I turned my back to the cottages again and checked my timepiece. The sun would sink low in the west before too long. Then the Hungry Mountain would swallow up the blazing light, the land would finally cool off, and the risk of nefarious beings seeing us would decrease exponentially.

Intermittent trees blocked the sun every couple of steps, causing a flashing effect as I hiked. It was obnoxious to my eyes. My gaze naturally fell to the forest floor, sheltered beneath the brim of my hat, in want of relief.

A purple star caught my eye—one of many pastel flowers on a lacy vine growing up a half-fallen tree. As I gazed at the intricate yellow stamen inside the flower, it reminded me of my beloved garden at home. Oh, to have been in my garden at home instead of that cursed wilderness.

I'd tended grapes that grew up trellises like those purple stars climbed that tree. Except, unlike my well-managed garden, there was no one to tend this floral constellation. My daydream broke from that one flower, and my gaze flitted over the whole plant, then over the myriad sprawled throughout the forest. Where the purple stars ripened to seed heads, the stars faded—though one could hardly call it that—into shining white starbursts. It grew in gossamer abundance, using any willing trunk as a framework. Purple and silver stars as far as the eye could see.

Franky waited patiently on a rise in the trail ahead of me, smiling slightly. "It couldn't have been all bad, could it?" he asked when I caught up with him.

He spoke of my childhood. In the past, we'd both reminisced with critical sarcasm. But there was a gentleness in his voice that I'd never heard him use before. Was he manipulating me?

"Everything good is overshadowed by the danger my parents put me in and the things they hid from me, as if nothing could be good for me but *their* life."

Franky sighed and shook his head. "Maybe you could just try to remember some of the beautiful things? It could make this an unforgettable evening."

When he'd ensured I'd followed, he continued onward again and disappeared over a small hill. I gave the flowers—I think they were called clematis—one more look. Remember the beauty? It seemed like a slippery slope to me.

Howls and barks sounded ahead, and my blood ran cold, stopping me in my tracks. An instinct prodded me to unfreeze, and I ran a few steps back toward the city. More yips and baying reminded me that Franky was out there somewhere, and he needed me more than ever. Swinging my crossbow off my back, I nocked a bolt and wound the crank. Weapon poised, I crept quickly up the trail.

When I crested the hill, I should have been thankful that I'd found him. Hope was hard to muster, though, when I saw Franky surrounded by foxes. They were everywhere. One wouldn't have been frightening, but ginger and gray canines carpeted the forest floor. *Where do I even start?* The foxes leaped toward Franky, away and back at him again in anticipation. I relaxed my aim slightly, trying to take it all in and formulate a plan.

Surely, these little things hadn't released that deep, loud howl before. There had to be something else out here, and I needed to do something quickly. I scoured the forest around us, trying to spot what other creatures we might be up against. It seemed unlikely that a wolf would be there too, but then maybe the evil of the forest drew them to us. The boisterous howl sounded directly in front of me, and I hugged my ears to block the noise. Until I realized the source of the howl.

"FRANKY! Stop that madness!" I yelled over the racket.

He fell into maniacal laughter. My heart thumped loudly in my chest. *What is wrong with him?*

"Control yourself, man," I hissed.

His laughter decrescendoed, and he sounded nearly normal again, though a nutty smile ran from ear to ear. He motioned me toward him. "Here, bring me the food, you killjoy."

I lingered, watching as many foxes as I could keep eyes on, and turned around slowly so that we stood back-to-back. Without sudden movements, I slid the thermocylinder off my shoulder and set it behind me, next to Franky.

The fact that I was the only sane person on Earth, the only person who could bring Franky back to his clearheaded Citizen self, was the only thing that kept me from crossing the ever-close line into panic mode.

Franky used no caution. He haphazardly bent to open the thermocylinder. "Put that crossbow away. It would not do well to shoot one of these for no reason."

"No reason?" I eyed the pack closing in on us. When Franky unbuckled the thermocylinder, the foxes charged. I fired a bolt into the nearest one and reached for my revolver. All the foxes except the one I shot leaped into the nearest bushes, and a deer spooked from nearby.

"NO! Nico! Didn't I just tell you?" He sounded desperate. The bolt had pierced both hind legs, but didn't seem to have hit any vitals. The shot went through and through, meaning my bolt was lost somewhere in the dense foliage. Franky knelt and examined the fox, grumbling all the while.

"This is bad. He'll be upset, won't he? You poor thing... Maybe he'll understand that it was an accident. Well..." He looked at me, shaking with some kind of wretched emotion. "I guess it wasn't, but I never thought you would be so rash. Oh, Nico, don't you ever think? Or at least feel?"

The scattered creatures circled closer again.

"What are you rattling on about? You need to explain if you have a set of mysterious rules I have to play by! *You're* the one who taught me to hunt."

"But you can't just go shooting every living thing that crosses your path." Franky shook his head.

"You can't be mad at me for protecting you!"

"I don't need *you* to protect me. Just… take the poor thing and go sit over there." He motioned to a boulder out of the way.

"You want me to pick up that creature?"

He didn't explain further, just waited with eyebrows raised.

I obeyed, mostly because I felt like Franky bordered on instability. When I scooped up the fox, I expected a fight. Instead, it leaned into me. I grabbed a handful of leaves to line my lap before I sat down so he wouldn't bleed on my trousers.

For several minutes, I avoided looking at the rust-colored bundle. I watched Franky slice pieces of venison off for the foxes, though much more stoically than before. The foxes swarmed in front of him again, each trying to get a turn. Every fox who caught a piece darted to a secluded place with it.

Without thinking, I looked down at the fox in my lap. His eyes gazed helplessly back at me. I thought I saw emotion in his eyes—fear or pain—but I caught myself. *It's just a beast.* The forest had played tricks on me again. The magic was always at work, and the lingering light of day made it all the worse. I'd have to be on guard like never before until I could get back to the city, until I could get both of us off that bewitching mountain.

The mob dwindled, and finally Franky spoke as if to a queue of people. "Sorry, I'm all out." He dumped the juices on the ground, and a few foxes jumped and scratched at the decaying foliage that soaked it in. He smiled woefully and stared at nothing in particular, as if his memory replayed the times he'd come before. *I bet he brought Raina here.* But his smile fell when he turned to me.

"I thought the forest would… would snap you out of it."

"What do you mean?" I asked.

"It's different for everyone. I know you crave the beauty of the untamable places, or you wouldn't garden. I just thought, with how much you obsess over your plants, you'd come out here and remember what the city is missing, but… Never mind. Let's get where we're going. And at some point we'll have to explain…" He eyed the fox.

"Could you at least finish your sentences coherently, please?" I couldn't hide my frustration anymore. It almost seemed like he was *trying* to get me killed out there, like he tried to draw me into the same sorcery that eroded his senses.

"No more shooting anyone or anything. In fact, give me the crossbow."

"Absolutely not. Unless you think the Council is going to come down and see us safely back to the city. It's just us out here, Franky! Who could I possibly shoot?"

"Then give me the bolts."

Always evading questions. "Best I can do is put it on my back again."

Franky glared at me. "Fine. But from here on out, you are a spectator. You will not fire any weapons for any reason. We're going to the star cliffs, and you're going to see things that… well… I think you'll be scared. But I promise when the morning comes we'll go back to Sanctius."

"You want me to stay out here all night again?"

"Yes. In fact, I want you to help me keep watch. We'll go to the star cliffs. You can sleep for a few hours and then we'll switch."

"Why would I keep watch if I'm not allowed to shoot anything?"

"You ask a lot of questions for someone who knows everything." He started straight west up the mountain, deeper into the forest. "Bring the fox."

"Wait up! Even you said the mountains basically eat people. How do you know we won't get eaten?" I said as I trotted a few steps to catch up, cradling the little beast.

"Simple. The mountains 'consumed' those who chose to walk the paths through them. Same with the sea and stars, and even the rivers I've heard. Many people have gone. They never return except in shadows and dreams, calling us to where they are. Citizens said those people were swallowed. If you ask me, the most dangerous thing on this mountain is *you*." Franky stabbed his pointer finger toward me.

The psychological battle ahead of me would be monstrous. Years and years of eyewitness accounts said there were real dangers in the mountains. If the Council said to beware of mountain trolls and sea serpents, there had to be some kind of beasts out there. Plus, I had scars to prove it.

I had only to hold on to my wits and resist the spells the wilderness put over people. Then, after I got him safely home, I needed to find the holes in Franky's defenses amidst his weakened state of mind. If I could just reason with him, show him that his tales didn't add up, then I could quarantine him from all the wild places and their evil enchantments.

Franky hiked upward with determination, but I proceeded cautiously. When he was clear-headed, he knew the mountains swallowed people, no matter what wild stories he'd come up with to justify it since. I watched for suspicious movement around us, but also for caves and mine shafts from days gone by. Repeatedly, I felt eyes on me. Every time I turned suddenly, only long shadows whisked to and fro in the evening sun.

"Perfect timing." Frank threw the thermocylinder where the clifftop met the mountain, as if he'd just arrived home. The sun hid in the west, but the sea still sparkled in a warm palette of colors around the shadow of the mountain. "I never knew what she saw in this place until I came early one night."

I was surprised to hear him speak of Raina here in the place he'd seen her last, where we'd both seen her last. *His psyche must be a tangled mess of fantasy and reality.*

"Don't pity me, Nico. I'm not the one who needs it. Raina will be just fine."

My compassion must have shown on my face as I set the fox near his pack.

"Franky." I walked over and put my hand on his shoulder. "Raina's gone. And she's not coming back."

"You're right." His gaze fell. "She's not. None of the evanesced are."

"Exactly, chap. That's why you and me, we have to stick together."

Franky sighed and looked long into my eyes, so long that I fidgeted. "You're right," he said. "So as soon as the sun sets, you can sleep first and I'll keep watch. We'll finish this crazy day like we started, together."

We sat a few arm-lengths from the edge and waited for the sun to sink behind us.

"Hey, I forgot about this." I pulled the flask of grappa out of my satchel and handed it to Franky. While he took a swig, I checked my pocket watch in the fast-fading light. I watched the second hand make its faithful path around the ivory face. *Steady as time.* That's what I had to be. I wasn't going to let Franky forget why we were still alive. *One more night out here.* I soaked determination in with the view of the city. The last light bathed everything in a rose-gold hue.

"See? Isn't it amazing?" Frank sighed.

"Absolutely marvelous." I surveyed the silhouette of Sanctius City. "Everything we could ever want."

"Mmmmm." Franky exhaled as if he were enjoying a delicious spoonful of soup as he gazed at the mingling of sea and sky. The peach glow turned to magenta shadow and then an eerie blue as the sun disappeared for the day. Franky laid back. "More than we can ever imagine."

The darkness finally hid us from any more beasts, and I relaxed some. As much as I loathed being out there, ignoring the Council's edicts, it was neat to see the lights of the city from up high. Slowly though, the buildings blinked out, and the cars shut down. A wave of darkness crept from the harbor to uptown. Melancholy silence hung heavily in the air.

"Ah, now they come."

"Who?" I scanned the skies for flying monsters.

"Nah-ah. No shooting, remember? This time, it's their turn."

My breath quickened. I vowed to leave my crossbow on my back, but I would use my revolver if needed. I watched Franky for a clue, but he still stared straight up.

"See?" He pointed way back over his head, almost to the top of the mountain, and handed me the flask with his other hand. There, in the darkest part of the sky, a dot of fire drug itself through the indigo-black.

"A shooting star," he explained.

Or a fire-breathing dragon. I kept my opinion to myself.

"And here come the constellations. That will turn into a lion." He pointed vaguely upward; I had no idea at what. He moved his arm to a different patch of sky and traced a cross.

"That will turn into wings and a head and tail, a swan or a goose or something." Again, his pointed finger changed locations. "And that will turn into a king on a throne."

Every moment, another star or twenty appeared. They just seemed random and chaotic. I could have made more out of splattered paint.

"Well, if I ever decide to escape on an airship, I nominate you for navigator," I said jokingly, trying to keep the mood light. "How many of those star things do you know?"

"Only a handful. Raina knew so many, I wondered if there were any stars she *didn't* know."

"You speak of them as if they're people."

Franky chuckled. "Maybe they are, and they're calling us to join them in some empire in the skies. After all, where else would we escape on your hypothetical airship?"

The depth to which he was deceived weighed heavily on me, and I resumed plotting his extraction from it. Franky interrupted to continue sharing his delusion. I drank more from the flask, thinking it would be better than Franky adding alcohol to his current state.

"No, it's the ocean for me," he continued. "The smell, the animals, the magnitude of it. Whenever I'm away from the water, something's just not right with the world. Even though I can imagine every part of it, every scent and taste and the crash of the waves against my shins, I still get this ball in my stomach. I miss it. Almost the way I miss Raina."

"Unfettered emotions only bring grief."

"Imprisoned emotions only hide what's already in our hearts. You're lying to yourself," Franky responded calmly and matter-of-factly, not inviting argument.

The spirits added to the heaviness of my eyelids. Good thing Franky planned to take the first watch.

"Can you hear them?"

Some part of me remained conscious enough to respond. "Who?"

"The stars. Their songs are so beautiful."

But I was already too far gone to register his last words.

WORLDS COLLIDE

I dreamt I was lying face up, using my forearms as a pillow. I was in a strange, dry place. Glancing around, I saw a barren yellow-white desert that ended abruptly over a crashing sea. A bright moon reflected off the sand, and stars twinkled in the sky. In this desert dreamland, the constellations Franky had pointed out were clear to me. But to my dismay, they each moved in formation. First, the cross. Then, the swan suddenly flapped its wings and banked to swoop down toward me. Its eyes burned red, and it tucked its wings to attack with the greatest velocity.

Unable to move, I tried to cry out for help, but nothing came out. The lion constellation galloped forward and grew enormous as it approached until it leaped, mouth gaping, and consumed the bird. Then the lion lowered himself before the king on his throne. The king tilted his scepter toward the lion, who leaped at him. I winced, thinking the beast would consume the royal constellation. Instead, they collapsed into one ball of stars and careened into the desert. There, a fountain arose in the wasteland.

Stranded there, I lay on the rock, unable to think of anything but the parchedness of the place and the great distance to the fountain. The air itself seemed to leach the moisture from my body. *Why won't the sea just share some moisture with the air?* I thought in my dream state. My tongue swelled with thirst. I managed to move my fingers and toes. I would have to choose between two deaths: wet in the sloshing sea or shriveling up in that dry place. In the agonizing dream, I rolled to my side to try to get up. A shrubby plant accosted my hand. I ran my hands up the thin, woody stems and inhaled the fragrance—a young cypress. Nothing to relieve my desperate parchedness.

The scent made me aware of my breath. Inhale. Exhale. Inhale.

Somewhere far beyond the cypress and the desert, I heard voices—voices that debated my fate. They spoke of the city flattened and swallowed up by the mountains and the sea. Callously, two men discussed how I would make my exit from this life. The way Raina left? Into the crashing waves below me? I heard weeping. Looking around as best I could, neither the rugged landscape nor the vast, turbulent sea showed any sign of life. Who discussed my fate?

But I will survive. I know my way, and *I will go my own way*! Breathing in new determination, I smelled the cypress again.

Inhale. Exhale.

The weeping continued. And the voices. Desperation. Consolation. Exhaustion.

Inhale.

The scent of cypress pervaded my sleep. It was close. On the cliff. Not the cliff in the desert by the sea; on the Hungry Mountain.

I blinked my eyes open but found no light. I heard the low rumble of a man's voice and muffled crying. Groping the clifftop, I tried to find my bearings.

Finally, my eyes collected enough moonlight to make a picture of the star cliffs. I followed the sound of that strange voice. Strange, but not completely unfamiliar. The sound of Franky stifling tears came from the back of the cliff, closest to the mountain. I moved slowly and slightly to look. I made Franky out, but someone else held onto him.

Remain calm.

The fox at Franky's feet moved. *Surely he'd be dead by now.* But there he sat, gently waving his tail back and forth, looking up at Franky and his captor.

I would have to solve that mystery later. *Think, Nico. What's your plan?* Whatever held Franky hostage must have been some ghoulish creature of the wilderness. Without sudden movements, I moved a hand to my revolver. I feigned restless sleep to better position myself.

Franky faced away from me. The form behind him reminded me of a bear. All I could see were furry bulges, wider and taller than Franky. Time to act.

Slowly, slowly I maneuvered my shooting hand toward them.

Inhale. Exhale. And before the stubborn scent of cypress registered in my brain, I jumped up and yelled, "Don't move!"

Franky wheeled around and put his hands out toward me. "Nico, what are you doing? Don't. Shoot."

The fox slinked behind them both, hiding close to the cliff.

Though the beast had let go of Franky, he remained in the line of fire. I sidestepped around them, following the crescent edge of the cliff. When I reached the northernmost edge, where the cliff met the mountain, I used my peripherals to find the trail Franky had led me down only the day before.

"You're going to let Franky go. He's going to walk to me, and we're going to leave here. Any sudden movements and I'll shoot."

"And what makes you think that'll do any good, son?" Up close, his voice sounded like rolling thunder. Franky walked slowly towards me, and the form stepped out from behind him. The glint of its eyes shone out from the tower of hair and draped furs.

"Franky, run. I'll follow you."

"Nico, just wait a minute. Let me—" he said casually.

"I said, 'Run!'"

Unhurried, Franky bent to grab his things.

"What are you doing? Let's go!"

"You can't outrun him, Nico. At some point you'll have to confront reality."

"I'm *not* giving in, Franky. I won't. We're going to survive."

The entity started up with an odd huffing noise. As soon as Franky set foot on the trail, I leaped down too. When the monster was out of sight, I grabbed Franky's hand and dragged him onward. Behind us, the huffing grew until the thing bellowed with laughter. Chills ran down my arms.

"What *is* that thing?"

"He, Nico. *He* is the Wilderman."

"That's the Wilderman?" My tower flashed into my mind—my refuge. I had to get there. Even the first street in the city would do.

"We can make it. We have to make it," my voice fell to a whisper between breaths.

Franky ripped his hand from my grasp. "We'll make it if he wants us to make it. I'll come. Just stop dragging me!" We trotted down the mountain, letting gravity help us along. The sound of footsteps echoed the thumping of my heart.

"You should have apologized, you know." Franky trotted behind me.

"Excuse my lack of manners, Franky. I'm only trying to save your life."

"No, for shooting his fox."

"*His...* fox?" My breath came in sharp gasps from our hurried pace. Maybe Franky ran out of air too, because he didn't answer.

We came to the River Umbra, and I screeched to a halt. Franky had dragged me to see nearly everything that the Council had warned us about, only proving to me that he was going insane and the Council was right all along. *So what about the nymphs and water sprites in the rivers and streams?* Franky didn't hesitate. He just plunged in and trudged across.

I wanted to close my eyes for fear of yet another frightening encounter. But walking works best with some amount of sight. In the limited light of early morning, I stepped into the shadowy creek. The frigid water grabbed at my pant legs and pulled me downwards. My pulse raced, and I did my best to hurry through. I stumbled up the bank and tripped over my soggy feet until I caught up with Franky. He waited where the uneven ground transitioned to the hard, paved border of Sanctius. *Safety.*

I jogged ahead of him, but he didn't follow. I turned to see Franky looking back across the creek, staring at the Wilderman, who stood amongst the rustling trees. He was like a man, but covered in skins and furs from shoulder to shoe. In a flood of moonlight between the trees, I saw a weathered face behind a graying beard. Thick eyebrows knitted together, sending wrinkles from the bridge of his nose up his forehead until they disappeared under a dark wool hat. But under those eyebrows, his eyes—eyes that penetrated the soul. Eyes that penetrated *my* soul.

I felt like that steam car from yesterday morning, as if vines crept around my body and tightened around my chest. Could this be one of the malicious gods from Tino's scroll? *Don't be silly.* I tried unsuccessfully to wrench my gaze away. The effort left me shaking.

When Franky saw that the Wilderman's stare held me fast, his head wagged slowly from the monster to me and back.

"Franky," my voice scraped.

"Nico, he can help you. If you'd just—"

"Franky, save me." I struggled to breathe, but I couldn't tear my eyes away.

"Can't you see I've been trying? The Wilderman is the—"

"Make it stop!"

Franky looked at the Wilderman but didn't say a word on my behalf.

"Well, which way you headed?" Though he didn't look away, the Wilderman's question was clearly directed at Franky.

"I—" he stammered. "I think I'll go with him."

The Wilderman nodded and grunted. "You're almost out of time. You'll know when, though."

Then the Wilderman spoke to me. "You too. Even your precious temple clock is 'bout out of time."

I mentally prepared myself to draw my gun as swiftly as possible, but as soon as Franky stepped foot safely within city limits, the Wilderman dissolved into the forest.

That evening, the peace of the city didn't settle me right away. My eyes darted from shadow to shadow. One block in, I was alarmed to find that the flora from the edge of the creek had somehow seized more vehicles already. The sidewalks cracked anew, and scraggly weeds forced their way through. I quickened my pace.

Block after block, the predawn light outlined the clean silhouettes of the towers. Their massive strength prompted me to tame my fears. I breathed deeper with each step and stepped livelier with each breath.

You're safe at last.

Franky dragged his feet through the middle of the street with his head down, eyes far away in thought. I backtracked and slowed to his pace, waiting for the sun to breach the horizon and wake the city. As soon as the engine tower roared to life, I directed us toward my tower.

"Come on. Let's get you a bite to eat and some sleep."

When we stepped out of the elevator, I was disappointed to realize that I'd left my hat on the starry cliffs. In my rush to get Franky out of there, I never even thought about it. I supposed a hat was a worthwhile trade for Franky's life.

After getting a few fresh things from the garden, Franky settled on my couch with deep sighs and shaky mumbling. I lay awake in bed, unable to sleep. What was the Wilderman? I thought of my brother, Valentino. Was he on to something? Was he warning me that the Wilderman was something like the ancient entities in his tales? My restless mind sought answers in the leaves of his scroll.

Luminary Tale
RAMI AND THE ANAGARR

In the far Blue corner of the world, some of the gods descended from the five highest mountains of the Blue jungles. Originally, they impressed the people in the villages tucked within the jungle, over whom they towered, nearly twice their height. With their sorcery, the gods from the heavens controlled the beasts of the jungle. The shapeshifters among them dazzled the people, roaming about as majestic and powerful serpentine creatures. The people honored the Luminaries as the sons of Rajdayamnech, their high god. They called them the *anagarr*.

The anagarr became powerful in the land. The people built temples, offered sacrifices and formed intricate statues and carvings in their honor. The anagarr taught the people of the jungle advanced stone-working so that they might be venerated with long-lasting monuments. A few of the most prominent anagarr slowly rose above the others in honor and power. Of course, the others were displeased, and tensions rose. The Luminaries required sacrifices in higher numbers and of greater value to increase their prestige in the land. They demanded that the local villagers battle against those who served any other anagarr. In this way, they turned all the people in the Blue jungle against one another. War and strife consumed them until the number of people dwindled.

At that time, there was a faithful priest of the god Rajdayamnech who lived high in the mountains. His name was Bundit. When he had fasted and meditated for many days, he had a vision. He walked many miles to a place where several villages fought for their Luminaries. He interrupted their warring to deliver his vision.

Bundit called for all to hear. And seeing his holy garb and his utter exhaustion, everyone quieted. In his vision, Rajdayamnech declared the anagarr were no longer welcome in the Blue jungle. Though the anagarr could have lived peacefully among men, even as chiefs among men, they acted wickedly, and Rajdayamnech could not allow it. He would imprison them under the sea, *except* when men were wicked. Then, he would release an anagarr to poison the life of a wicked person until they changed or succumbed to evil.

Now the anagarr had lived long above the Earth. There were those who doubted that Rajdayamnech or any other being was strong enough to imprison them. Others feared. Some waited anxiously for their punishment. A few ran away.

There, in the Blue corner, not far from the mainland, there were five islands spaced like stepping stones in the Western Sea. Upon hearing the prophecy of Bundit, a few of the anagarr took some of their loyal subjects by raft to the far islands. The chief of these was called Rami, after his fathers before him.

Each of the anagarr claimed an island as his own, naming them after the five high places on which they had originally appeared in the Blue jungle. They roosted with pride atop the waters while the other Luminaries lived caged underneath them. The people of the jungle who had come with the anagarr soon felt at home on the islands.

The islands were sparsely populated with peaceful fishermen. And though the followers who traveled with the anagarr testified to their greatness, the fishermen still doubted them. To win their hearts, the anagarr shared the ancient knowledge of the stars. The Blue islanders learned to navigate the great seas. They caught new species of fish in greater numbers than ever, and harvested sea plants at distances they had never dreamed of.

Whether the Blue islanders worshiped or merely tolerated the anagarr and the new settlers, we do not know. But we do know that the anagarr and their followers built towering monuments of stone for themselves. They built them with masonry, and they built them with their magic. If you fly a steamship over the Blue corner of the world, you will see the massive pillars of stone that pierce the palmy jungle islands. And if you look closely, very closely beneath their raiment of vines, you will find the shape of the hooded viper and the serpentine eyes carved into their faces.

LOVE AND WAR

"Good afternoon, sunshine." I welcomed Franky to the awakened world, though he looked nothing like sunshine. From my room, I'd heard him muttering in his sleep on and off for hours.

"Did you formulate a plan for two lone men to ward off the wilderness invasion of Sanctius while you were tossing and turning on my couch?"

Franky shook his head. "Haven't you learned anything? The wilderness isn't the problem, Nico. It's the city. The Wilderman isn't evil; he's good."

My chest tightened. Part of me had hoped a few hours of sleep would change his attitude. Deep inside, I knew it wouldn't be that easy. "He's an alchemist, Franky. The power he holds over you in the forest—it'll wear off soon. Don't worry."

"Can't you see that the City Council and their goons have been poisoning you? Literally. Why do you think I taught you to hunt? The food, the ampgas, everything in Sanctius was perfectly formulated to turn you into an obedient minion and poison you against beauty and goodness!"

He paused, and his stare bored into me. "Look at you. You care about what happens to me. You never would have felt brotherly love if you were still eating the factory's food. It began with your garden. *That* saved your life. Your garden is the only reason you've had half a chance, and now you're going to throw it away because you're too stubborn to admit that you've survived *despite* the city. You're too obstinate to admit that the day you left the Borderlands you made the biggest mistake of your life."

"Oh, my poor friend." I fell back a step. He was truly unwell. How else could he believe such things about the Council? About his own father? In former days, there was good care to be had for him. Delusional Citizens were brought to caring professionals. *Now, it's up to me.* I declined to say anything more.

Instead, I focused on cooking breakfast while Frank used the restroom. Several days ago, I'd found a nest of quail eggs. They made a pretty dish served with fresh greens, pâté and sliced pears. It was the least I could do for the lad. As I finished drying and putting away dishes, I rekindled some conversation.

"Well, Franky, ole pal, it's been a wild couple of days, eh?"

"Nice pun."

"My point is, I think you need to stay here for a couple of days."

"If that's what you want to do."

"Well, *I* have a couple of things I need to take care of." I moved closer. "But this is the perfect place to clear your head." I motioned to the perfect order of my suite.

While Franky gazed around, I seized the opportunity to wrench his arm behind his back and stuck my revolver into his spine. "Just hold still, mate."

He reached back to whack me with his free hand. "What are you doing? You wouldn't shoot me."

He felt sickly within my grasp, fighting back so weakly. But I didn't want to let my guard down.

"I would never kill you. But don't push the shooting part."

Franky put his free hand in the air in surrender. "Why? What on earth are you doing with me?"

"It's for your own good. I'm going to live a long and happy life by sticking to the safety that the city and the Council have provided for us. I'd really like you to—"

"There's something you need to know, Nico. There's more behind the Council than—"

"I'd *really* like for you to have the same chance," I continued over his interruption. "Can't let you go traipsing through the woods like this is one of your whale tales or fairy tales, or whatever contraband you've been reading." I thought of Tino's scroll. Should I have even opened it? But this was different. Franky was chasing after ghost stories. "You know most of them have terrible endings, right?"

"So you're taking me hostage? That's my happy ending?"

"I'm just going to keep you safe for a few days. We'll get this whole thing sorted out," I promised.

"Oh yeah? And how, do you suppose?"

I pulled a rope from the drawer closest to me. Franky didn't argue, just walked with me willingly to one of the dining room chairs. I tied his hands together with the metal tubing on the back. Wary of his knees so near my face, I tied his ankles. *This is going surprisingly well.* I looked into his eyes and tried to evaluate whether he would try to escape.

"You're running out of time, Nico."

"Is this about that kook in the woods? Your haunted woodsman?"

He ignored me and randomly jumped topics. "Did you ever wonder why the clock in the Time Temple keeps going? They don't run without a keeper, you know."

"You take care of it, just like you do the engine towers. You, of all people, should know the truth. Your own parents aided the intricate operations of this city and the Time Temple."

"You're so wrong. I'm not the keeper. And neither was my dad or any of those sick henchmen. Dad intended to bring me into the inner circle, to join the next generation of emblem-holders. He thought he could train me to assume the power he held, power that he was a fool to wield. He failed to figure in me seeing through it. When my dad showed me the secret of the clock and the Council tower, my eyes were opened to who he really was and whom he really served. They lied to us, Nico. Their armory and their tower—it was all so that humanity could be governed and controlled. It took me a while to sort it out, but it's the Wilderman who holds it all together."

"If that were true, I wouldn't be here. My survival is proof of my faithful citizenship in Sanctius City. I am living proof that the Council is right."

"Your survival was prolonged by your inability to see reality. The rules are everything to you until they grow inconvenient, then suddenly it's okay to do whatever you deem best." Franky's voice rose as he spiraled out of control.

"We have all been tasked with survival. I seem to be the only one willing to do what it takes. As soon as things get tough, people jump ship," I responded calmly.

"You are so obstinate!" Franky growled.

"You say that like it's a bad thing. I see it as an asset. It's why I'm sane and you're delusional."

"You mean disillusioned."

I only huffed in response while I double-checked my knots.

"The Wilderman will come for you, Nico. But unlike you, he won't force you to do what he thinks is best, even though he's right—*also* unlike you. At some point, you *will* have to choose—freedom or slavery, life or death."

"You say he won't force me, as if it's so noble. In reality, he couldn't if he tried. I'll stay in the city forever if I must. And after you're cured of his spectral influence, you'll help me keep Sanctius safe forever. We'll partner in combating the evil creeping in at the borders."

"You only have a few days," he continued, as if I hadn't said a word. "I don't know what will happen to Sanctius. I know it sounds crazy."

"Franky, I'm keeping you here because I care." I interrupted his crazed rambling. "If there were any doctors or any other way, it wouldn't have to be like this. I'll be back in a bit to make sure you get refreshment and a chance to use the lav."

"What a gracious host you are." Franky rolled his eyes at me as I shut the patio door. In the elevator, I turned the challenge over in my mind as I descended toward the street below.

How do you fight an evil magician? I needed to access all the research results and accumulated information that the commissioners had. I decided the Time Temple was the best place to start. When I stepped out onto the landing beside my building, I chose the nearest steam car to get me there.

Ages ago, when superstition and ancient philosophies died at the hands of good science, the Council turned the cathedral that formed the foundation of the Time Temple into a museum. I hadn't been there since my time in school, but I remembered many exhibits cataloging the process of man and his inventions. Supposedly, there were research and literature archives on some of the upper floors. It sounded like that's where Franky found some of his fantastical beliefs. There must be a remedy on those shelves somewhere, clues as to how I might snap Franky out of his hypnosis.

I hate downtown. Everywhere I looked, invasive plants, droppings from small rodents, and snake holes declared that this was a war zone between tamed land and wilderness.

Seagrass exploded through the stony pathway to the entrance of the Time Temple. The solid iron double doors were much taller than necessary, three times the height of a man. The pair of doors arched to a point in the middle, with intricate metalwork over every inch. Brass flowers and vines inlaid into the lower end created a mountain, rising toward the middle, far above the handles. An oxidized copper river snaked its way through them, growing wide at the bottom of the doors. On the top portion, small stars were riveted all over the iron sky. Following the arch of the door, eight larger, many-sided stars were cut sharply into the door so that a deep point receded into the middle of each.

Nowhere else was such miraculous workmanship seen. Even the massive hinges were made of countless twisted strands of iron that had been melded together in some places and maintained their individual lines in others. I pulled the handle of the right-hand door. It didn't move.

Yes, I hate downtown. And I hate Franky's precious sea with its salt that ruins everything.

I planted my feet as best I could and put all my weight into pulling on the handle. Finally, the door budged and flung open, depositing me, breathless, on the walkway.

TIME STANDS STILL

I stepped into the Time Temple, and the thick brown darkness comforted me. By nature, the first floor had the oldest windows. They were Gothic arches with latticework, stained glass and a *lot* of dust. Slowly, through the dusty haze, I made out the interior of the centuries-old cathedral. Things weren't quite as I remembered them from my school days.

Between each set of towering flying buttresses, a display had been set up. In grade school, the displays had been so intriguing that I hadn't bothered to look at what lay behind them. Each booth explained an aspect of the culture during a different era: pre-steam, the vertical-piston coal days, the steam revolution, and the modernization collaboration that took place on this very spot and produced the magnifying tank and the closed steam system. For each of these epochs, there were models, illustrations, and basic explanations. But I needed more than an appetizer. I needed all the juicy details about Citizenship if I was going to help Franky. Real research.

I wandered into other areas of the Time Temple. Irregular layers of the building were connected by awkwardly positioned staircases. The floor above the original cathedral contained administrative offices. Dilapidated wooden desks were arranged like a maze. Parchment, pens and ink sat out on many, as if employees had left for work as usual one day, not knowing they'd never return. *Remember the evanesced.*

I unrolled scrolls from a few of the desks, but they pertained to the running of the museum. I weaved my way through the maze. Partway through the room, I found another staircase leading upward to the left. It took me to a smaller addition with a steeply pitched roof.

Religious people in the pre-steam days had attempted to take the building back for the religious societies of the day. The poorly funded addition was nothing but a storage closet for modern Sanctius. Between the chairs and boxes, there was a path through the center of the room where the ceiling was high enough for me to walk upright.

At the far end, I climbed another staircase that jogged up to the right. I stepped into a large room with tall windows between thick iron posts on three of the walls. *This is more like it.*

Whereas the lower office floor had antiquated wooden desks, the fourth floor had sleek metal-framed workspaces. On the inside wall, there were floor-to-ceiling scroll shelves instead of windows. Most of these had modern handles with internal gears to wind them up, much more sophisticated than the administrative scrolls on the second floor.

Diagonal lines formed individual rhomboid cubbies for the well-organized scrolls. An etched brass plaque clearly labeled each shelf. There were mounds of scrolls on history, religion, sciences and even tales of fiction. I felt as if I stood in an airship station holding a ticket to anywhere. *Where do I even start?*

My fingers bounced over the brass ends of the scroll tubes as I walked along the wall, sampling titles.

The Advent of Steam: The True Record of the Life and Death of the AC Magician Nikola Adze

 The Council's Official History of Sanctius City
 The Greatest Empire: The City That Saved Humanity
 The Rise and Fall of Religious Zeal
 Psychology's Role in Citizenship and Governance
 The Demigods Among Us
 100 Days in an Airship
 Fairy Tales of the Southern Continent.

I pulled the fairy tales out of their stack. A few scrolls fell at my feet, so I replaced them neatly before I unrolled the leaves from the tube. There were talking animals, incoherent riddles, moral interjections… *I have enough of that garbage trying to sort through Valentino's collection.* I wound the handle quickly and replaced it.

Next, I found a thick work of fiction. I settled on my knees to examine it more closely. The story described a hero destined to save the known world. I skimmed the beginning and quickly determined it to be completely unrealistic. *What's the point of reading such an unlikely— nay, impossible—story?*

Yet several hours later, I found myself flat on my belly, winding all the layers of the scroll back into the large tube. It was a ridiculous notion that only one person could have the skill set required to bring a positive result. A far more likely story would contain a formula that many people could learn and perfect. No wonder fiction had dwindled down to the small collection prescribed in school to learn good Citizenship. I turned the scroll over in my hands and thought about the tale. *It's just a bundle of words.*

Wondering how I could have wasted so much time in futile reading, I set it back on the stack and dragged my eyes to a different diamond-shaped cubby with the label "CITIZEN STUDIES." The stamped brass labels held crowded descriptions of the contents of each. *A study of the consequences of religious fervor in adverse conditions.* The end cap nearly ran out of room for the lengthy subtitle.

The tightly wound scroll hesitated to unroll. I carefully tugged harder until the mass of parchment broke free. The first layer was an abstract and brief description of the study. Four doctors performed covert observations, each in a separate community. Each doctor entered their selected village through some pretense. One made and repaired leather shoes, one wove linen cloth, and two others operated market stands, falling in with the local tradesmen. The full study laid out in detail the subjects' responses to adversity.

I flipped forward to each of the individual reports included before the evaluation and conclusion of the study. Three set out by airship to the Northern Reaches, the Western Tablelands and the Southern Continent. The fourth…

Doctor Faber set out on [redacted] by submarine to seek human life on the Eastern Isle. He, his team, travel companions, captain and crew were never seen nor heard from again, adding credence to the commonly held belief that the Eastern Isle is a subject of conjecture and exists only in myth. Let the record state that the Council strongly advised against any exploration of the Eastern Sea, warning of the potential dangers therein.

It was unthinkable that Franky enjoyed spending so much time by the sea, even in it. All manner of danger lurked in those waters. Swarms of poisonous sea vermin. Chaotic tentacles. Visions of a giant serpent crushing the submarine invaded my mind as if someone were reading me the missing piece of the story. I shivered.

The research, Nico. I had already wasted too much time and needed to focus on what the other doctors found. In all three of the other studies, I found similar reports. The doctors made themselves at home in each community, befriended the outcasts of society, and tested their mettle with difficulties, both engineered and chance occurrences.

Subjects demonstrated lack of reason increasing with duration of challenging circumstances.

Dire and life-threatening situations produced greatest hysteria.

Joyous singing and ceremonial chants increased as quality of life diminished.

In no less than four households within the Northern Reaches study village, hallucinations and inability to accept reality occurred.

One household, after running out of food, had even set the table and recited a religious poem as if a feast were present.

Hallucinations likely. Upon questioning, each member insisted food would arrive somehow. No tradesman was compensated. Villagers appear to believe in some kind of magic.

I grew more concerned with every word. It sounded so much like Franky. But how had the doctors cured it? I flipped to the back layers of the scroll where the results were summarized. Page after page of thick medical jargon grew hard to read. Skimming was nearly impossible. I'd flip to a page and start at the top. *You'd think there was a competition to use the most words and syllables.*

I found a page listing treatments. The doctors attempted many treatments, even bringing subjects back to Sanctius with them. Copies of those individuals' records were attached to the bottom layer of parchment. They had attempted to reset the brain through hospitalization, the removal of food and concurrent food-based rewards, mind-altering experiments with electricity and pharmaceuticals, industry, confinement—the list went on. The results were poor at best, and I grew more discouraged than ever.

One clinical study restored a small percentage of patients to their pre-symptomatic lives. *How? I need to know more!* But I couldn't find any more details except that even that study was ultimately deemed unsuccessful.

I scoured the scroll for any sign of the doctor involved or similar research. In the back of my mind, I heard thumping upstairs, but my subconscious dismissed it as regular sounds from the enormous clock several floors above my head. Had I not been desperate to find an answer for Franky, I would've realized sooner that they were footsteps.

Aha! Here's one by Dr. Faber. My senses returned, and I tried to digest the thump, thump, thump of footsteps slowly descending a set of stairs. *Impossible!* Footsteps required feet. The only other pair of feet on Earth were tied to a chair in my penthouse. Unless… I thought of the wild man, the Wilderman, the sea monsters and the mountain trolls.

There was a set of stairs a few arm-lengths to my left. I went to the foot and leaned forward. It was unmistakable. Someone had come down the stairs to the level above me and crossed the floor as I listened. A waft of earthy air brought with it a cold wave of fear.

I ran to the shelf and scanned for the scroll by Dr. Faber. *I just saw it. It has to be here somewhere!* The footsteps started down the nearby stairs just as I spotted it. Several scrolls tumbled onto the floor when I jerked the one I needed from the cubby. I bolted, leaving the mess.

"Don't worry. I'll get them," the old man's voice rumbled above me when I reached the storage chapel.

That witchy woodsman, I growled inside. But I had to be sure I wasn't imagining things. *Of course, you're not.* Right. If there was one thing I could be sure of, it's that I was the last sane human on Earth. Rushing through the remaining floors, I burst outside.

I had to fix Franky, which meant I had to remain calm. I hid myself around the corner of the temple and waited, hoping with all my might that the scroll I took held the information I needed. My heartbeat, my breathing, everything slowly settled.

But then the Wilderman stepped out and returned the massive iron door to its place. *What is he doing here?* I never thought he'd venture into the city, especially not the Time Temple in the heart of downtown.

"I knew you couldn't live with yourself if you'd left a mess. So I put 'em in the right places and everything. I wouldn't want 'em haunting your thoughts later." He chuckled.

I peeked around the corner to find him staring straight at me. A cold sweat washed over me. *If I feel like panicking, then I just need a plan.* I reminded myself to be logical about this. I just needed to get to Franky and spend the next few days setting him right and figuring out what to do with the Wilderman. Simple.

He tipped his hat to bid farewell with a mischievous twinkle in his eye. Then, he turned and walked downhill toward the beach. I watched him, laden with furs and a wool hat, walk toward a sunny beach in the middle of the afternoon.

How ridiculous. But man or monster, there he was.

I couldn't deny that a second narrow escape from the Wilderman left me agitated, but I had Franky to consider. I jogged to the steam cart and returned to my building, trying the whole way to leave the puzzle of the Wilderman at the temple clock for another time. On the elevator, I distracted myself by attempting a peek into the scroll I'd borrowed. It was at least five inches thick and stuck shut. I held it under my arm and jiggled the crank. Still unsuccessful when I stepped off the elevator and made my way into my flat, I tried my best to make cheerful conversation. "Hey, chap. I bet you need to pluck a rose by now. I'll make some food while you take a break in the lav."

My eyes darted around. Franky wasn't in the chair nor anywhere in sight. I checked my bedroom and lavatory. Both were empty, though the mess of soapy water on the counter betrayed the fact that he'd been there.

As a last resort, I went to the patio. Only after weaving in and out of every raised bed and the entire greenhouse did I give up. I plopped on the bench Franky and I had set up together only two days ago. This time, I faced south, the way Franky had before. I ran my hand along the wood, like he had. Light and dark alternated in oval pathways. It was beautiful in a way; I suppose. It just wasn't my taste. I bent over to admire the perfectly matched gears supporting the seat. I considered the fabrication, the miracle of human ingenuity.

Compared to those cogs, what was the plank besides a precisely cut hunk of dead tree? Franky was so far out of his right mind to prefer it; I had to find him. I gazed out around me, looking for answers. I followed the slope of the mountains to the white cliffs and their abrupt end in the glaring bright sea.

The sea. Of course, Franky would go to the sea. He thought the forest would cast some kind of spell on me, but it was the sea for Franky. Somehow, everyone seemed more susceptible to some aspect of the wilderness or another.

I dropped my face into my hands. Was it hopeless? He had submitted to its power for so long. It sounded like something had been going on even before I'd first met him. But I had to try; I owed it to him. I rose from the bench. No, I owed it to myself and the leaders of that great city to try to bring him back. I would honor Sanctius' ways by preserving her Citizens as long as possible.

I gazed at the sea from my garden haven and breathed in determination. The scent of sweet pea flowers and the high-altitude view cranked my brain into action like steam in the cylinder of an engine. And something dawned on me.

The Wilderman had headed toward the beach from the Time Temple. He could be luring Franky to his death. My hand gripped my revolver.

I'm going to need more weapons.

ONE

Downstairs, I sought the Dan-Doyce from among the running vehicles. I threw the top back. Plenty of room for weapons. I tucked my crossbow next to my leg like a security blanket. It was a good start. More than once, Franky had mentioned an armory below the Council tower accessed by a secret elevator. Based on the mess he made in my penthouse, I knew Franky hadn't been gone long. There was time to grab a few things if I hurried. I knew the Councilmen would want me to go to any length to prevent the Wilderman from catching Franky. The engine purred, settling me as I sped to the Council tower.

Inside the tower, I ignored the regular public elevator and took a hallway that followed the rectangular shape of the building. After I'd turned two corners and thought I'd end up circling the whole central shaft of the building, there it was—another elevator. It looked as if it were made of silver. *Surely not.*

There was no time for closer inspection. The elevator was just as strange inside. Only one button directed the elevator upward, set apart above the others. It had an odd symbol, like a sideways zero. Below, there was a button labeled "B" for the basement, which I hit, and then a series of numbers with downward-facing arrows.

The elevator opened directly into the armory, where rows of cases and bins contained weapons and defensive gear. I took a couple of long-range rifles, extra bolts for my crossbow, plus a few different blades. A pair of gauntlets caught my eye. One had a miniature crossbow built into it, complete with a quiver of tiny bolts loaded with injectable poison. The matching gauntlet had a retractable blade. I strapped them onto my wrists. They felt like they were tailor-made for me. It was a comforting confirmation that I was doing the right thing.

Time to go.

"Please let me get there soon enough," I said to no one. Loneliness hung over me without anyone to commiserate with. I used to complain about Franky whenever Raina came around, and vice versa. Since the day I graduated from school and became an official Citizen, I'd resolved to persevere, even if everyone else abandoned Sanctius City's safety. As I drove, I was determined to ensure that I had someone to survive with.

I screeched to a stop directly behind the wall, where the Wilderman's fur coat lay. Immediately, I saw them standing waist-deep in the surf. The Wilderman, still wearing a lightweight knit jumper, held on to Franky, who stood slightly in front of him, with one arm. I reached for a rifle with a tank glass scope mod. I turned a knob, and brass gears moved the glass until the Wilderman was in focus. As soon as I had him in my sight, he pointed straight at me. Franky looked at me and then back to the Wilderman with a pleading look on his face. The shot was too risky.

I replaced the rifle in the back seat and loaded a slender bolt into the mini-crossbow on my left wrist. I felt my belt for both revolvers and trotted down to the beach. The Wilderman grasped the back of Franky's neck. Franky held both his hands out toward me. I stopped a few arm-lengths away from the lapping waves and drew a handgun.

"Nico, wait a minute. You don't understand."

"Oh, I understand completely."

Franky shook his head, his lip quivering.

The Wilderman spoke. "Nico. You and I need to discuss some things. But Franky's done trying to explain it to you."

"I will not let you hurt him."

"And I won't let you stop him."

"Stop him from what?"

"Nico," Franky answered weakly. "I can't do this anymore. It's like

I've been two people for you for so long. I wanted you to have every chance at a real life. But I'm so tired. And you just won't listen. There's a way out. I tried to tell you. There's a path out of this wretched place, and I have to take it."

"He can't see what you see, Franky. He's not willing," the Wilderman patronized me.

"Don't indulge his hallucinations," I spat. "I don't know who, or… or what you are. But you're going to give me back my friend, and no one will get hurt."

Simultaneously, tears poured down Franky's cheeks, and the Wilderman chuckled. "It's time, Franky. Say goodbye, son."

"Nico, it's better. I promise." He took a second to still his shaking voice. "Please come… before time runs out. Goodbye, chap."

"Go on. I'll look after your friend. Huh, huh, huh." His guttural laugh was anything but comforting.

"And just what do you mean…"

Without further warning, Franky dove into the water. He swam along the sea floor until I lost sight of him.

"…before time runs out?" The words intended for Franky escaped my lips as I stepped helplessly toward him. The tide washed over my shoes, and a shiver ran from my heels to my head as the saltwater infiltrated to my skin.

"He means out of Sanctius. It's all coming to a stop." He nodded to my waistcoat pocket and motioned with his hand toward the Time Temple and the city beyond.

"It would take one powerful woodsman to shut down the whole city of Sanctius. You'd have to stop the very sun from rising in the sky."

The maniac chuckled again. "Now, I think we both know that's not true. A good backup plan, though. I'll keep that in mind."

Another wave washed well over my boots and drew my attention downward. An even stronger wave followed and hit me at the knees. The crashing waves fell higher each time. My gaze met the Wilderman's. He smiled and stepped toward me. The menace was making the tide rise. How was he doing it?

"I could teach you how to swim." He laughed again, jolly as ever, and I grew sick to my stomach.

The water receded with a low rush I felt through my whole body. I ran toward the quay, but I was too late. A massive wave gathered itself, thundered forward, and threw me into the sand, receding as fast as it came. I fled up the stairs to the car. I hopped over the door, apologizing to the vehicle for getting seawater all over the interior. As I did, I looked back at the Wilderman. He floated on his back in the angsty tide, still smiling like a lunatic. The water had already risen partway up the quay, flooding the stairs.

Monster. Magician. Beast. And yet he had the face of a man, the wrinkled and darkened face of an old airship captain. Or was that just the face he wore today? I wondered if he could change his appearance. It seemed unlikely since I'd only seen this form. But it was no more implausible than the fact that I was sopping wet when it should have been low tide. An entity that could manipulate the entire Eastern Sea should be viewed with the highest possible suspicion.

My heart pressed outward against my chest. The Wilderman had dared to come into Sanctius. He had invaded my border of safety. I could no longer plan an escape; I had to defeat him.

I gripped the steering wheel tightly. Tears threatened to form. But I refused to succumb to my emotions. I refused to be vulnerable to his invisible weaponry, like those calamitous fools who left this city empty. It was time to do something.

I jumped back out of the car, snatched a long-range rifle from the rear seat of the Dan-Doyce, and ran toward the Time Temple. That was *it*. I wasn't going to mess around anymore.

You shouldn't. Take him down.

Was it solitude that gave my thoughts a conversational quality?

"You'll always have me, Nico," the Wilderman called from the rising surf. Or did he use mindspeak again? It was hard to tell. I shook off his voice.

Don't let him poison your mind. He can't find you if he's dead. You will survive. Your way is the only way. These empty streets are proof.

That narrative drove me up the block, into the Time Temple and across the museum floor. What kind of lawlessness would consciously steal my last companion from me? It didn't matter what his face looked like. He was certainly more monster than man. No, I'd had quite enough of his evil campaign against mankind. I would avenge Franky.

I hastily planned my attack. The east side of the temple clock would face the sea where the Wilderman swam. It would take only a moment to set up the bipod or find support for my rifle. Aim and fire. Simple as that. Those wretched waters can have his body, just as he'd given Franky's to them.

Up each set of stairs and across each floor, my steps fell in sync with my pounding heart. I inhaled for three steps, exhaled for three steps, relishing the adrenaline rush. My confidence grew as my senses sharpened.

I took two steep stairs at a time into the tower. Left, left, left again up the narrow square obelisk. When I finally reached the spire, I skidded to a stop at the sight before me.

There was the Wilderman—standing before the clockworks inside.

"Fascinating, isn't it? Time?"

His words woke me from my shock. I reached for a pistol from my leather chest holster.

"You humans think you live and die by it," he continued. "But time is peripheral, an unimportant measuring device like arm-lengths. But you can't measure what you don't have."

I closed my left eye and pointed my revolver steadily at his chest. *Choose. Life or death.*

"So, you admit you're not human," I said as I squeezed the trigger, comforted by the confirmation that I was killing a beast.

"You cannot solve your problems by hurling metal at them." The Wilderman was unfazed. The bullet seemed to pass through him as if he were a ghost.

"You're a specter," I gasped.

I replaced the pistol and wound the tension on the miniature crossbow. Maybe a poisoned arrow would do the trick.

"Ghost. King. Wilderman. People have called me many things."

"You're not an uomo *salvatico?*"

"*Do I look like some kind of ape-man?*" His lips did not move, but I heard him loud and clear.

"Mindspeak, furs, lurking about the forest killing people left and right. You seem more beast than man to me."

"It would be unwise to accuse me of sins I haven't committed. I am no hybrid abomination devised by lesser gods," he said.

"Awfully big words for a wild man," I spat. *How dare this creature try to indoctrinate me with some kind of made-up history?*

"The wild men are an obscenity," he continued. "It was dark magic that made them, and wicked for them to usurp my power."

"*Your* power. Who died and made you the king?"

"Funny you should ask."

The Wilderman flickered as if he were a night sky illuminated momentarily by lightning. For one instant and then another, I saw the stark white picture of a king draped in a white fleece. He wore a crown made from sun-bleached branches and stood in front of a whitewashed throne carved from a massive tree. The vision snapped back and forth a few times, leaving me haunted, standing with the same old bearish Wilderman clad in skins. His eyes, as deep as the abyss, sucked me in from behind the folds of his weathered skin.

I blinked and shook my head to shake off his gaze. "You're a phantom. A sorcerer. I refuse to succumb to your witchcraft."

"Now, believe me, son; I'd rather no harm was done here. But the thing is, it's too late for that. I'm drawing back the curtain of time now, so that reality can take the stage." He reached out and touched one of the barrels of the clockworks. The barrel ground against the intersecting gears. A cascading cacophony traveled across the platform of clockworks, gear after barrel. The going train screeched, and the hands quivered. "I told you that time is up. Now how about you start listening to my offer?"

He's insane. He looked at me like a wildcat who'd finally cornered its prey. *Cornered but not caught.* I saw one way of escape and took it without a second thought. No means were unreasonable to escape his clutches.

I drew my handgun and fired a shot through the glass on the south face of the temple clock. I tucked my face into my arm and leaped through the shards.

The steel roof was long, covering several floors of additions. I dug my heels into the roof to slow my descent. My handgun went flying past me. It hit the flat metal framing holding down the roof and flew off. I turned onto my stomach, still trying to slow myself down, unsure if I'd go the way of my pistol. But the steel frame was just thick enough to grab onto. My body swung a few times before it steadied enough to drop a story to a smaller roof, and then shimmied onto a windowsill before I could use a fire escape ladder mounted to the wall to get to the ground.

Though my heart thudded in my ears, I was pleased with my relatively smooth escape. A few scrapes from the glass and a sore hind end from the roof weren't bad.

I scrambled up the hill toward my tower uptown. Behind me, the entire Time Tower imploded. The Time Temple—weights, bells, metal and stone—crushed itself. One thing was clear. I needed to fortify my refuge.

"Niiiiiccoooo," the Wilderman called as he emerged from the cloud of debris. "When will you understand? I've rent time. Your precious timepiece is of no use."

I couldn't resist. I pulled out my pocket watch. It didn't reassure me with a polite movement of the second hand, but then I was running for my life. Or maybe I'd forgotten to wind it with all the drama of the last few days. *Faster. You have to get home.* I hurriedly stowed it and ran on.

"Listen, Nico. We just need to talk. There is a way out of this."

"Death is not an option. I will not listen to your lies." I could feel the anger emanating from the Wilderman as I threw a rebuttal behind me without stopping. Chills went down my spine when he laughed that lunatic laugh again. His ability to find humor in the severest of moments grated on my last nerve.

"It's your *only* option."

"I choose safety."

"And where might you be safe anymore?" he called after me.

His menacing tone drew my gaze over my shoulder as I ran uphill. He paused by the engine tower, reached his hand out toward the iron frame of the building, and closed his eyes.

I took advantage of his delay to gain ground toward home, but even two blocks ahead of him I heard the steam tower's rumble rise. Higher. Louder. Higher.

My blood turned cold.

It began with a whine rising above all the other noises. The lowest tank floor burst first with a sickening crash; if one could call them crashes, they were so thunderous. The clamor rocketed upward as, floor by floor, the condensed water exploded through the glass as thick as my hand. And that wasn't the end of it. Explosions of a different kind followed as the engines themselves blew to pieces. I turned the corner north toward my tower as brass, copper, aluminum, and steel rained down around the Wilderman. Maybe he'd be caught in his own snare, crushed by his own cataclysm.

"You go on home and have a good night's sleep, Nico. I'll be in touch tomorrow to settle the issue." His mindspeak broke through the tumult and dashed my hope of finally being rid of him.

My eyes suspected every shadow that darkened the last few blocks toward home. When I arrived at the foot of my building, the reality of what had just happened hit me. I had no elevator. No power. No water pump to care for the garden. And no way to get to it anyway.

This was not the end. Centuries of human evolution didn't bring me here to give up. I stared at the elevator cage. I scrutinized the street in front of my building. There was an abandoned city maintenance truck with bags and boxes of tools left, as if the repairman would return tomorrow for work. Though a fair few of them were rusting, there had to be something I could do to get to my rooftop sanctuary. My vision tunneled to a simple steam bike.

I can't. I'm a gardener, not a mechanic.

But there was no other option. What better way to honor Franky's memory? I retrieved the steam bike from across the street and asked myself, as I would hundreds of times in the next few hours, what would Franky do?

First, I needed to disconnect the elevator cage from the cables. But then what? I couldn't move the entire thing. I gazed over the gaudy metal cage, scrolling decorative finishes and delicate glass. And then I spotted it—a sledgehammer in the back of the work truck.

I began matter-of-factly, swinging hard at the nearest corner post of the elevator cage. To gain access to the cables and chains behind it, I needed to remove the elevator. Destroying it via sledgehammer was the most efficient method available to me.

With every blow, I thought less about modifying the elevator and more about the events of the last few days, the past few years, all of it. What a twisted series of events that led me here. By the time cracks spidered through the glass panes, my eyes blurred with hot tears.

You think you're the only one who can break glass and bend steel?

The sledge landed solidly on the center cross-frame, and four windows on the cage shattered.

That's for Franky.

I didn't shade my face from the shards, only blinked hard as I turned to wind up for another blow. The sledge whistled as I drew it around. Smash.

And that's for Franky.

Again, smash.

And that's for Raina.

Smash. The bulk of the remaining elevator buckled.

And for my family. For all the people you stole from me, everything you've ruined.

One more swing landed hard against the last corner post, and I broke down with the last of the cage. On my knees in the pile of rubble, I fought back angry grief. Glass pricked at my knees through my trousers; physical pain reminding me I had physical problems to deal with. After all, I was the survivor. I could not crumble under the weight of solitude. I sucked in a deep, shaky breath of air and wiped the moisture from my eyes.

Fate favored the brave. I would be brave.

Besides crying, what would Franky do? I re-centered my thoughts on the task at hand. With gloved hands, I hammered and tore scraps of framing away from the cables.

Franky would not clean up the mess of glass.

Then I would have had to mop him up when he cut himself to shreds. Taking a shovel and broom from the work truck and sweeping, I focused on the work. I focused on the growing pile of rubble—the length of a man—from the elevator cavity. It took everything in my power to ignore the voices battling in the shadows—voices I'd heard in my dreams, voices I'd heard when I read Tino's tales, and the voices of the Wilderman, the forest and the rushing waters around Sanctius—all fighting to invade my thoughts.

Nothing set me right like a job well done, and the tidy bottom of the partial elevator shaft did the trick to renew my strength. Now, to rig up the bike. There were multiple pulley systems. Chains seemed too difficult to integrate into the bike, unless I could find the perfect chain wheel *and* a housing of some kind, and then I'd need a way… No, that would get too complicated for me.

The cables, on the other hand, were already there, attached at both the top and the bottom of the shaft. If I could find a way to use them to hold the bike against the building, I could just drive it up. Unlike chains, cables needed fewer specific parts—any kind of channel to run them through that I could also attach to the bike.

I dug through scraps in the back of the maintenance truck for a piece of iron large enough to prop the bike on to work. While I was there, I hunted for anything that might help me make the necessary modifications.

"Oh, perfect!" I exclaimed to no one. I hauled a pulley wheel out of the bottom of the pile. It looked to have been part of a belt assembly because it had sidewalls to keep a belt in place. It would be perfect for feeding a cable over.

Piece by piece, I mocked up a solution to the puzzle, digging through everything on the maintenance truck for bolts and nuts that fit where I needed them. There were a couple of arms to attach to the frame, each with an eye to guide cables and pull the bike frame toward the building. I found cam-shaped gears and a pipe to fit on as an emergency brake handle. I stared up at all eighty-four floors of my tower. *Maybe I should rig up two of those.*

What might have taken Franky a couple of hours took me most of the day. The sun drew dangerously near the silhouette of the Hungry Mountain, and I still needed to stock up on more weapons from the city armory and see what other supplies I could find.

I tested the bike a few times, driving it up a few stories and using the bike's brakes to lower myself back down. I wouldn't be able to do that too many times before the brakes wore out, so I tested out my emergency brake as well. I was incredibly proud of my efforts, but I'd have to wait to brave the entire building until after I'd found more supplies.

The Wilderman would find me. When he did, I would be ready.

ROSA

It would take strategic fortifications to defeat such a powerful enemy. I needed to be prepared for anything. Since the maintenance truck had provided for me so well that day, I gathered my things and drove it to the northwest quarter of the city where there were many factories. Although I knew they would have been scavenged through already, something told me I hadn't found the last of Sanctius City's protections. The factories had been shut down and vandalized for so long that I couldn't recognize which was which, so I parked in front of the first one I came to. All the doors had been ripped off the hinges. My eyes collected the fading daylight streaming in.

Conveyor belts ran from end to end and floor to ceiling of the cavernous building. There were large machines stationed intermittently along the belts. Obviously, the lower conveyor belts had been robbed of their products long ago. I climbed a pulley system until I could peer over the third level of belts and see cans and paper bags. *Food.* How did I forget that this was the provisions factory? After it shut down, people stole most of the remaining food, and then the population plummeted. *Thank you, Mr. Wilderman.*

A faint answer of "You're welcome" pricked my ears. But it had to be my imagination and paranoia working against me.

Hanging from the pulley chain, I swung my legs back and forth until I could grab the nearest machine and haul myself onto the belt. The line of cans had been picked through and discarded haphazardly. Some were opened—rotted and dried up, of course. I walked carefully down the belt until I found a fresh tin.

Oh! It was veggie mash with a packet of protein crunch topping. I used to love that stuff. I pulled a blade from a sheath on my thigh holster and pried it open. The vegetables seemed a lot softer than I remembered. I used the knife to draw out a scoop, sprinkled the protein crunch on top and timidly took a bite. *Absolutely nasty. How did I ever like this stuff?* I caught myself in the traitorous thought. Having a garden of fresh vegetables must have changed my food preferences. How else had my loyalty slipped without realizing it?

I was wasting time, and there were supplies to collect. I tiptoed along the belt until it ran near to a catwalk and jumped over. The expanded metal walkway led to a door in the exterior wall, which opened onto a bridge of similar construction. It was one of several raised walkways connecting the various factories. I trotted across and opened the door, but I wasn't prepared for the next factory.

The Human Life Tower. Or at least it *was.* It looked more like a harbinger of death than anything else. The tower had a square footprint. Offices lined all four walls for at least ten floors. In the hollow center, a miniature railway spiraled up, in and out of itself as far as the eye could see. Intermittently, like lonely mine cars, there were human infants in various stages of development.

A human factory. Sanctius City—food, education, healthcare, all of our many advancements—had long removed the need for physical procreation.

I had entered on the second floor. I walked slowly around the balcony. A platform jutted several feet into the center of the building where parents could summon their pods for visiting and inspection.

There were many advantages to the system the Council had settled on. I knew that. I'd been well-educated on its benefits in preparation for my own match date. Primarily, it allowed the increased survival rate that came with marriages without requiring the risks of emotional attachments.

The possibilities that this factory provided excited me. If I could get the power up and running again, even if I had to use smaller engines for local supply, maybe I could use my own genetic material to make more people. Surely there were instructions somewhere. I had a vision of Sanctius repopulated with Nicos of all ages. A deluge of pride, fear, disgust, excitement, and anxiety washed over me—grogged emotions. I closed my eyes for a moment to beat my feelings into submission. *Breathe.*

What was it about that place?

I tried not to feel, not to look too closely. My gaze hopped quickly from pod to pod, spiraling around the track coiling through the core of the building until it landed on the pod parked in front of the visiting platform. I tried not to look at it.

At her. The child was a girl. I had to look again; something about her humanity demanded it. Her body had only decayed a little, the process slowed by the pod fluid. The serial number read ROS934, the first three letters of a last name and an identification number. Some of my grade school friends from Citizen families used to refer fondly to their serial numbers. Being a Borderlander, I lived with the dual humiliation of having no serial number and having a belly button. I was born. They were formulated.

"I'll call you Rosa," I said out loud. The person in front of me deserved to be named. No matter how I tried, I couldn't avoid the tragedy of the place. Emotions threatened to bloom one by one.

Anger. Cut it down.

Sadness. Shut it out.

Suspicion. *How can this be anything but wrong?*

Grief. *Am I less of a human or more of a Citizen for refusing it?*

The supplies I needed were not there. I needed to keep moving if I was to defeat the one responsible. Him. It. That monster.

I continued around the second-floor balcony and used one of the office windows to seek an avenue to the next factory. It was very close, nearly touching, so that I couldn't tell much about the building. There seemed to be a well-used walkway between the doors on the ground floor.

On my way, I passed meeting rooms and official-looking offices. A door labeled Dr. Scibey, Program Director, caught my eye. Inside, shelves full of scrolls begged me to find comfortable answers to my uncomfortable questions. Surely there were ample studies that would put me at ease.

I found a small scroll, a patient file, sitting partially unrolled on the desk. In the evening light through the office window, I skimmed over it. Surely there was no invasion of privacy when all the patients and staff were long gone. Just a peek.

It wasn't a standard couple profile of a Sanctius Citizen matched with the genetic information needed to begin embryo germination. There were various medical drawings of the woman, abdomen swollen. She was with child. Someone had sketched a fetus in various positions.

I wandered behind the desk to a pile of scrolls of similar records. All the patients had come by watership from other corners of the Earth. Men, women, and children from less sophisticated civilizations sought refuge in Sanctius. Some scrolls traced the movements of pregnant women who refused treatment in the Human Life Tower. Most of them had moved to the Borderlands or the harbor area and were eventually lost to the knowledge of the Citizen staffers. No doubt, they had succumbed to the spells the Wilderman employed in those areas and evanesced. *Like Raina. And now Franky.*

I redirected my hardly containable feelings into renewed zeal for my purpose. If it weren't for that monster, this place would still be chugging along, multiplying humanity. I used to think all the cryptid beasts of the wilderness were the problem. But it was him. The Wilderman seemed to be the overseer of everything wrong with this world. Fumes bellowed through all my inner workings, and I rushed out of the building to hunt for something useful. I ran to the next building and burst through the door.

I was astounded to find myself in the Council tower. The door opened directly in front of the alternate elevator. Instinctively, I pushed the button, but immediately turned to hunt for stairs. It wouldn't work, of course, because the Wilderman had destroyed the last running steam tower.

But it opened.

When the doors began to close again, I stopped them and jumped inside. The Council must have had its own steam tank and engine somewhere. Or some other power source. The doors sat closed, and the elevator waited. But where was I going?

I wanted some answers. What was the Council doing? How did they still have power? There had to be more information that could help me take the Wilderman out. I selected the highest button, the sideways ellipse, and the elevator surged upward. My heart raced at the thought that my heroes might be waiting for me when the doors opened. But after a couple of seconds, it came to a gentle stop.

I pressed the ellipse. Then I pressed the B button and all the numbers. Nothing happened.

I paced for a while. I banged my head against the stamped metal on the walls. For a moment, an idea gave me hope. I wedged a knife behind one of the thin brass wall tiles, anticipating access to some of the mechanics. Not that I knew what I would do with it. But then I'd turned a steam cycle into a rideable elevator that day, so my confidence was brimming. Unfortunately, I found nothing but framing. Even when I used my crossbow to move a ceiling tile aside, all the mechanical bits were encased and out of reach.

And then I sank to the floor, head in my hands, willing away the helpless urge to flee. *I'm losing control.*

"You never had it." The temptation to give in to the overwhelming odds against me slithered into the elevator and pervaded my thoughts. The space suddenly felt tiny, like it was squeezing the life out of me. I needed a distraction.

I reached for Tino's scroll from my satchel. What was it that drew me to read it in so many moments of restlessness and solitude? Was I clinging to my last feeble connection to my family? Again, something silent whispered to me to open it, to search its pages, to solve the puzzle within. My exhaustion from the day caught up with me, and my head fell to my chest, dozing intermittently as I read. Tino's next story wove in and out of my sleep like a vivid, nightmarish vision.

Luminary Tale
SLAYING THE GIANTS OF BARAK

Nico, I think this will be hard to read. I hope it is, that you're not so hardened. It was certainly difficult to rescribe it here. Don't take for granted how much truth is in this mythology. It's terrible, but true just the same.

A long time ago, here on the great Orange plains, after the clans migrated here and scattered abroad, there were still giants and beasts rampant in the land. All the people knew the dangers of the evil creatures. Though we spoke different languages and lived in different houses, all men performed the secret sign to prove their humanity whenever they came upon a stranger. It was passed from the elders to the young when they came of age, so that the giants and those-who-could-change-form would never learn the sign and fool the people. We do not say the name of those-who-could-change-form, for to name them is to call them.

Often, messengers and traders visited other villages and tribes, making the sign as they entered. They heard ominous reports throughout the land with uncomfortable similarities. From the windy lower plains to the towering forests, people all over the Orange corner of the world went missing. Skilled hunters had not returned. Water jugs lay by the rivers, with no sign of the women who had carried them there. Worst of all, children disappeared with unsettling regularity.

When the messengers had carried this sad news all over the land, all the elders in the many clans and villages knew it was time for action. They met in a village in the center of the Orange corner of the world and called many brave men to hunt out the evil creatures and giants to kill them, and if possible, find out where the missing people had gone. No one had ever gone looking for these beasts before. In fact, they carefully avoided all the pale giants' known haunts. But those brave warriors were up to the task.

After several months, a few of the chosen men returned to the village of meeting, ragged and injured. They told a tale that shocked the elders and angered the men of all the plains and forests, high and low. The warriors had killed many evil beasts in many different forms before they made it to a strange and terrible place. Stones stood unnaturally on their ends and atop one another in enormous stacks. Where the land had been flat and peaceful, hills and mountains built with earth and stone tore the sky. Giants roamed about, and those-who-could-change-form came to meet them, but it was unclear what they were doing.

The men remained hidden to find the purpose of the place. When the moon rose, so did the activity in the strange area. The warriors gazed in shock as those-who-could-change-form dragged people from all directions to the place. Giants forced some of the people to work as slaves—carrying, cooking, and all kinds of work. There were confused but healthy-looking men and women brought in that night, whom the giants shoved into line with others who were gaunt and bent over. The entire area was a flurry of activity.

Then, all the hearts of the brave men swelled hot in their chests. The giants took the children who had been brought in that night and dragged them all toward one of their built-up mountains, chanting the name of Barak. Barak's star-children and fabrications—giants, beasts, two-legged, four-legged, horned, antlered, hairy, every known evil and more—slowly gathered around an altar. As soon as they realized the children were to be used in an evil ritual, several of the warriors simultaneously signaled an attack. They rushed into the encampment and attacked the giants, each with the weapon of his people, freed the captives and destroyed the altars.

In the heat of the battle, the men divided themselves. One group was to escort the captives home, and the second was to fight as long and as hard as possible to allow the others to get away. But the giants were too many for them.

When the pale giants saw their captives escaping, they ignored the warriors in the camp and went after those in flight. Though the brave men chased the evil creatures, so many spread out or changed form that they could not find them all. The attack party searched the area for days. Besides a few in the form of the sly dog, they did not overtake their enemy, nor did they find any captives. They returned to the village of meeting, exhausted and frustrated.

Now the council of elders was greatly angered at this story, for each one understood that similar atrocities occurred near their homes. Every elder returned to their clans and villages. They told the heart-breaking truth to their people. At first, most people did not want to believe their elders. Those who had lost loved ones did not want to believe such evil could have been done to them. But the elders chided them, reminding them of their duty to oversee the land, to uphold good.

When the people accepted the truth, they too were angered at the atrocities committed against the children of mankind. Then, all the people prepared to battle the great evil, for it would take them all to defeat such darkness.

Every village sought out the giants and provoked them to come and fight. When the giants saw the people united against them, they were afraid. They ran and hid. But the people chased the giants and killed them at the altars where they had sacrificed children, threw them off the mountains of their divination, buried them in the mounds of their sorcery, and burned them in the caves where they had lurked.

And so, my children, that is how all the men of our Orange corner of the world united against great evil. Remember it well. For though the few remaining monsters may have retreated into cave and hollow, today darkness disguises itself in clothing of light and walks about in broad daylight. Our sons and daughters are still taken captive, and it will take many wise and discerning warriors to fight it.

STRANGER THAN FICTION

The elevator surged upward again, jarring me from sleep. How long had I been in there, sleeping and reading in turns? My spine prickled. Could it have been a coincidence that the cage moved after I had finally finished that tale? The butterflies returned to my stomach. I was about to enter the Council's secret chamber, the glass half-orb that overlooked the entire city.

The doors opened, and my suspicion mounted. The sun had risen over the Eastern Sea like a spotlight on the scene. From the inside, the orb atop the Council tower looked like a command station. A brass dashboard encircled the room under the thick, tinted windows. There were ivory buttons and leather-handled levers at workstations every few arm-lengths. At each station, there was a chair, and the elbows of regal violet Councilmen's jackets poked out on the sides. But the room was startlingly still.

I circled the room, turning the chairs to face me. *No, no, no.* In nearly every chair where I hoped to find a Councilman and answers to my questions, there was a dry, decaying body in a purple jacket. My heart pounded.

This is the Council. They drop communication banners and preside over the city with supreme wisdom and authority. Dead?

My certainties withered like the rotted flesh scarcely clinging to the

Councilmen's skeletons. The sight was appalling, and I was affronted by it. How dare the Councilmen die without leaving word or anything?

The events of the week were more than I could bear. Raina. Franky. The Wilderman's appearances—quickly becoming incessant and beyond annoying. And here was the Council, rotting at their stations.

My aloneness closed in on my mind with high velocity. All the messages and edicts on the banners—clockwork? What happened to these men? How long had they lain here? And how in the wilderness did this tower still have power? I didn't know what to do, but nothing wasn't an option. I needed answers.

If the Council couldn't provide answers, then I'd find them myself.

In the center of the room was a large square desk surrounded by four more chairs, high-backed and upon closer inspection, hiding four more skeletons. I scanned to and fro. There were no obvious signs of violence. Many of the bodies had weapons, but they were all holstered.

Between the desk and the eastern windows of the orb, a cylinder hung from the ceiling. It was enormous, too large for me to wrap my arms around, and beautifully gilded. Artfully made brass handles and gears extended from the wall, the cylinder close to the central desk. I walked around the machine, trying to ascertain what it might be. I turned one of the handles a quarter turn, and the whole contraption tipped back toward me slightly. A glimmer of light slipped across the floor. I bowed low to peer through an extension off the side of the cylinder.

Of course, a telescope. It was pointed at the sky, which was growing brighter as morning bloomed into midday. Maybe they were looking at something at night.

I walked around the room, slowly taking in each workstation. Two of the men at the central desk were slumped over their work, but I could see schematics and maps among the various papers.

"Excuse me." I pulled a thick, open scroll from under one of the bodies. "Don't mind my tug."

A cloud of dust puffed out with the stack of papers, and I hid my face in my arm until it settled. Each of the layers was a map of the city and surrounding areas. I felt pretty lost. A map seemed a comfort, however small. I laid the scroll out on the desk.

There was a regular street map, a layout of all the steamworks and underground drive assemblies, and even a layout of all the ampgas stations in Sanctius. A few pages contained detailed drawings of some of the buildings. Several maps had markings and symbols I couldn't make sense of. Architectural schematics. Traffic planning. Flip, flip, flip. Until something caught my eye.

On one map, the streets and buildings were marked in pale gray, hardly perceptible. More boldly, some kind of canon was stamped in red ink here and there throughout the city. Scattered around the sea east of the city were blue-stamped steamships. Instinctively, I looked for them outside the large, curved windows facing the sea. Of course, the sky was empty. There were no captains; there were no crews. There could be no airships. On the far-right side of the map, there was a roughly crescent-shaped blotch labeled Eastern Isle.

There is no land in the Eastern Sea. The memory of my grade school field trip on the airship came surging back.

I looked through the telescope again. Nothing but the sky. Relief hovered over me but couldn't settle.

My eyes swept over the map again. It dawned on me that I had clumsily bumped the handle and redirected the telescope. I lightly touched one handle and then another, trying to remember which I'd messed with. I nudged the left handle, and the telescope moved horizontally. *Wrong.* I inched that handle back to its place. When I rested my hand on it, the right handle moved clockwise a quarter turn like a downhill walk toward home. The refraction of light on the floor skipped toward the desk. I stepped onto it so that the light illuminated the toe of my boot with a full shining spectrum. And then I bent to look.

Why did I hesitate?

Because I knew. I knew the island was there. I knew there was an emerald gem breaking the horizon line. But if I knew it, why then, when I finally rested my face on the eyepiece, did the silhouette of it on the blazing morning horizon knock the wind out of me?

The island was real.

So what? Well, the telescope was poised directly at it. So the Council had known about it too.

I thought for a moment, but as always, an answer was provided for me from the emptiness around me. It only meant that a great evil lay out there. Weapons around the city and heavily armored airships had guarded Sanctius for many years; they were protecting us. It made sense then that their deaths coincided with the escalation of the Wilderman's attacks on Citizens.

"They died protecting you." I didn't register the whisper from the shadows. My thoughts followed suit without skipping a beat.

They must have died protecting us. The thought offered a little comfort.

"And fighting the Wilderman."

They must have been actively fighting the Wilderman. I looked again at all the steamships mapped out around the Eastern Sea, obviously a defense against whatever was on that island. There were more air balloons, ships and guard stations marked on the Hungry Mountain. Why? I had never noticed them since I'd been hunting. But then they were further up the mountain than I preferred to go.

"Higher."

There, nearing the highest altitude of the Hungry Mountain, was marked in tiny bold red print: WILDERMAN CABIN.

Mentally, my gears spun at max revolutions.

"I have his location," I whispered through my bated breath.

"But so did the Council," the shadows argued.

So either they chose not to take him out, or they couldn't. I churned over what I knew about the history of Sanctius—which didn't feel like nearly enough.

"How can I learn from the Council's mistakes and formulate a better tactic if I don't know what their mistakes were?"

"I can tell you what their biggest mistake was." The direct offer made it impossible to write off the whispers from the darkness as my own thoughts.

I stood rigid, still looking out the window, searching the reflection of the room. My eyes darted to the corpses, their occupied holsters.

"None of that now." It was a man's voice from the back of the room, deep but a little scratchy, like he'd just woken up. "I'm here to help you, Nico."

"How do you know who I am?" I turned slowly to face the speaker. He was very tall. So tall, in fact, that his head, dotted with a few brassy hairs that betrayed red hair in days gone by, nearly touched the ceiling. He wore a nice suit, though it hung loosely on him, and his face looked a little gaunt.

"You're the last man on Earth. You're our last hope."

The audible statement that I was the last man on Earth made something in my chest feel swollen.

Wait. "Our?"

"Yes. We're interested in the future of Earth. You could say we're the council behind the Council. We work, and have worked, throughout history in concert with mankind to ensure a future that is… mutually beneficial."

"How's that going for you?" I retorted. Nothing was going my way, and it didn't seem likely it was going his way either.

A dry chuckle was his only answer.

"Well? What mistake could have left *all* the Sanctius City Councilmen dead here at one time?" I glanced around at the remains of the greatest men of my era. And then I scrutinized the sallow form before me. I should have felt happy to find that there was another human—or something like it—there with me. But although I knew all too well that there were other "things" out there, something about his sudden humanesque appearance grated against something inside of me.

"You are obviously a wise and well-educated man."

"Oh, well, I have tried to learn and grow ever since I became a Citizen. But I—"

"You know this is a complicated world that contains much more than meets the eye."

"Well, of course; I've been dodging monsters since I was a mere boy."

"Let's avoid labels such as monster until further discussion," he hissed, as if he held in pressurized steam. "We'll use 'entity' to avoid any misplaced connotations."

Where was he going with this?

"You're well aware that not all the entities on this planet are friendly to mankind. Nor do they all get along with one another. I would like to introduce you to my associates. We have worked alongside men, sometimes in a… governing capacity, for many centuries. For much of that time, we did this publicly and with splendid results. Some extenuating circumstances forced us to move underground, both figuratively and quite literally. Would you accompany me, Nico, to our deep underground council chamber?"

"I don't even know who or what you are. You could be a cave troll or a forest rake luring me to my death like so many before. I'm not the last surviving human for nothing."

"Oh, please forgive me. I forgot to properly introduce myself in my expeditious efforts to form a collaboration. I am Magnus from the tribe of Aza."

Aza?

"Yes. You recognize the name of my forefather. I'm so pleased to see that you've been studying the extraordinary histories of our gallant alliance."

I wondered if he noticed the twitch betraying my sudden urge to devour Tino's entire scroll. Surely he wasn't some sort of demigod. No matter what he was, it might be best that he remained unaware of the scroll. Magnus looked anxiously out the window before continuing.

"I'm sure you're wondering how this could be true. It's a very long story, best told by the entire lot of us. I would love to introduce you to my comrades. And I'm sure you'd enjoy some companionship, maybe over some supper?"

My stomach prompted me to accept his offer, but I was still suspicious. "I don't understand why any of this concerns me."

"Why, Nico! You're the survivor! I know that the gods—oh, none of that now—we as *entities* have been somewhat absent, but we're in this together. We can help each other."

"If you're some kind of deity, how could I possibly help you? And what makes you think I would?"

"Because I know we want the same thing."

I raised my eyebrows.

"The final and absolute defeat of the Wilderman."

I tried to look unfazed. But my pulse pounded at my temples, and my hands shook. I thought about playing it cool and pretending I might not need their help. Desperation for victory over the Wilderman at any cost won out.

"And you think we can accomplish this together?"

The appalling presence of royally jacketed corpses slumped in their chairs only deepened my desperation.

"I'm positive. Come, let us discuss the matter in full." He opened his hand toward the elevator, but then stopped and pointed at the loosely rolled maps sitting on the desk. "Oh, and you might as well bring those."

Should I trust this 'entity' that considers himself a god? Up to that point, I had devoted my life to the principles of Sanctius Citizenry, the edicts developed by Councils past. But the Council I trusted lay rotting around me. And apparently, Magnus's council was in some kind of partnership with them. Maybe they pulled the strings along. Essentially, they've always had my loyalty. Why should it change now? Surely, they would only want to continue the City Council's good work. The Wilderman was my enemy. And he was their enemy, too. Didn't that mean we were on the same team?

For a second, I looked at the bodies of the Council I'd trusted. Then, I evaluated Magnus, waiting for me to board the elevator with him. His sallow form, his thin red hair—nothing about him screamed deity. Otherworldly, possibly. But divine? But then, any "entity" that could assist me in getting the Wilderman out of my way could be worth a partnership. I stepped under Magnus's arm, extended to hold the elevator door open, and walked into a partnership with one monster to defeat another.

GODS AND MONSTERS

The giant Magnus pressed the eighth button below the "B," and we descended. The elevator worked perfectly. Had he disrupted the elevator service to the Council room before? Or maybe the Wilderman? I fiddled with my satchel and adjusted the strap on my shoulder, wondering if either 'entity' would want me reading Tino's collection. I peered up at the giant through the corner of my eyes. His head bowed forward, and the few hairs on the top of his nearly bald head still tickled the stamped metal ceiling tiles.

What kind of underground base would self-proclaimed gods operate from? It turned out to be something straight out of a fairy tale.

The elevators opened into a massive oblong conference room, complete with a comically large table. The domed ceiling appeared to have been gilded at one time, though even from far below I could see it was chipped and tarnished by moisture. Perfectly round tunnels radiated into the distance in every direction. The elevator was situated in a wall between two such tunnels. From one tunnel, I could hear slow-moving water. Another emanated an inaudible hum of energy, hinting at the hidden power source. All were black as night, even though the main hall was well lit, revealing the strange scene in front of me.

Nothing could have prepared me for the attendees convened around the table. Every face gawked at us. All seated around the table were similar to Magnus's size and humanoid appearance. There were a couple with darker complexions; the rest were fair with blonde or red hair.

Even crazier was the myriad of standing attendants. Gathered around the giants, creatures—normally reserved for myths—carried trays, tablets, and drinks, apparently for their masters. There were small dragons, wild men, minotaurs—all the beasts about which I'd been warned by the city leaders. *See? I knew they were right.*

The towering men sat in high-backed chairs that, though solid enough to hold their occupants, had the appearance of shining liquid mercury. Each chair's back featured an emblem near the top. Magnus introduced them while I attempted to take it all in. He stretched his hand toward our left. The first chair had the emblem of a crossed hammer and sword with icicles dangling from them in the back.

"Nico, may I introduce you to Lars of the warriors of Yomi? And this is Edi of the line of Rami."

Edi had a cobra carved into his chair. Magnus's hand politely gestured around the room at the seats with emblems of a cheetah, a jackal, a bull, a walrus with massive tusks, and the mermaid emblem from Franky's cane.

"This is Omar from the line of Mârôs, Mato, a son of Barak, Ali of the sons of Ezek, Pasha of the line of Batai, and Finn of the large and illustrious family of Arach."

I stared at the familiar mermaid emblem and the giant sitting in front of it. Something about the menacing smile he returned broke my gaze.

"And finally, as I said before, I am Magnus of the distinguished house of Aza." He pointed toward his own seat, which carried the emblem of an eight-pointed star resting on a mountain peak.

I stood there awkwardly, wondering what I was supposed to do. For some reason, I had a desire to back slowly onto the elevator and leave. As if he had read my mind, Magnus placed his hand on my shoulder. His hand was so large that it engulfed the upper right corner of me.

"Come, sit with us, Nico." He pointed to a large stone block next to his chair. "Let's discuss a future that would be advantageous to us all."

I glanced around the table and wondered how that was possible. They stared back at me with eager eyes. But what were they eager for? The cold stone stool beneath me sent a chill up my back. Their hungry eyes didn't help.

"You said you could help me take out the Wilderman."

"Yes, yes." His voice sounded more tired than it had at the top of the Council tower. The words hissed out from between his teeth. "In fact, you're the one in the position to help. We're quite obliged to you."

He looked expectantly at all the other giants around the table. Nods with "Oh, yes, yes," and "Much obliged," met him in response.

"How do you suppose I could help you? You seem to be a powerful lot." I gazed around at the monsters at their beck and call.

"But we're not human, you see. And matters are complicated in our… realm, you could say."

"If you're not human, what are you?"

"You are, of course, a well-educated young man. You will have read from the mythologies from across the world?"

"Of course." My mind fled to my satchel.

"And you know of the demigods, the heroes of old?"

"So you're—" My eyes widened in honest surprise that he implied this once again. The pieces were all there for me to figure out, but how could I be anything but shocked if they were actual demigods?

"Yes, we are the descendants of the Luminaries. We reign over the kingdoms of the Earth."

"Are you immortal?"

"Not quite," he answered with staccato regret.

"But weren't your ancestors, the Luminaries, immortal?"

"In a manner of speaking, yes." Magnus looked down at me out of the corner of his eye. Maybe he wondered if I knew too much. I decided to back off a little.

"I just wonder, why do you need me to kill the Wilderman? If you are god-kings, why haven't you destroyed him already?" Besides being skeptical regarding how I could help, I felt a little angry that they hadn't done something about the Wilderman and his evil beasts. How many lives could have been saved from evanescence? But then…

I looked around at all the servants of the giants, just then able to spare them enough thought to take in the utter weirdness of them all. The minotaur, some kind of small dragon or very large lizard, and a centaur all brought food and drink to their masters. I shrank when the hairy wild man set two goblets and a large platter of cheese on the table next to Magnus.

I had never been more confused about the moral position of the beasts of the wilderness. If they were against the Wilderman, then surely they couldn't be all bad. But then, the Council had warned us… Did both sides have their own armies of monsters? Thankfully, Magnus interrupted my thoughts before my brain overheated.

"That's quite a long story, Nico. But I suppose you must hear some of it. I know you will understand our plight." He took a sip of the deep red liquid in the goblet, settling into his chair. "You see, long ago, the Wilderman himself, though he went by another name, tasked us with caring for the kingdoms of the Earth, for he was also a king like us. But it wasn't long before he grew jealous. Because of the love the people had for us and the accomplishments we achieved, he tried to steal our kingdoms, the inheritance of the Luminaries, from our fathers and from us.

"The Wilderman caused great destruction; the face of the Earth was never the same again. All the kingdoms were in tumult and fought against one another. You must understand, they had to in order to survive. He even imprisoned our forefathers deep under the oceans!"

Murmurs and sighs of concurring pity levitated down the long table, which I noticed for the first time had an intricate pattern of inlaid wood beneath its congealed layer of grime. A suspicious stain darkened the floor near the entrance of one of the off-shooting tunnels. I looked at the floor of worn and broken mosaic tile, wondering what else lay this far below ground that I was unaware of.

"He made war against us to take back all the kingdoms of Earth for himself. The Wilderman recruited men to help him, lying and deceiving them to hate us and our servants. He had his own army of fierce, inhuman beings."

All the giants joined Magnus in shaking their heads. Some even shook their fists at the chipped gold ceiling, uttering curses at the Wilderman somewhere above them. Anger for all the friends and family I'd lost mounted with their jeering.

"But what can *I* do?"

"Since he collects humans, you can get close enough. Our best efforts have had mankind at the forefront. We thought we'd beat him once, sentenced to execution for his crimes. But losing a little blood isn't enough to kill him. We must disintegrate him!" Magnus pounded his fist on the table as the words hissed out with extra pressure.

I jumped, and my heart raced.

The rest of the giants laughed darkly and jeered some more. This did nothing to soothe my racing pulse. But disintegration... Their vengeful energy drew me with them, and I smiled; this might actually work. They must know a way. My thoughts ran ahead of Magnus's explanation.

"Can you actually do that?" I burst out in my excitement.

"The human wonders if it's possible."

Dark laughs radiated around the room.

"Soon enough, Nico. You must allow me to explain some more of our history to better prepare you."

I nodded, but I would have preferred that he'd gotten to the point and sent me back up the elevator with whatever secret he intended to impart.

"Besides giving many gifts to mankind, we maintained intimate relationships with many influential families. In the early days, we could live openly among your kind as allies and governors. As times changed, so did humanity. It became prudent for us to work closely with... select humans."

"The Council." The words escaped my mouth as fast as they dawned on my mind.

"Yes, very good."

"So the Council's recent activity, like the banners?"

"Occasionally us. Mostly clockwork. Once a few simple banners were loaded into each tube, they flipped out one by one and didn't require any work on our part unless events warranted a special message.

"Like all sentient beings, humans have a certain pride. We knew some things would be better received by humanity from their fellow men. We allowed select *men of interest* to bestow our gifts to mankind. Sort of a 'charges d'affaires ad interim' situation, if you know what I mean."

I didn't. I had so many questions, still stuck on *all* sentient beings. How many races of sentient beings were there? But it was rhetorical, and Magnus didn't pause for discussion.

"As you've worked out, governments such as your Council, monarchs, dictators, as well as leading thinkers and inventors worked in close relationship with us to benefit the sons of the Luminaries and humanity alike."

"So steam power—was that a collaboration?"

Snickers answered.

"Oh, Nico. Surely, you don't think men like Franky's father made Sanctius what it is today. Throughout history, we have been providing your kind with the tools and technologies needed for beneficial advancement. You may have gotten there eventually, but we get impatient sometimes. You know, waiting around for generations and all."

If I, a gardener and food enthusiast, could make a steambike drive up the side of a building, surely ingenuitive men like Franky could have revolutionized steam. I tried hiding the defiance on my face, but it must have shown. Magnus reached out and patted my back.

"Yes, you understand the human pride we discussed. And we do care about your feelings. So you can see why our kindness led us to work more covertly in the modern era, to preserve your dignity." His last sentences seethed out in a creepy but patronizing tone, almost as if he were speaking to a child.

There was no use arguing with a room full of hungry-looking giants. So I waited for him to so kindly bestow whatever gift would help defeat the Wilderman. I placed a thumb and forefinger in my pocket to reach for my watch. I hesitated to take it out for fear that it would offend them or that they might take it from me. Still, the feel of the cool gold icon comforted me as he went on.

"Although you are not an emblem holder, it seems fitting that one with solely human blood would receive our gift and carry out our final victory."

Solely human blood. Only human. "Do you mean that the Council members were something other than human?"

"Not just the Council members, but all emblem holders… among others. The Luminaries and many of our predecessors took human wives and husbands. Our bloodlines are just another of our gifts to humanity and… worth preservation, however diluted they might be by now." Magnus peered greedily into the darkness of the stained hallway.

I thought back to Tino's scroll and the tales of the Luminaries. So far, this all lined up. But there was something about the tone of these stories that made me wonder what else my brother was getting at. And why would Tino have let the Wilderman get to him if he knew all of this about the Luminaries and their descendants? How could he have still evanesced? Perhaps the gift of the scroll was his last act of sanity.

Magnus rose from his chair and walked toward one of the tubular hallways radiating from the main chamber.

"Though the Wilderman succeeded in hiding the technology of our first fathers from us, we have rediscovered some of the ancient ways."

The giant named Lars rubbed his hands together in greedy anticipation. They all shifted in their chairs as Magnus disappeared down a tunnel for a few moments. Magnus's absence made me shrink on my stool. Though I had but little trust in him, I had much less in the rest. The seconds felt like hours waiting for Magnus to return, hoping his demi-god buddies and their monster side-kicks didn't get hungry in the meantime.

THIS IS OUR FUTURE

Magnus returned with an oddly shaped gun in his hands. It was much more rounded than the revolvers I was familiar with. But after all the anticipation, just a gun?

He placed it gingerly on the table in front of us. On closer inspection, the front didn't seem to have a barrel, nor did I see a chamber for bullets. On the contrary, something like an antenna protruded out the front. Much of the gun was white, but it had metallic marbling throughout. At the back of the gun, something like a dinner plate formed a sort of shield between the gun and the shooter. Besides the relative shape and a trigger, it looked nothing like any gun I'd ever seen.

Confused but unimpressed, I turned to Magnus for some kind of explanation.

"This is a high-frequency collection and emission weapon. Sometimes we call it the life-taser."

More nefarious chuckles from around the table.

"But," Magnus continued, "we just refer to it as a frequency gun."

"And you think this can kill the Wilderman once and for all?"

"The Wilderman thinks *he's* the king of everything up there, except some of our known loyal servants." He motioned to the chimerical menagerie standing behind the giants.

I wondered how many more might be lingering down those dark hallways.

"So we turned that against him." He gently laid his hand on the gun to explain its functions. "When you pull this trigger, the materials in this gun create a sort of vibrational vacuum. In doing so, it collects energy from everything within range. As long as you hold on to this trigger, the gun will charge. When you release the trigger, it will emit the entirety of that charge. So, the longer you hold the trigger, the higher the frequency the weapon will emit. This ceramic shield encourages the gun to draw from the plane in front of the shooter. *But* we don't recommend frequent use for extended periods."

Before I could get a question in about the risks of doing so, he continued.

"You must hold it down for several seconds to do any damage. A quick burst will collect only a hundred hertz at most, which will often help your enemy rather than harm them. Remember that. It may come in handy in an emergency.

"Now, there's no use dilly-dallying down here anymore when you could be ending all our troubles for good. Let's get you—"

"Wait a minute. I have some questions."

Magnus looked around at his buddies, annoyance on all their faces. He forced a smile. "I'm sure you do. And I wish we had all the time in the world to fill you in. Do any of them pertain to your mission? If not, the rest of your questions can wait until we initiate you as one of us upon your victorious return." His encouragement was obviously forced as impatience dominated his mood.

"Well, up in the Council chamber, it seemed like the Wilderman's headquarters are on the Eastern Isle. How am I going to get there?"

Incredulous protests erupted from each of the sons of the Luminaries. Magnus held his hands out to silence them.

"You are not to make any attempts to reach the Eastern Isle. As long as you are here, the Wilderman will be as well. Take out the scroll I instructed you to bring."

My heart raced when he mentioned a scroll. Though I was relieved he was referring to the maps, my hands still shook as I unrolled them and flipped for the layer he'd want.

"I believe you saw a map with his cabin labeled."

I found the correct one and set the whole thing on the table. Holding the tube with one hand, I used the other to smooth out the map and hold the curling right edge down.

"This map labeled strategic military offensive positions we assisted the Council in setting up."

"What happened to them?" I interrupted.

Magnus looked around at his comrades before answering, pleading for patience once more. "In short, they tried to steal this weapon." He patted the gun. "And, shall we say, scale it up. They tried to outdo us, and it did them in."

Ali and Finn laughed through their noses. Magnus glared at them with wide eyes.

My indignation flared at their flagrant insult toward Sanctius. "Is it funny to you that the greatest men of my time died all at once because of you?"

"Oh, ho ho—the little man still defends his little city," Ali retorted. The rest of them burst into laughter.

"Silence!" Magnus yelled.

"We don't have to listen to you. You're not the king of us," Mato spat at Magnus.

The other giants and their servants all muttered agreement.

But Magnus ignored them and spoke directly to me. "Now, Nico. It's important that you listen to *me*." He cast a sidelong glance down the table. "We cannot join your mission, but we will keep an eye out for you."

"Why—"

"Let's just say it would only make things worse for you, you know, draw attention. And the sunlight doesn't really agree with us these days. We're giving you an extraordinary gift with this weapon. You must promise to use it well." At the word *promise,* I looked once again around that cavernous council chamber and its ridiculous occupants. I wondered if it was even possible to make a gentleman's agreement when no one else was even a man.

"What's in this for me? I mean in the long run."

"Oh, Nico," Magnus took on a patronizing tone again. "You

will be a king among men! Walking this Earth, with no other man to contend with, you are the first to use this technology in full. And no man can steal it from you. Once you kill the Wilderman, you'll be the legend that begins a new era for mankind. And then, of course, we can make *arrangements* to keep you from loneliness."

"Are you saying there are other people somewhere on Earth?" Hope rose that I wasn't truly alone. They could help me kill the Wilderman, and then I could start anew.

"I'm saying there are more of *us* on the Earth. And that includes women, of course. Such a king as you, Nico, would require a queen—a goddess to rule beside you. Indeed, such arrangements have been made before with great success. With the gift of our frequency technology, you'll be indomitable."

A king. After all that time remaining loyal and refusing to let go like all the others, I would finally be rewarded. This was so much larger than a penthouse suite. It was dominion. I let myself imagine the immense comforts, rewards, even preeminence. Meanwhile, a disagreement had broken out again amongst the council.

"Well, it *won't* be my corner," one giant protested. His antlered companion nodded and huffed in agreement.

"If you'll recall our original discussion, *Pasha*, you have no need to worry," Magnus spat with hidden meaning in his eyes. Then he turned to me.

"So Nico, let's get you on your way. You have everything you need and we—"

"Hey!" the one called Omar interrupted. "We agreed! We want a full commitment! Take him to the inner room and spill—" Chaos erupted as the others cried out in agreement until Magnus threw his hand out to stop them again and continued.

"Nico, do you remember the boyish tradition of exchanging blood to seal a promise or friendship?"

My chest felt tight, and a cold tide of new fear crashed over me. What would they do to me?

"We do a similar little thing here, just to prove we're all in this together. Okay?"

My breath came in short huffs. They wanted my blood. But then, they certainly couldn't kill me if they wanted me to do their dirty work.

"Yeah, okay," I shrugged to feign a casual assent to whatever terrifying ritual they required. What choice did I have?

Immediately, Lars, nearest to my left, jumped and threw his arms around me.

I let out a yelp, but Magnus reassured me there was no need for a struggle.

While Lars held me tightly, Finn and Pasha pressed my hand down on the table so hard I thought they might crush it.

"Now, boys, you needn't be so dramatic," Magnus said as he approached with a knife in hand. "It only stings for a second, Nico. Do you promise on your life to take this weapon and hunt the Wilderman with it?"

"Well—I mean, I do but—do we really need to—AAAAHHHH!"

Magnus slit my wrist open. The wild man handed him an empty goblet, and he caught some of the blood. "That's not so bad," he said as he wrapped my wrist tightly with a cloth bandage. The wild man set the goblet on the table, causing me to hold the contents of the first goblet he'd brought in with appalled suspicion.

"Now, we all send you out against the Wilderman and wish you every success."

"Here, here!" shouted all the giants. They raised their glasses while Magnus led me to the elevator doors, tucking the frequency gun and map scroll into my satchel. "Best of luck, Nico. If worst comes to worst, we will come to your aid. We will do everything in our power to help you. But *you* are our best chance at success."

****

The elevator closed between us and deposited me on the ground floor of the Council tower. I didn't remember walking around to the front doors or circling the block to get back to the maintenance truck. I had a strange sense of relief—like most people who entered that chamber probably didn't reemerge. When I passed the ampgas station, I mindlessly strapped on a mask and inhaled deeply, trying to force some ampgas through the mask. Nothing. There was no clock to signal the hour and no steam tower to power the station. With my mind reeling, but unable to land on any coherent thought, I drove home, simultaneously dazed and tempestuous. If only there were a way to access ampcrystal to level me out.

The shock of all that had just occurred still clung heavily, dulling the excitement of my first ride as I rode the steambike elevator up to my penthouse suite. It was tricky to brake at the top without rolling back downward. And then, even after I set the cam brake and hooked it to a solid part of the frame, I had to climb from the bike to the patio over eighty-four floors of open elevator shaft.

Indescribable comfort washed over me as I walked safely around that haven. I meandered around my garden, taking time to tend a few plants and look over the city.

Poor Sanctius. She had cared for humanity so well. The wounds of neglect and the abuse the Wilderman had inflicted on her showed, even from eighty-four floors above. From the end of a raised bed of strawberries, I stared at the crumpled steam tower and debris littering the street around it.

In the absence of steam rising into the engine chambers, anger rose in me. I couldn't rebuild the tower myself. But maybe with the help of the giants… I pulled the frequency weapon from my satchel and examined it. The white material forming the bulk of the gun seemed ceramic to me. The metallic ribbons coiling through the gun looked copper and silver, possibly aluminium.

I pointed it to the west toward the cliffs that stole Raina from us, and then a little northward toward the nearest trees. It was the part of the forest that had tempted me so often, the forest that Franky had purposely used to deceive me. I would have to go back tomorrow, but I would be strong. It would be worth it to stop him.

I squeezed the trigger, taking my vengeful anger out on it. Magnus hadn't mentioned anything about range. Not until the gun made a faint whine did I release it, hoping it would affect the forest at such a distance.

I saw it before I heard it. The trees buckled as if someone had hit them with a cannonball the size of a building. Branches and needles flew, and then the deep, monstrous bang hit my ears, followed by the crashing of tree pieces crumbling down the mountain.

"Well, that should do the trick." I looked at the little handgun in awe. Just in front of me, the strawberries had all wilted and blackened like a cold winter frost had struck. A deep depression fell over me at the sight of them. It felt like all happiness had been sucked from my body.

"You can grow more," I consoled myself. But the dark, empty feeling remained. "Finalize your plans and finish this."

Talking to myself had become too natural, and I made a mental note to work on it after the Wilderman was dead. I removed the maps and Tino's scroll from my satchel and maneuvered the bulky gun gently back inside, allowing the shield to rest on the opening. I spread the scrolls out on my bed and formulated a plan.

Luminary Tale
THE ARAGHENÁNN AND THE FIGHTERS

Do you know why they call us fighters, my child? I will tell you.

There was a time when many tribes, led by heroes, dotted our land. These children of the Luminary Arach were fierce warriors and indulgent rulers—the Araghenánn. They taught us the art of bountiful hospitality, but they also taught our forefathers to look at humans as commodities—capturing, stealing, and enslaving men and women from other tribes and foreign lands. The Luminaries had passed their fiendish ways to their descendants.

In those days, life was brutal—starvation, shapeshifters, slavery. Death lingered around every corner. But our people have always known how to enjoy the moments between hardships. So, there were perpetual cycles of feasting and fighting.

One day, a sage appeared in the Green corner of the Earth. He stood unafraid of our warriors. He said he'd come to help them and teach them. Never before had anyone dared to come in peace. It shocked the people.

Our ancestors were tired of trying to walk in the shoes of the heroes that had come before. They had sacrificed their brothers and sisters, who had died willingly to earn favor from the gods for those they left behind. But they feared the dark magic of the heroes and their gods.

And then the sage came and told them something they'd never heard before. He told them to *fear not* for he knew an even greater power. The sage taught them a higher magic than the one they had practiced before. He taught them magic *over* the herbs rather than from them. Best of all, he taught them magic that brought life instead of death. It was a power that freed them from dependence on the heroes and the spirits that their fathers had served. Our people found a new hope.

The creatures in the shadows raged. The Araghenánn and their evil pets lost their firm hold over the Green corner of the Earth. Some of them retaliated. They attacked the people with new vengeance. They whispered violence into the hearts of the few men who despised the sage for the changes he brought to our land. The evil entities and angered warriors attacked the sage's followers, but they met with failure. The sage spoke as if there was a shield all about him and his followers. And they acted bravely accordingly. Thanks to the sage, the people of the Green corner of the world carried a light that could not be contained.

And things were good for a while. Not perfect, but good.

If there's one virtue the Luminaries and their evil children have, it's patience. So the Araghenánn waited. When the enemies of our people arrived, the Araghenánn empowered them in their attempts to conquer and subdue our forefathers. The advancements of the invaders combined with the sorcery of the Araghenánn nearly broke us. But alas, the light in us still could not be put out. The song on our lips could not be silenced, and our spirits could not be crushed. To be from the Green corner of the Earth is to be unconquerable. This, my son, is why they call us the fighters.

But take care, my child. For the Araghenánn only hid underground, and the dark magic still lies heavy in this land. This is why you must be careful to listen, with your ears *and* your heart, to stories of old, and why you must learn to be brave like the sage's followers, with the shield of light about you. For who knows when the darkness and the magic will reawaken and find the light dimmed in the hearts of men?

THE FALL OF THE GILDED CAGE

I woke from a deep and dreamless sleep fully dressed, with my head on a stack of parchment and the frequency gun on my bedside table. Tino's scroll laid open over the maps, which were unrolled to the strategic military layer with the Wilderman's cabin on it. Last I remembered, I'd plotted a swift path to the cabin that would pass by some of the marked previous locations of air balloons and defensive outposts. Maybe I could find something there to help me.

A couple of hours of rest had done me good. I breathed in the tension of the day, convincing myself to use the anxiety for my own ends. First, my garden. I'd care for my haven like every other day because I intended to return and enjoy it in peace for the rest of my days. Nothing could get in my way once the Wilderman was gone.

As if someone had prodded the laceration on my wrist, the fact that giants lurked underground awaiting the moment they could replace the Wilderman popped into my mind. *They're helpful. They'll let me go my own way once we all get what we want.*

I packed up my satchel and tried to smarten up my slept-in clothing. *It only makes sense that you would take him out. You're the best Citizen there's ever been.* I wasn't sure whether the thoughts originated from my own self-assurance or an actual voice in the shadows, so I just kept moving rather than thinking too long about it. I replaced all my weapons in their holsters and homes, donned my satchel and jacket, and made ready to leave as soon as I'd tended the garden.

Outside on the patio, the sun intermittently hid behind the clouds, alleviating me of both heat and brightness. It felt like a beautiful day to embark on a victorious campaign.

"You really should treat these grape vines with some pine needles once in a while. They like a little bit of acidity." The Wilderman's voice halted my thought.

The glimmer of the morning sun on the Eastern Sea silhouetted his bulky form. He stood near my and Franky's bench. "I know where there's a lovely old Aleppo pine shedding plenty of needles if you'd like me to show you."

"The only thing I want is for you to disappear off the face of the Earth forever."

"I don't doubt you mean that, but you're seeing things all wrong."

He moved around the bench. My hand twitched ever so slightly toward my satchel.

"Ah, yes. I noticed you've found one of the Council's many secrets. In fact, that's why I decided to pay you a little visit. Now, there might not be any more people for you to destroy, but I'm still going to have to ask you not to go firing that contraption into the forest. I'm sure you'll understand how I feel about the whole situation since you have your own little forest here that you care about so much."

My breath came hot out of my nostrils, and my lips were glued together. I'd never planned to encounter him here. And he had the audacity to compare my garden to his wicked woods. I stepped slowly around the garden toward the glass walls of the greenhouse to maneuver around him. If I needed to shoot this thing at him, I didn't want my conservatory or my flat obliterated with him. The best-case scenario was for me to bait him back out into the forest and away from my haven. Even though it was his home territory, I could engage him without risk to my suite.

"How's your man-eating mountain doing? If I fire this at it a few more times, will it puke Raina back up?"

"Raina walked across a bridge willingly to the Eastern Isle and wouldn't ever want to return. She pret-near danced across."

"Is that some euphemism for the death that comes to everyone who falls victim to the enchantments of your Wilderness?" I spat the words and immediately regretted it. I needed to keep my emotions in check, and this discussion wasn't helping.

"Now, I can see you're hurt that your friends have left. But you see, they tried to help you. Especially Franky. He warned you that time was running out. And it is, Nico."

"*Your* time is running out. Now I have a frequency weapon." I rested my hand on the grip of the gun sitting inside my satchel. "I *will* defend my home. I haven't outlived the rest of humanity for nothing."

The Wilderman laughed.

I stood aghast. Why was he always laughing? I thought my head would explode. *Breathe, Nico. Stay calm.*

"You're right. You're the most stubborn, self-righteous human on Earth." He chuckled some more at his own irony and then continued. "But I would like to offer you freedom from that—freedom from yourself and freedom from this city. It's a liberty that the sons of the Luminaries would hide from you. They would convince you there is no more freedom than the slavery you're in."

"Is this the spiel you always give before people evanesce? How inspiring."

"I can explain it some more, Nico. But you'll never hear me out as long as you're holed up in this tower where you've enthroned yourself. I know this is going to be hard to understand, but I care about you. So I'm going to have to take the tower. You can have another garden, Nico. But this one has to go."

I looked around in horror. No words would form to try to stop him.

"You've been trying to make sense of this ever since you took to reading Valentino's scroll. It's been especially difficult to wrestle with since you lost access to ampgas. But even without the poison in your veins, whispering to the ears of your heart, you refuse to see the truth. I will tear down all the high places, destroy every obstacle between you and me. Just like I did the steam tower and the Time Temple."

The leaves on the sweet peas in the nearest garden bed trembled.

A slow rumble resonated from deep below me through the soles of my feet. My eyes wrenched wide as my body tensed from skin to core.

"If you'll look at that little timepiece of yours, I think you'll find your time is up, son."

I tore my eyes from my enemy to pull it out of my waistcoat. My hands shook, but the hands of the watch stood perfectly still. *No, no, no.* I tried to wind it. *It can't be broken. I—I can fix it.* I shoved it away and refused to fall captive to his mind games. Heat filled my chest. I pulled the frequency gun out, indignant that he casually threatened both my last safe place and my prized possession.

But my aim found no target. He was gone.

The building quivered. *He couldn't. He wouldn't.*

But he had. He had destroyed the steam tower with a touch, and he would do it again to my home. I looked frantically about, desperately trying to think of a way to stop the demolition or save something of my rooftop paradise, everything I'd worked for.

The tower groaned a warning. I ran to my makeshift elevator and leaped into the seat, stowing the frequency gun in my satchel as I went. I released the lever on the cam brake and let the bike down one speed short of plummeting.

Three-quarters of the way down, the elevator cables swayed. *I can make it.* I willed the ground closer.

A deep twang echoed as the cables snapped. I leaped off the bike as I neared the ground floor. I landed hard, recovered quickly, and ran as fast as I could away from the building. My lungs burned as dust filled them.

A sickening crash sliced the air as the windows shattered from top to bottom. The walls crumbled until a deafening roar filled the air. I covered my ears and ducked as I ran. It rained glass and concrete. A cloud of dust chased me onward. When it settled, I turned to see the last of the iron framing bend over like folded laundry and then fall into the heap of rubble.

The dust continued to roll, but I didn't want to go any further away. This ruin was all I had left. I wanted to curl up in the wreckage that used to be my home. Or maybe I could find another. I'd find a little crevice to hide in and search for a new tower tomorrow.

As if in response to my thoughts, the earth shook under my feet. All the skyscrapers in Sanctius swayed. Cracking and popping warned me that the Wilderman was bringing the whole city down somehow.

I had to choose between surviving without the city or dying in it. The Council chose to die in it. I would not make the same mistake. I would survive. Where, I did not know. But memory sent me out of the city on the same path I'd run thousands of times. Upstream, along the creek, around up the mountain.

I didn't stop until my legs begged and pleaded and threatened to strike. My head swam. I sat at the base of a tree and resolved not to pass out. I leaned against the tree and failed.

While I lay sleeping, I dreamed I was in my garden. I wandered around, taking in the fullness of it, knowing in my subconscious mind that it had all been taken from me. Ripe peas were ready to explode out of their pods. The weight of their abundance caused the vines to fight against the twine guiding them up the trellis.

I pulled the hem of my shirt up into a basket and picked peas until it was full. Something about a plentiful harvest always made me feel like things were alright in the world. But everything wasn't right. A bell rang, just like the ones at the ampgas stations. My nostrils flared, searching for satisfaction. I looked at the peas in my shirt, and in my dream state, I knew they were the answer.

I fell to my knees and let the pods fall onto the patio. My thumbnail dug into the blossom end of a pod and tore the string off. My hands shook as I cracked open pod after pod. I tossed the peas into my mouth and waited for the satisfaction to settle me. Each time, just as a set of peas slid down my throat, the bell rang out.

More. I need more! Chew, swallow. DING! Open another pod and toss peas in.

A thundering roar and dust cloud erupted from the northwest as I repeated the compulsory ritual. I gathered pods in my shirt again, then ran to the edge of the patio to investigate. The bell rang, DING! But I ignored it as I watched dust roll up from the collapsing steam car factory.

DING! The abrasive alarm dared me to look away, not from ruins, but from a black hole in the earth where the building used to be.

DING! My mind could no longer resist. I sat on Franky's slab of wood and spilled the pods in a pile next to me. I ripped open one pod, threw the peas in my mouth and then ripped open another one as quickly as possible.

DING!

I closed my eyes while I chewed and waited for the peas to do what the ampgas had done. But the rush of confidence didn't rush through my veins.

DING!

More peas and another rumble, this time straight west. DING! I continued to rip pods open as I watched the block uphill from me disappear into darkness.

DING!

With every mouthful and every ding, another black hole opened up in the city. I grew ravenous, sure if I could just finish the peas, I would be satiated. But the clanging continued. Peeling and opening fell by the wayside, replaced by tearing into the pods and eventually just chewing the tough outer shell with the peas. But they only slowed me down.

DING!

I shoved handfuls of peas into my mouth until I nearly choked. Amid the clanging and dinging and bonging, the walls began to crumble. Then, like a wave, the center of the patio followed.

All around me, black caved in upon black, and I fell.

DING! Even in the dark emptiness, the demanding toll continued. I curled into a ball, falling, falling. But there was nothing I could do.

"Help!" I cried into the empty darkness. "Help me!"

And suddenly, I was a child in my father's arms, as if I'd fallen asleep during a long night by the fire. He laid me on my small feather mattress in the corner of our Borderland cottage. Next to me on the wooden floor, he set a tumbler of crisp, cold water freshly drawn from the forest well.

He laid his hand on my shoulder. "You are not in this alone," he crooned. The sharp, woody aroma of cypress wafted over me, and he walked out the cottage door. The scent seeped deep into my lungs, where it quickened the blood in my veins.

I blinked my eyes open and breathed deeply. The sun peeked over the Eastern Sea, casting a golden light through the trees. Overhead, clouds milled about the sky, daring the sun to light the land.

I slowly unfurled my aching body and attempted to stretch out the stiffness. The pressure of my father's hand still weighed on my shoulder, and the scent of cypress sparkled thinly in the forest air. I brushed the dust off one arm and then the other, each puff a reminder that the world's great city of refuge had been leveled.

Tears ran down my face, although I tried to prevent them with all my might.

You can't let him break you. You cannot succumb to your emotions.

I breathed deeply in an effort to stop my chin from quivering. The sharp coolness of the mountain air cleared my head. No sooner had it taken effect than my senses were on high alert.

The Wilderman and his wilderness had many tricks. I could not fall for any of them. No, safety demanded my restraint.

When I set my right hand down to push myself up, it landed on a familiar object. My heart fell like an elevator cut loose. Another cup of water. The Wilderman had been there.

On cue, I realized how dry my mouth was. My parched throat begged for relief, just like the bell had demanded ampgas and then, strangely enough, peas. What a dream.

After such a vivid and unsatisfying dream, I couldn't resist satisfying my thirst. I grasped the handmade bark cup and slurped the water messily. I leaned back against the tree, waiting for a poison to take hold of my body.

My eyes closed, heightening my other senses. A few birds chirped and twittered. The musk of pine and cypress pressed in on me, and the leaves of birch and beech trees whispered eerily. If I had been out on a normal hunting trip, I'd be home and safe by this point in the day.

Home. The word was empty. Worse than empty. It was some kind of vacuum threatening to consume itself.

With my head against the tree, I realized there was only one thing to do. I pulled the tube of maps from over my shoulder. Survive. At all costs. All I had to do was erase the Wilderman once and for all. Then I could return to Sanctius and start over.

And a kingdom, I was reminded. *And allies.*

Yes. I would not sit there and mourn for Sanctius when an even bigger empire was due to me, if I could just get rid of the Wilderman. After quenching my thirst, I squeezed the bark cup, willing it to break. When it didn't, I tossed it angrily out of the way and weighed down the corner of the scroll with rocks.

Apparently, there was a time when airships and defensive balloons were stationed all over these mountains. Airships would have been used as large patrol vehicles. Balloons, with an open steam system to lift their envelopes, were more likely used as guard stations. They would have been lowered regularly for more water and fresh guards. If I could ascertain my approximate location, perhaps I could find one between here and the Wilderman's cabin.

I puzzled out roughly where I was on the mountain and the most efficient route to check the old balloon anchorages. This was my last campaign. I didn't care how much effort it would take to cross the mountain and double back either by air, if I found a balloon, or on foot if I didn't. Nothing would stand in my way.

I eyed the former steam balloon stations one more time, trying to memorize their positions on the mountain's ugly face as best I could to avoid constantly needing the map. With any luck, I would not only surprise the Wilderman at his cabin, but do so silently from the air. *He probably suspects me dead in the city, anyway.* I set off hiking northward, pleased with my advantage. I hung on to that last thread of hope and tried not to think of the work it would take to rebuild in Sanctius again. Failure was not an option, but I needed to take one impossible task at a time.

IT ENDS TONIGHT

The direct route I had planned turned out to be completely impassable. The topography on the map was deceptive. Simple lines on a page materialized as a jagged landscape. If ravines and cliffs didn't obstruct my way, thick bracken gated my path. I hiked up and down and up again, all the way around the east face of the Hungry Mountain. A year ago, such an encounter with the wilderness would have driven me home. But my instinct to leave the rugged, strange place was easily squashed by the knowledge that there was no home to run to. Not mine, nor anyone else's.

Of course, there was the Wilderman's cabin. I wondered whether the wilderness would still hold any danger after the Wilderman's defeat. Could I take over his cabin? Or maybe the giants would help me construct a palace right on top with all that technology they mentioned. A symbol that I had helped them conquer our mutual enemy. I couldn't imagine living out there on the mountain, but the possibility that it might be tamed cheered me, nonetheless.

I zigged and zagged and slashed my way to the place where the third balloon was marked on the map without seeing a sign of any vessels. Another dead end. The hot fuel of revenge alone drove me onward.

The fourth mark on my planned route was directly west of the third, straight up the mountain. Midway between the two points, I saw a thin strip of olive-green canvas hanging from a tree—a balloon envelope. Where was the rest of it?

I stopped short and scanned the forest. To my left, southwest up the hill, a wall of rock weaved in and out of the mountain, dappled with gray light through the trees. Hanging over the edge of a crag twice as high as a man, was another tuft of canvas. I'd mistaken the olive and cream canvas for shrubbery and rock. I must have looked over it three times before I spotted it.

The hike around the cliffs to reach the balloon on top was brutal. Thick thorn bushes tempted me to climb the wall to avoid them. It wasn't as high as the star-watching cliffs, and rebellious souls had climbed those for enjoyment. Surely I could scale a smaller one.

Subsequently tempting was the weapon in my satchel. One well-aimed blast could clear the way, possibly even bring the balloon to my feet. But it would also alert the Wilderman. Stealth was one of my few advantages. I could not risk losing it.

Scratched and belligerent, I reached the envelope of the balloon. I held my breath as I dug through the canvas in search of the steam tank. If it wasn't intact, the envelope was of no use to me, whatever its condition.

The heavy cloth went on forever. At the bottom of the heap, I found the steam tank lying on its side. It was five or six arm-lengths tall and still half-filled with water. *Perfect.* There were a few surface abrasions in the glass, but Sanctius' steam tanks were made of several finger-widths to an arm-length thick convex glass, depending on the size of the machine. The thick-walled tank on a steam balloon could withstand a surprising amount of abuse.

The vessel's basket, which would have dangled below the steam tank, appeared to have taken the brunt of the impact, preserving the integrity of the tank. The wicker basket was nothing more than a shredded pile of branches, but it had cushioned the steam tank from the rock below. I was grateful it had served that purpose in its end.

Still, I had to make it usable and quickly, if I was going to harness enough sunshine to be airborne that day. Moving a small section of the heavy canvas at a time, I laid the durable fabric over the brambles that had guarded the cliff so well. Once spread out, I found the tear. A thin diamond, a couple of arm-lengths, was missing. There wasn't time to patch it properly. So I set out to sew it closed as quickly as possible.

My chest holster of braided leather was the nearest thing I had to the thick, multi-stranded thread holding the rest of the balloon together. Because Franky had made it for me, I hated to part with it. But there wasn't time to be sentimental. I removed my pistol, which seemed old and underpowered next to the frequency gun, and buried it in the bottom of my satchel with my extra knives, pens, and tools.

Several strands made up the braided straps of the holster. It took several sewn one after another to mend the seam. I stabbed holes along both sides of the tear and threaded the leather through with my fingers. A few holes, a few stitches. My stomach growled. My hands shook, and the cut on my wrist throbbed. Blood stained the bandage. But I couldn't stop until I finished this conflict with the Wilderman for good.

I searched the few trees accessible near the cliffs. Thankfully, one of them was a pine spitting resin from an injury. It took some digging in the basket wreckage to find something to heat the resin with. *A pair of goggles!* After a little cleanup with my shirt, they worked to magnify the sunlight, which softened the resin until it was thin enough to handle. A flattish stick served perfectly to scrape the resin over the stitches. It was no long-term fix, but it would work for the day to keep the holes from ripping open and only worsening the damage.

While the resin solidified over the rent envelope and the uncovered tank warmed slowly in the sporadic sunlight, I cut all the cords that had formerly attached the basket to the envelope and tank. There were a handful of very long ones that had dropped all the way from the envelope around the bottom of the basket. The rest were shorter—some more and some less than the length of a man—and had run this way and that, connecting various pieces and adding stability to the vessel.

Once separated according to size, I bundled the longest cords into a rope and turned them into a loop for my foot to rest in. I attached it to the uprights of the envelope. Next, out of the shorter cords, I made a support to wrap around my body and a couple of handles.

Estimating the positions of the rope handles was difficult, with the envelope deflated and all the rigging lying on the ground. There was no time to experiment because the sun burst through an opening in the clouds. Now that I'd uncovered the thick magnifying tank, it didn't take long for the water to dance behind the glass.

I packed up my things and dragged the envelope closer to the tank. The canvas was heavy, and I struggled under its weight. Slowly, I was able to prop and pull and position until steam lifted the envelope slightly. I dug my knuckles into a hem and drew a large section over my back. With every bit of my weight, I leaned forward to move the balloon over the exhaust port on top of the tank. As the envelope swallowed gaseous water, the tank supplied more in the glaring sun.

In a slow upward sweep, the envelope pulled skyward. A burning pain in my hand triggered panic in my gut. It was pinched in some of the rigging. I recoiled and wrenched my hand free to catch the handhold loops I had set up. My unsophisticated harness dangled below the tank which hung below the envelope as it shifted around, up and down, left and right, unsteadily taking to the sky.

The stirrup dodged my foot a few times before I caught purchase. As I shifted around to get settled, it became apparent that my right hand had gotten rope-burned when the balloon took off. I maneuvered the large "seat" loop around my body, trying to situate all my mess of ropes so that I felt secure as I rose above the trees. Only when I readjusted everything a bunch of times did I decide things couldn't get any better and took a moment to inspect my hand. My palm was blistered, even oozing near my little finger. To make matters worse, blood completely soaked the bandage on my left wrist. *Managing these ropes certainly won't be easy.*

My heart soared as the trees sank below me. As I gained elevation, the balloon drifted eastward, opposite the direction I needed to go. I had never ridden in a steam balloon before. Theoretically, if I continued to rise, I'd find some kind of stream of air to push me in the right direction.

It was there, floating above the trees with no idea how to get where I wanted, that I realized I was wholly unprepared for that part of my plan. Going up in a ship or balloon with the vessel intact was one thing; hanging on to a makeshift harness with one rope-burned hand and no basket was quite another. With my burned hand gently closed into a fist, I adjusted the set of cords around my middle. I found it to be most comfortable as a seat running diagonally underneath me. I could lean on it with less concern about falling. Still, I gripped the stirrup and the rope above it tightly with my calves so I could grasp the steam vent cable gently in my blistered right hand.

The forest became an emerald blanket interrupted by patches of cream-colored cliffs. Beautiful as it was, I looked forward to the moment I could pull the cord to let steam out and return to Earth. My balloon's direction shifted from east to north, and then suddenly southward. South was better than east, but it would do me little good for any length of time. I needed to find that elusive western breeze.

I passed through a few wisps of clouds. The cables and cords soaked up sweat from my nervous hands. I could no longer make out any details besides land and sea. A gray-brown blot was all that remained of the area where Sanctius City should have been—the glory of the landscape. It was disorienting, both the height and the bird's-eye view of the destruction. I set my jaw in indignant resolution. Anger steadied my hand and dulled my sense of caution. In fact, I had lived through so much and was determined to make it through so much more that I felt nearly invincible.

I'm flying. Who can stop me now?

Light gray clouds gathered below me. Past them, the sea in the east pulled away from me. *Finally, westward.* I smiled victoriously at the bright blue water, but the darkest green lump in the distance, the island that didn't exist, reminded me of the task at hand—westward, to erase the enemy that had polluted humanity's existence for all time. Without the Wilderman, the mountain might not be hungry, nor the sea angry. *Maybe I'll rename them.*

The clouds made it difficult to navigate. I tried to picture the map in my head. When gaps in the clouds allowed me to see, I tried to compare my distance from the sea to the location of the Wilderman's cabin on the map. It would take quite a bit of time to reduce altitude and land. But then there was the contrary airflow. I decided it would be best to overshoot the cabin and hope there was still a strong eastward wind at lower altitudes.

I pulled the steam vent cable. It took more force than I expected to open the flaps high on the envelope. The vents redirected some of the heat outside the envelope. The balloon floated downward.

It almost worked.

By the time I slipped among the trees, my rope-burned hand screamed for relief. Although the air movement pushed me east, closer to the cabin, it also sent me farther south than I'd planned. The forest was unrelentingly thick, and there was no such thing as a good landing spot.

The cabin was very high on the mountain, and tendrils of clouds followed the curves of the land. They were moist as I descended through them. It didn't seem like I'd have any sunshine anytime soon. Once I landed, I would be stuck.

"Landing" was an inappropriate term for my entrance. There was never a chance of anything graceful, but I planned to replicate the balloon's first crash, being sure to move out of the way of the tank. It survived the first time; I expected something similar. The balloon itself descended quite gracefully. Just above my head, all the ropes suspending me beneath the tank, however, caught on a branch.

The envelope continued past me, deflating with a long fuh-rump, and then settled with a light rustling. Meanwhile, the rope of my waist loop stuck to the branch, and the falling balloon pulled my arms away from the tree. With my bottom half attached to a tree and my top half pulled toward the wreckage, anyone walking up on the scene might have thought I levitated nearly horizontally at first glance.

Okay, I'm sure there's a way down from here. If I let go of my handhold loop, I'd be left hanging upside down. I pulled against the large steam tank. Of course, it was too heavy to budge toward me.

Not only did I find the weight unbearable, but so did the branch from which I hung. There wasn't even the slightest warning. My stomach flew to my throat, and an ear-splitting crack chased me to the ground. I fell onto a bed of pine needles and rotted leaves near the steam tank. Of course, the branch followed me to the ground, bludgeoning me before I had time to catch my breath.

ENCHANTED

It took a long time to convince my body to move. I'm not sure I *could* have moved if the branch had been any larger. Though if it had been, maybe it wouldn't have broken in the first place. For the first several minutes, I reminded my lungs how to move air in and out. For a while after that, I told myself I was simply strategizing. *No need to rush off without a plan.*

I mentally replayed my descent to estimate where I'd fallen in relation to the cabin. From where I lay, I couldn't see anything in the way of landmarks. By the time I accepted that my best guess placed me a short way south of the cabin, pine needles and dry branches stabbed me in the back and arse and left calf no matter how I shifted. My discomfort finally overruled my exhaustion, and I set to getting out from under the log.

It wasn't nearly as challenging as I thought. The momentum the branch carried as it fell on my abdomen made it feel huge, but I lifted and shifted it until I could shimmy out. I crawled a couple of arm-lengths away. Several parts of me demanded I lay back down—my back, my hips, and oddly enough, a sharp pain screamed from the back of my left knee.

But to lie still any longer would leave me feeling things—emotionally, that is. It was of no concern to me what those sentiments might be. I didn't have time, and I couldn't risk what they might do in concert with the forest enchantments. I told myself that after I stood, the battle would resume. No procrastinating. *You will go straight to the cabin, even if you have to blow your way through this forest. Stealth be tossed.*

I finished my prebattle pep talk with soaring optimism about the new life I'd start with the sunrise, a life *without* the Wilderman.

And then I did it. I stood up, pretended I wasn't painfully stiff, and walked north and slightly downhill to the east in the direction I hoped the cabin would lie. Westward, the mountain rose through patches of mist. My steady pace quickened my breath. I tried to slow it, shoving down pain with each exhalation.

I inhaled the cold, deflated breeze of the high-altitude air. The trees seemed to echo my breath, whispering and groaning as if alive. Deer trails ran like veins in every direction, following the path of least resistance. The forest was like one creepy entity, shrouding the deadly Hungry Mountain in funeral garb.

The landscape grew intermittently dense, then steep and rocky. It wasn't raining, but the trees dripped with moisture. The dampness in the air reinforced the cold until it penetrated to the bone. I pulled my jacket collar up around my neck to no avail.

The only warm part of me was my rope-burned palm, to which the numbing air was a welcome relief.

I alternately made my way up steep, bare paths and then clambered up boulders as steps. Every time one foot fell with a dull thud, it reminded me to lift the other and keep moving. The rhythm was a welcome distraction from my body begging me to sit and rest. I watched my feet fall safely on uneven ground and then glanced ahead for my next steps.

This mechanism for coping with my exhaustion, pain and hunger turned out to be over-effective. A high-pitched rush of water woke me from my trance and froze me in place. How much ground had I covered? It wasn't the thunder of a huge waterfall, nor was it a trickle. It sounded as if an entire brook came from one large faucet, rushing out and falling hard.

How had I not noticed it sooner? I blamed the magic of the mountain.

I stood there, looking for anything that stood out. Not far ahead, maybe half a city block, I caught sight of something out of place. One patch of wood didn't match the trees. I crept slowly toward the object, and Franky came to mind. He always intended to make a mountain man out of me. *Look at me now.*

The rush of water increased in decibels as I inched closer to the odd wooden object. I veered off trails and peered around trees until I could make it out. A spring rushed out of the cliffside onto a waterwheel.

How odd. But the noise made sense after seeing it.

My entire body remained tense and ready for action, but I indulged my senses for just a moment, allowing myself to stare at the water bubbling along the wooden wheel as it turned. It seemed to come out of nowhere, running over the wheel to a small pool and then continuing in a little brook down the mountain.

There were cypress trees radiating from the sopping wet ground near the wheel into the surrounding forest. They were absolutely beautiful. Ages ago, archaic technology like this waterwheel moved bulky, inefficient machines. I guess I should be thankful. Perhaps those ancient versions of factories paved the way for my own modern Sanctius.

But it was no more. And any hope I had of rebuilding a new city could force me to continue my alliance with the giants. I unconsciously rubbed my satchel, inside of which Tino's scroll was buried. Of course, I'd accept any help to eradicate my world of this pest. But was a long-term allegiance wise? I gulped down an uncomfortable feeling of being small and outnumbered. *Worry about tomorrow when it comes.*

The Wilderman had proven to be a powerful enemy. Would he rely on such primitive technology as a waterwheel?

A slight movement drew my eye to the right of the wheel. For all my heightened awareness, the sprightly flowing water had distracted me from properly observing my surroundings. I mentally scolded myself.

Be on your guard, Nico! There are no scenic excursions today.

There I was, closer than ever to my goal, and I stared at an outdated power plant like a buffoon. I could not let the magic of the forest dull my senses.

A rod attached the wheel to the Wilderman's cabin and then disappeared inside. The siding was made of wooden shakes. I gave myself a break for ignoring the setup due to its camouflage. Vines and moss had long adopted the building as part of the forest.

The roof was slightly rounded, and I guessed it was also made of wood, though it was no longer visible. Behind the cabin, the mountain rose steeply upward. Trees growing up there had spread their roots over and even into the roof. A coating of mosses—pea green, chartreuse-yellow, and the bluish color of iodized copper—topped layers of pine needles, cones, roots, and branches. At a glance, the house could be mistaken for a massive boulder nearly swallowed up by the mountain.

The only door was on the south side of the cabin, hugged by two small windows that were so dirty I hardly noticed them. There certainly wasn't any light shining from inside, but a thin ribbon of smoke rose from the stone chimney.

That same, barely perceptible movement repeated itself and called my eyes toward the ground. A stag lay under the left window, the one closer to the wheel. His antlers blended perfectly with the colors of the cabin and the forest. Steam shot out of his nose as he breathed.

Somewhere in the back of my mind, a warning dinged to suspect everything where the Wilderman was involved. It warned me that this was not what it seemed—an enchantment.

The stag's head rose proudly, and his eyes met mine. If this was his guardian, the Wilderman should have picked an animal without strikingly long eyelashes. I half released the tension that had mounted in my body but remained alert. The deer's coat rippled from front to back, shaking water droplets in every direction. He turned his head toward the waterwheel, but never broke his gaze toward me.

I glanced left and right for any sign of his owner and then lifted a foot to inch closer. As I set it down, the leaves squished more than usual, but then I was off-trail. There was only a brief moment when I realized there was no solid ground beneath. I was too late to stop myself from falling through the thin branches supporting the leaves and into a pit trap.

My nightmare flashed through my mind for a moment, falling through black emptiness. Quickly, my landing at the bottom of the pit erased all thought except for pain augmented by my previous plummet. Then quickly, panic gripped me by the throat. *How am I going to get out of here?*

Many hooves thundered off to the east, probably spooked off by my graceful descent. As I collected my breath for the second time that day, I evaluated my options. Ground level was out of reach, but not terribly far. The walls of the pit weren't smooth. Surely I could get a foothold and climb out.

Leaves rustled above me, alerting me to nearly noiseless footsteps growing closer. I quietly unbuckled my satchel, lifted the flap, and set my hand on the frequency gun.

The stag's antlers appeared first, then a dewy black nose followed by his short, silky beige fur. Up close, his dark eyes angled forward with a black, pointed outline. His presence was majestic, commanding.

"Hey, there. Easy, buddy." The whispers caught in my throat. He was far more intimidating standing above me than he had been lying in front of the cabin. "I just need to get out of this pit, okay?"

I turned around slowly and felt the opposite side of the pit for any sign of a way out. In two bounds, the stag moved around the hole and towered straight above me again. This time, he craned his head down and stuck his nose uncomfortably close to my face. More than his nose itself was the intimidation factor of his antlers, which arched above either side of my head. He exhaled hot steam and blinked slowly, unfazed. His eyelashes were even lovelier up close, but they no longer abated the threat of his presence.

I backed away and spoke in a soothing voice. "Well, here's the deal, chap. I need to get your—whatever he is to you—Wilderman guy so that I can live the rest of my life in leisure and prosperity if I play my cards right. Therefore, I really need to get out of this pit. Now, if you leave me to it, I can do that on my own. Unless of course, you'd like to offer your assistance."

The stag snorted. By that time, I had felt around for rocks or tiny ledges that would help me escape. Still explaining my every move to the deer in a calm voice, I reached for a knife in my holster, which of course, wasn't there. My holster was part of the steam balloon. Digging around in my satchel was more conspicuous, but the deer seemed to watch calmly.

He jerked his head upward a little when I stabbed the knife into the densely packed earthen wall to use as a foothold. Still using slow movements, I turned to put a foot on my knife handle.

"So now, I'm just going to hop on out of here and—" But it was too late.

The stag leaped the entire pit, directly over my head, and pivoted to face me at the corner. Although I ducked and then backed away, I felt his warm breath above me and his gaze peering down into the hole. I crawled to the opposite corner and ripped the frequency pistol out of my bag. I uncurled slowly, but confidently, and pointed the weapon at the beast. He raised his head defiantly, as if daring me to challenge him.

"You're an awfully handsome beast, so I hate to do this." I had just offered the animal my sincerest apologies when its ears shot backward on high alert.

I heard humming in the distance.

What had I been thinking, apologizing to a deer? The forest bewitched me, no matter how hard I resisted. I shook it off, pointed the frequency gun square at his chest with my finger curled around the trigger, and squeezed.

MY ESCAPE

"Let go."

From beyond my view, the Wilderman's deep voice shot the command over the edge of the pit like a cannonball. Why did my finger obey? The gun hadn't had a chance to charge, and besides standing erect and looking toward his master, the deer hadn't reacted.

I recovered quickly though, and pointed the weapon in the direction of his voice. The Wilderman took several more steps before I saw him over the edge of the pit. He stopped next to the stag and rested his hand on its back.

However sentient I'd imagined the deer before, he simply turned back toward the cabin and disappeared out of sight like any other deer striding through the forest.

"So, you came to shoot me, huh?" The Wilderman sounded more than entertained to find me in his trap. "Seems like I already warned you that I can't have you shootin' those things off in my forest."

"And I thought it was socially unacceptable to level a person's home." I stared at him through the barrel of the gun.

He only shook his head. "Let's get you out of there, shall we? We've got a lot to talk about."

"I don't need your help."

"Here I thought we were gettin' to a better place. I was out lookin' for you, and you were out lookin' for me. Seems like an improvement in our relationship, don't you think?"

I only huffed at him.

"Well, son. The problem with your stubborn independence is that it always costs something, a lot of somethings usually."

"You don't make any sense. My independence, *by definition*, has nothing to do with anyone but *me.* Except that you... *you* insist on stalking me like some crazed human-hunter. You mess with people's brains. You drive them crazy until they somehow evanesce! It's worse than if you'd just killed them all right away. Instead, you take their sanity and everything else. They give up everything because of you!"

My eyes burned with hot tears, and my breath came in tight gasps. But I couldn't stop myself. He had done everything I feared he would. He took everything from me. I spat my anger at him, letting myself lash out before I destroyed him.

"You're a monster. You change people until they're hardly recognizable. And you drive them to the mountains to be eaten, to the sea to be swallowed up, and to the sky to be snatched away."

"Well, I suppose you could see it that way. And to be quite honest, your mate Franky would have taken his dive sooner had it not been for you. But your little kidnapping stunt was the final straw."

"How dare you imply that *I* had anything to do with Franky's evanescence? It was *you*! It's always been you. Every friend and everyone more. My brother. My parents. My—" The faces of the people I loved flashed through my mind: Mama and Papa, my brother's nearly twin face, Franky's wild and free rebellion against his emblem-holder destiny, and a dark-haired girl from across the western ocean who'd abandoned the city and me for the very monster standing over this pit. Though every muscle in my face flexed against it, my chin shook as I stiffened my aim at the Wilderman.

"This is good. Get all this stuff out."

"Aargh!" I yelled at the sky as my frustration mounted at his encouragement.

"Nico," another voice came panting from the forest behind me. "Don't worry. I've come to help."

Magnus strode over to the edge of the pit opposite the Wilderman, with one leg dragging a little. Whereas my heart had risen into my throat with anxiety at the approach of the Wilderman, it sank low into my gut at the sight of Magnus. He was there to help. So why did I dread him joining our little rendezvous?

"Always sticking your giant feet where you have no right to be." The Wilderman rolled his eyes.

"It's fortunate I *have* feet after your temper tantrum," Magnus said, motioning down toward the rubble of Sanctius.

Then he turned to me. "Nico, let me help you out of there. You've waited too long to use your new toy there. It's time we ended this and rebuilt our life without *him* in it."

Our life. I looked from Magnus to the Wilderman and back.

"It's almost as if you're not elated that I came to rescue you."

The Wilderman ignored Magnus and spoke directly to me. "You'd do right to think carefully, Nico. You won't get out of that pit until you make a serious decision."

"I didn't expect such ingratitude from you—the one man who'd outsmarted everyone else," Magnus said.

"It's the most important decision you'll ever make. Could be your last if you're not careful," the Wilderman threatened.

"See? He's threatening you," the giant accused.

"Why do you think he wants you to pull that trigger? Why doesn't he do it himself?" the Wilderman asked.

"You deserve this revenge. I can help you out if you just complete your mission," Magnus prodded.

My mind reeled with so many questions. Finally, I resumed yelling at the Wilderman. "You're a trickster. You've been hunting me. Why would you help me out of here? To kill me?"

"You're not all wrong. I have been after you. And yet, you sit here right in my trap, and I haven't killed you. Nor have I killed anyone else."

"If it weren't for you, everyone I love wouldn't be gone. I wouldn't be trapped between you two in a *hole* in the ground!"

Magnus made a disdainful hiss.

"Well," the Wilderman chuckled. "I suppose that's true. Though it's the least I've done to get you here."

"You knew I would come?"

"I don't mean here, to the cabin. I mean to *me*. And *with* me."

"He wants you to follow the rest. He wants to ruin you!" the giant said.

"Always the half-truths with your lot." The Wilderman pointed at Magnus, who recoiled in response.

Then he went on speaking to me. "I do want you to follow the rest. In fact, I want to take you to them. Not to ruin you, but to renew you."

My right hand, grasping the frequency gun, had slowly fallen. I'd let my guard down, and as a result, my eyes raised in hope. Franky and Raina? Farrah? Tino and my parents? Could they possibly be alive?

Magnus sensed my weakness and spoke up. "He's getting to you, Nico. He's bewitching your thoughts. There is only one way for us to survive."

Us. Survive. And more… power, companionship, there were so many possibilities.

But to my surprise, the Wilderman didn't deny the accusation. "Bewitching? Well, I suppose so. Everything out here is absolutely enchanting. Remember the clematis vines, and the galaxies of purple stars you admired in the forest, Nico? Spellbinding, mesmerizing? Yes! But fear is the only reason any of it seems dangerous."

What did that mean? Surely, I should fear danger. It's more likely a highly evolved self-preservation. To do otherwise would be madness.

I drew a hand to my aching head. Out of the corner of my eye, the Wilderman startled me by leaning into the hole. He hung a small pail of water on a root poking out of the wall.

"Don't drink it. It's probably poisoned," Magnus cautioned.

"I've already had some. It's not." I looked at Magnus through narrowed eyes, the little trust I had in him wavering. I thought back— the giant seemed no more accurate than the Wilderman—possibly even less so.

The Wilderman continued. "For many generations, Citizens have served fear just like they served Magnus and his fathers before him. What I offer is an escape from the trap you're in. Not just this pit, but from fear itself."

Magnus exploded. "I am a divine king! And we are worth serv—"

"You're nothing but a poor, abominable descendant." The Wilderman laughed blatantly at Magnus.

My chest cinched and my eyes blurred. "If you're saying there's nothing dangerous out here, you're wrong. I've seen them, I've—"

"Yes, you had a run-in with one of Magnus's friends' little experiments."

"Creations," Magnus corrected. "He thinks he's the only one who has the right to be creative. That's probably what drove an artist like Franky to be a crazy hoarder."

"How do you know that?" I asked hurriedly, anxious to know anything more about Franky.

"We know things, Nico. We have our ways," Magnus answered elusively.

The Wilderman spoke to Magnus once more. "Creativity is one thing. Diabolical recycling is quite another."

And then he turned to me. "Do you remember that there were two on the mountain that day? Do you remember that I protected you from the wild man?"

I reached into the deepest recesses of my memory, to the one place I'd tried hardest to forget. The day I'd run into the wild man, the second hairy monster and the dream of the two horsemen flooded to the forefront of my thoughts. The familiar sight of the stag burst upon my mind's eye, but Magnus quickly interrupted.

"I know you've been taught about us. Remember your education, how it gifted you with the knowledge of ancient, superior beings. We have served and aided and taught humanity. And you have the makings of a great king, Nico."

But the Wilderman couldn't let that offer stand. "And *I* know it was your brother who brought you everything you needed to see through that education and find the truth. I made sure of it. You have seen glimmers of the truth, but you will have to lay down your fear to grasp it."

I shook my head. I hated him. Right? There was no way he could be anything but my enemy.

The Wilderman continued. "You thought you could control your circumstances and avoid all the things you feared. You even convinced yourself that you didn't need to deeply mourn the loss of all those you loved. I have gone to great lengths to prove all of that untrue."

"He's tortured you for his own ends. Why would you give up ruling on Earth with us?" Magnus taunted.

"To what end?" I spoke directly to the Wilderman. "Why would you do all of this?"

"Because when you are ready, like Franky and all those before you, I wish to take you to my land beyond the sea."

"What do you mean, *your* land?"

"I mean, I'm the King. It's an abundant land. Like this should have been." He motioned around. "Like this one was before my servants betrayed me."

My eyes shot toward Magnus, who mounted his defenses.

"You have no idea what my fathers went through, some of the things we suffered at the hands of mankind. He *imprisoned* my first father. Did you know that? You could be a part of bringing about justice!"

"To be entirely accurate, Magnus—I know that's not your forte—*I* am your first father. The Luminaries are *my* family. Those who abandoned their posts abandoned me. Now Nico, you must choose whom you will trust."

I watched the giant for a moment. He held out his hand and curled his long fingers inward a couple of times to beckon me. His complexion was pallid. The few faded orange hairs poking out of his thin skin were reminiscent of the corpses in the Council tower. How old was this thing? I recoiled at the thought of living the rest of my life in partnership with him and his hungry-looking partners.

As I leaned away from Magnus, the Wilderman reached his tanned and calloused hand down to help me out. I wasn't ready for that either! How could I possibly make a decision like that with both of them staring down at me in that dirty hole? I turned from one to the other and back again.

All the emotions of the past decade and more rose to the surface, and I wept into my hands, ashamed on top of it all that Magnus and the Wilderman both saw my emotional outburst. And I was mortified to find that the emotions had been there all along, that I had not conquered them. I'd only masked and manipulated them. Tears flooded my hands, and sobs shook my body, but even that was not enough. I collapsed into a ball, overwhelmed with feeling.

"You're stronger than this. Get up!" Magnus wheezed.

Just like in my nightmare, I had fallen into a dark blackness, and voices rang out like ampgas bells around me. *Do more! Do better! Get up! Keep going!* Once again, I felt the hand of my father on my shoulder. The warm weight of it quieted my violent sobs.

As the weight materialized from a reminiscence to a reality, I looked through bleary eyes at my captors, for to escape one was to be apprehended by the other. Magnus glared over the edge of the pit. If anger and disdain had propulsion, he could have lifted me out of that hole with the levels he exuded. But they seemed to me negative in energy, drawing life from me with every second that he stood there muttering at me.

Or *was* it at me? Maybe his mumbled curses were meant for the Wilderman, who knelt beside me with his hand resting on my shoulder.

That touch.

I'd avoided any contact with him. Surely that hand should burn. Or chill. I waited for it to start an implosion in me like the Time Temple, like all of Sanctius City.

But it didn't. It stilled my aching soul.

The giant seethed above me, his eyes boring holes into my subconscious.

The Wilderman knelt beside me in that pit, comforting me as I fell to pieces. I grew brave enough to look at him. His eyes were as deep as the starlit sky, but empty of malice. I saw in them the only light of hope to be found in that darkest of moments. It was a cerulean-blue spark reflecting the Eastern Sea.

"What do I do?" The sound of weeping still saturated my words. "What can I possibly do now? There is nowhere to go."

"Of course, there is," the Wilderman said gently.

"Don't be taken in, Nico. It'll be the end of you. Don't you want to continue to be the survivor? Until you have real power?" Magnus rattled on.

"Don't you worry about him. We haven't seen the last of him quite yet, but just like he was powerless to harm me, as long as you're with me, he can't touch you unless *you* allow him to. Now, let's get you out of here."

But how? My exhausted heart pleaded with him, but I couldn't utter the words. The Wilderman wrapped his arm around my shoulders and guided me to the side of the pit closest to his cabin.

"Here." He gestured to a rope ladder anchored to the ground above by thick wooden stakes.

"When did you put that there?"

"It's always been there."

"Lies! He's drawing you into his illusions." Magnus's wheezy voice had become an unwelcome noise, like the hissing steam from a busted engine. A warning to run. But then, where had the ladder come from?

"I searched all over this hole for a way out."

"To be fair, you searched for *your own* way out. You were unwilling to see mine."

He climbed out ahead of me and thrust his hand into the hole once more, beckoning me to join him. I didn't reconsider. Not then. There was no other rescue for me. I climbed the ladder and took his hand.

AT THE TABLE

When I joined the Wilderman at ground level, he grasped my hand in both of his for a long handshake. Again, with the physical contact, a blanket of calm settled over me. How was that possible?

"You have a lot of questions, I know. And for a little while longer, our adversary back there will have answers of his own. You will have to choose whom you will believe. The farther we get, the harder it will be to hear his whispers."

"Farther we get… where?"

"Toward my kingdom, of course. We'll take the entrance to the forest path just behind my cottage, after we get a little refreshment there, of course."

I had even more questions than before. "Your kingdom?" My eyes searched the heavy folds of weathered skin that threatened to bury his eyes for evidence of kingliness. Nope. He still reminded me of a weathered old fisherman.

"Yes, my kingdom on the Eastern Isle. It's a land of beauty and plenty." He motioned toward the elfish cottage, and we strolled in that direction.

"If you're such a good king, why didn't you invade Sanctius long ago and save us from the Council? If what you say is true, it's as if you just stood by and let them oppress humanity."

"Fair point. He couldn't possibly care!" interjected Magnus.

"I don't conquer and steal slaves. I liberate them."

"How is Citizenship in Sanctius slavery, but somehow being a citizen of your kingdom is freedom?"

"Very astute, Nico," the Wilderman said with a smile. "There is only one difference between slavery and selfless service, and that is love."

"I still don't understand what happened to them all. All those people… they were here and then they were gone. I watched Raina evanesce into the night sky. We both watched Franky disappear into those crashing waves. What have you done to them?"

"I will answer in part, only as much as pertains to your decision. After all, your story is woven into theirs; no one's story is theirs alone. I will tell you as much as will help *you* choose life as well."

Life?

"Every heart has its own unique needs. Like others you've known and loved, Raina met me where her heart was soothed, looking at the same stars she left behind in the Southlands. She learned to know me, and slowly, to love and trust me. In time, she found the bridge of light and chose to join me in my kingdom on the Eastern Isle."

"Bridge of… how could she walk on…?"

The Wilderman laughed once again. Though it seemed less manic to me this time.

"As for Franky, well, the sea was always in his blood. He's been growing to know me there since he was a boy. He'd come and swim or just sit by the sea and breathe. Later on, we went for walks together. The difficulty with Franky, being an emblem holder, was that my enemies had their own designs, beyond the general destruction of the average human."

"Are you saying that Franky is an above-average human?"

"No. No such thing. But there are some that would describe your friend as having noble blood, descended from the kings of old. But they were only stewards who sat on stolen thrones."

"He's saying you're all just average, worthless humans to him," Magnus spat. But I was too astounded at my realization to heed him.

"The Luminaries! So they really are gods, all the entities in the tales Tino gave me?"

"Like many things, the old tales are a container for truth. Stories are like baskets, woven with intricate language and beautiful ornaments to deliver truth to their recipient. Or like a tapestry, whose core of warp and weft runs strong and true throughout, though threads of mere adornment all but hide their existence."

I lost track of my path trying to understand his words. Even back in the Borderlands, I'd thought truth was supposed to be black and white. The Wilderman meandered at my pace, slowly guiding me to his cabin.

"Valentino has a gift for sifting the truth out of the wildest story. He assumed you'd be able to do the same. And you have, even though it's been a more laborious process than he imagined."

At this, the Wilderman turned around and looked at Magnus. His gaze didn't become intense or scrutinizing; he just looked and waited. Magnus cowered ever so slightly and slunk back a few steps.

Interesting.

The fragrance from the thickening stand of cypress trees engulfed me. Before, I was wary, as if it would suffocate me. Now, it felt more like a warm hug from a relative I hadn't seen in a while. The scent that I'd fled over and over became a nostalgic comfort.

We meandered up to the door of his cottage, which didn't lose any of its enchanting camouflage up close. The stag arose but passed us without a glance. I turned to see what it would do. Magnus stood a little ways off, where the cypress trees gave way to birch and pine. The stag stood directly in front of him with its head held high. I was surprised to see Magnus plop down like a defeated child, cross-legged with his chin resting on his propped-up hands. Mystification must have shown on my face because the Wilderman explained.

"He knows better than to pick a fight with my servant at my house." He motioned inside.

Part of me expected a palace to magically appear. But there was no luxurious mansion hiding behind the rustic facade. Inside, on the wall to my right, there was a large, open hearth. A black cauldron bubbled over a low fire. Along the back corner, there was a counter and cupboards in a small L-shape. Shelves on the wall above were packed full of jars and crocks of amber liquids, dried plant matter, unknown sticks, and other mysteries.

Was I right to trust him? As if on cue, I heard Magnus calling my name from behind his invisible fence. He certainly wasn't more powerful than the Wilderman. But was Magnus completely wrong about him?

I surveyed the kitchen area—several rustic wooden stools surrounded a table made with craftsmanship that outshone the rest of the house. That alone stood out from a setting that seemed to me everything a witch's haunt would be. In front of me, a simple featherbed lay against the wall with wool blankets folded at the foot. To my left, the door to the mill shed stood ajar.

While I examined my surroundings, the Wilderman took a bowl from a cupboard and ladled the mystery contents of the cauldron into it. He opened another cupboard door and took one of the many bark cups stacked neatly inside and disappeared into the mill shed. He came back and set the cup and a spoon on the table with the bowl.

"You can get started. I'm sure you're famished."

He was right. I sank onto a stool with such relief that I wondered if I could have gone an arm-length farther. He retrieved all the same for himself, as well as a round loaf of bread, and sat across from me. I smelled the thick stew, wary. At that point, he'd already had his chance to poison me. I was so hungry and emotionally drained that I hardly cared if it was my last meal. I devoured it by heaping spoonfuls. We ate in silence except for the occasional plea or shout from Magnus. I finished long before the Wilderman did and wondered at his lack of hurry.

"I thought you were in some kind of rush—all that 'time is up' talk."

"I was," he said, and then continued to eat his stew.

I waited in vain for further explanation.

"But you're not anymore?"

"Mmm, not really. We'll be on our way shortly. But you trust me.

Only a little, I know, but that's what matters." He chuckled and nodded his head toward the mysterious jars of herbs in the kitchen. "You have begun to tell light from darkness, and I know it's the beginning of wondrous things."

The Wilderman continued to eat his stew. When he finished, he took all our dishes to the kitchen, hand-pumped some water into the vessel sink, and washed our dishes in silence. Then, he came and knelt next to me, taking my left hand in his.

"Let's fix this up, shall we?"

The Wilderman ran his hand over the bandage Magnus had placed over the slit in my wrist. He carefully unwrapped the cloth.

The place where the wound had been had healed into a scar that looked years old. I looked from my arm to the Wilderman and back again.

"Thank you! But…" I remembered my manners and stopped.

"Go ahead, ask. I want to answer," he said.

"Well, if you can heal it, couldn't you heal it without a scar?"

"I could, but pretending the pain never happened isn't the same as healing."

While the Wilderman tossed the filthy bandages, I thought about that—about all the pain I'd refused to feel. I half-consciously ran my hand along the Wilderman's beautiful table, much like Franky had admired the wood slab on our bench. The intricate inlaid wood design stood out from the shabbiness of the rest of the cabin.

"I don't mean to be rude, but why is your table so elegant when your house is quite… rustic?"

"It's the only part of the house I made for others to use," he answered.

What could I say to that?

"Time for us to keep moving," the Wilderman said. He gestured toward the door. When we exited, Magnus leaped up and talked incessantly.

"He's turning you into a traitor. We had a plan, and now you're being a coward."

I scrutinized him while he continued accusing me and abusing the Wilderman. With his pale, sinewy form and his desperate attempts to sway my loyalty with his hands flying as he spoke, he reminded me of an overturned beetle desperately wriggling about.

The Wilderman, on the other hand, stood there in his quiet strength and waited. His eyes didn't plead or scold.

"Is there anything you can do for him?"

"It's already been done," he said quietly. "But you, on the other hand, your welcome celebration awaits. Are you ready to take the forest path to the Eastern Isle?"

"Wait. What did they want to do with Franky if he was yours, so to speak?" I said wait, but I willingly followed the Wilderman around his cabin, instinctively wanting to distance myself from Magnus.

The Wilderman sniffed and pursed his lips behind his beard. "The difference between a weapon and a tool is the heart of the man that holds it."

I strolled silently, trying to piece together how that applied to Franky.

"I'd have thought you'd figured it out by now. They want whatever I don't. And at this point, they thirst for the darkest evils. They'll scheme and experiment and use what Luminary knowledge they have left to attempt to usurp me and satisfy their never-ending appetites. But they operate on borrowed power and with stolen resources. Emblem holders were one of those resources. Their emblem signified Luminous blood, which they hoped to use to form legions for themselves. Now that you're here, they'll no longer have access to all that. Their reign of pretense is over."

Magnus's alternating threats and promises were only an ugly whisper in the distance. We slipped into a narrow walkway between the back of the cabin and the cliff. The roots above us, growing from the mountain onto the roof, shattered the sunlight, making our shadows leap at each shard of brightness. The alternating dark and light tired my eyes, much like the clash of evil and good had disoriented my heart.

From the front of the cottage, I thought this back corner had disappeared, almost morphed into the mountainside. But under roots, moss, and fallen leaves, the path led to an opening in the mountainside. My befuddled eyes took time to adjust as I peered into the dark, gaping hole.

"You're going to walk straight into his trap," Magnus's voice slithered through the roots from above. "You've always been afraid this mountain would eat you, and now you're willingly throwing yourself into the belly of it."

I looked to the Wilderman, wondering if he would argue with Magnus or command him to go away. Instead, he spoke to me.

"Well, ready to come with me and leave death behind forever? Here, you have been used; there, you will be loved."

"Loved, psh," Magnus scoffed. "You'll just be another soul in his vast collection. He'll love you the way Franky loved the books on his shelves. Even now, you're coming to the end of your story. Then he'll stash you away forever…"

Magnus droned on incessantly. But as my eyes gathered light to see more clearly inside the tunnel, I heard him all the less.

"I will give you a home forever, as I have for all those that I *love.*" The Wilderman spoke plainly, motioning into the mountain path, unconcerned with correcting all Magnus's fallacies.

The tunnel widened after the narrow opening. From what I could see, it was at least as tall and wide as an airship, but there only seemed to be enough room for two people to walk side by side. The passage was filled with a jungle. Vines draped from tree to tree behind leaves, dwarfing my body. The sound of birdsong echoed from deep within.

I felt as if I'd glimpsed the deepest longings of my heart. I moved to step forward, but he held his hand out to me.

"Weapons first."

With only a moment's hesitation, I dug for all my weapons and tossed them onto the forest floor. The Wilderman laughed quietly and simply motioned forward again as I triple-checked the bottom of my satchel. Along with my weapons, I dropped my guard and eagerly stepped away from my years of worthless strife and into a mysterious new life.

ZERO

I closed my eyes and reopened them, willing them to collect more light so I could see the magnificent forest around me.

"How does it grow without the sun?"

"It doesn't need the sun. It only needs light," the Wilderman said, and walked into the tunnel.

There he was—the White King I'd seen glimpses of before. His radiance illuminated the passageway and a magical scene beyond my wildest dreams.

The canopy of the trees lightened as they rose, as if the massive leaves outgrew serious shades of green in favor of a wild lime color. The giant branches overlooked younger trees, rolling waves of shrubs and flowers. I paused to take in the strange plants.

At first glance, the pathway appeared hemmed in by one kind of variegated bush rising to my waist. On closer inspection, it was a medley of plants growing in concert with one another. Shrubs formed a roundish frame. Tufts of sweeping leaves like wide blades of grass provided the bulk. Then, vines of every shade of green, plus white, and deep, dark red wove themselves into the amalgamation in an extravagant coat. Flowers rose through the mass on tall, straight stems, like spears shooting just above the waves of bushes. Pink, red, purple, orange, and yellow flowers dotting the flowing shrubbery gave a decorated effect, as if someone had pinned them there as party decorations.

These confetti bushes rolled on as far as the eye could see through the forest. Above them, vines draped from tree to tree and from tree to floor. Butterflies floated lightly through the air, and birds danced in the light of the Wilderman. Creatures skittered over branches and across vines.

I didn't realize how long I'd stopped to take it in. The Wilderman watched from ahead, smiling warmly, obviously enjoying my wonder. He no longer looked like the grizzled woodsman, but remained the King clothed in white. I joined him, and we meandered through the underground wonderland.

"It's paradise."

"Only the road there." He laughed that warm, joyful laugh. "But even the road to paradise is full of immeasurable beauty and joy if you have eyes to see and a heart to receive. Your eyes are well-prepared for this road, Nico. Your former life did give you that gift, one of the few things you'll be able to take with you."

We meandered through the sprawling forest tunnel on the singular path, as far as I could tell, which curved gently for the first quarter hour. The landscape had been steadily descending, the way easy on the legs. Gradually, the path straightened and steepened downward until we leaned back to balance ourselves. Though we seemed to travel steadily deeper into the earth, the forest only grew more colorful and noisier with life.

It dawned on me how intimidating the presence of the Wilderman was next to me. I had hated him, run from him, and worked to sabotage his plans my entire adult life. Yet, he guided me down the steep path with such care that I couldn't doubt his goodness. A weight fell heavily onto my shoulders. I had not only fled and fought for my vain life, but I had ruthlessly deterred others from following the Wilderman's voice.

"How can you ever forgive me? I think I may have done more harm in my short life than the entire Council put together."

"It's not a competition, you know." He smiled. With sincerity in his voice, he continued. "You need not apologize for the zeal that led you to do so; that was a gift. But I do forgive you for believing the lies that caused you to impede others."

As we walked, the Wilderman showed me those lies and dug them out like weeds from my heart. After the events of the last few days, many were plain to see and easy to uproot. Other lies had tendrils that wove around the most painful places of my heart. I didn't want to follow the shoots into the depths to find their root source. Even when we did together, parting with the lie felt like an amputation. And yet, each time I allowed the Wilderman to excavate the darkest corners of my heart, he replaced the poisoned, atrophied places with new life. Somehow, he took the worst pieces of me and transformed them into the very best.

All around, the forest grew more colorful and full of life. Light shone brightly throughout the tunnel, and colors I'd never seen before stood out from layers of the lush forest. The fairy tales and fantastic art I'd scoffed at and secretly longed for only hinted at the magnitude of the wonders around me.

Our steps turned uphill. The effort to climb grew, as did the work to remain pliable to the Wilderman's work in my heart. With tears in my eyes, I labored with every step until light from ahead joined with the light of the king—The White King of the Wilderness.

Hope filled my soul and renewed my strength. After a few more lengths uphill, the path leveled, and I clearly saw a doorway ahead. Instead of a crude hole in the cliff like the entrance, this doorway was made of two massive stone pillars with an equally magnificent lintel adorned with intricate carvings.

The Wilderman put his hand on my shoulder to stop me before we approached the opening in the mountain.

"Nico." He looked at me tenderly. "We're not quite finished."

I couldn't see anything but sand outside. The silhouettes of two men darkened the doorway and then stepped inside. The Wilderman held up his hand toward them, and they paused. They were clothed in simple, undyed clothing. The one on the left held a bundle in front of him.

"These men have fresh clothes for you. Clothing for your new life." I stole a glance out the doors to the bright golden sand. "This is where you leave your old clothes and your old ways. This jungle grows from the stained raiment and tattered tokens of past lives. Every lie you laid down enriched the flora of this passageway as they dissolved. The jungle itself will reduce these rags to mere molecules to replenish the glory of this wood. Are you ready, Nico?"

I searched the Wilderman's eyes. He seemed to imply that I might not be ready, that I'd missed something.

"Of course," I answered.

He waved the men over. The man on the right held his hands out, waiting for my old clothing. I slipped my shoes off and handed them to him. As I pulled at the buttons on my waistcoat, I realized what the Wilderman waited for. A cold sweat rose from my abdomen to my temples when he held out his hand for my watch.

I pulled it from my waistcoat pocket and removed the chain from the buttonhole. The watch tugged at my heart, as if the chain had been anchored there instead. I ran my fingers over the intricate clasp and the scrolling on the gold case. My thumb clicked it open, like it had a million times before. The hands sat motionless, even though my eyes willed them to move. I met the Wilderman's eyes but subconsciously pulled the watch closer.

"Until now, you have served your own purposes within the constraints of time. Even now, you cling to man-made order as a source of comfort. But this is the last thread binding you in slavery to your fears.

"I crushed time, Nico. And yet, you long for the system that gave you a sense of control. Your vices were breaking you, so I broke your vices. You may only walk through these doors when you empty yourself of your desire to take back the time. But when you lay that longing down to die and decompose, you can be truly satisfied with the delights of my kingdom." He thrust a hand toward the mysterious land beyond the sand.

I gazed at my watch, heavy in my hand. The metal was so cold compared to the warm golden light reflecting off the sand. I did want what was warm and good. The last stain of power-hungry willfulness exited my heart like a puff of black smoke, and I gathered the chain quickly, placing it in the Wilderman's hand.

I quickly removed the rest of my clothing and heaped them in the arms of the waiting man. He walked into the forest to feed the soil with the costume of my past self. The second man helped me into undyed linen similar to his own.

"Does everyone always wear this color here?"

"We do when we celebrate the return of the King."

He moved out of the way, and the Wilderman escorted me to the door. Lovely green land skirted with beach sprawled both ways in front of me. The sea crashed behind us. The doorway was part of a huge rock formation jutting out of the wet sand.

I could scarcely take it all in. In the distance, there were mountains with splashes of meadows between the lush trees. I squinted to make out intermittent buildings on the mountains. My gaze followed the increase in dwellings down to the small harbor. Only then did my eyes wander to the crowd lining the beach and the many docks hovering over the water.

Everyone cheered and danced. "The King has returned! The King is home!" Two different songs broke out, one from each end of the long, thick mass of people. Somehow, they were not discordant.

"Don't you have an actual name?"

He smiled at me and laughed heartily.

"Of course, I do. But I think you have known my name for some time now."

ACKNOWLEDGEMENTS

There are so many people who have served as guideposts and street lights along the way. First of all, Nic, thank you for the tender, loving care with which you handle this wild thing. Your kind "husbandry" helps heal my broken wings. And thank you Micaiah, Adriel, Eloise, and Caedmon for being a joy to know and grow alongside.

There are many people who have said or done just what I needed, when I needed it to keep me from wasting my passion for writing: Helmut Teichert and by extension Bill Bright, Marion Rose, and Ted Dekker; English teachers through the years; and Mark & Kerry Kellond. Everything I write is a direct fruit of the Mt. Fuji retreat. Stefani, Danielle, and all the authors in my critique group—Abigail Wilkes, Bryan Mitchell, David Joutras, Michelle Ami Reyes and Paul Regnier—thank you for being so encouraging! Shout out to Annika for being my first non-family young fan. I'm baffled and honored.

In fact, thank you to everyone who has ever said kind words to me, they're fuel for my spirit.

The good folks at Descendant Publishing have been an enormous blessing—Troy, Stacy, and all the Descendant family. Thank you Dawn, for giving me the best editing experience an author could ask for.

Thanks to all my blurry & fringey friends, Dr. Michael S Heiser, Nate & Luke and all the Blurry Creatures guests, for teaching me to read the Bible with my mind, heart and imagination, especially Dr. Judd Burton and his sultry southern voice.

Thank you to all the parents it took to raise me, Dad, Mom & Duane, Suzanne & Mark, and Crystal & Steve. Go team. I'm especially grateful for Mark, whose visage and fatherly love (I'm just now realizing) inspired much of the Wilderman's character. St. Francis himself would be impressed with your wordless sermons.

Most of all, to the true Wilderman—the perfect, caring Father, Creator of all the beauty that draws us out of our worst selves and Love itself—all praise, glory and honor to You.

ABOUT THE AUTHOR

Elicia Johnson is an author, Charlotte Mason educator and shepherdess. Though she has many interests, her passion is for the written word. When she's not reading or writing, you'll find her hiking, paddling or sketching in the mountains or along the shore. Her extensive bucket list includes a ride-along on a MotoGP track and a degree in anthropology. She loves studying cultures, languages and singing and playing music, especially those of her own heritage.

Elicia operates a small farm in Montana, focused on her flock of Finnsheep. She lives with her husband and their four children where the Rocky Mountains meet the high plains in Montana. They love to throw a good backyard dance party and share the freedom and joy found in God's love with those who need it.

https://eliciajohnson.page
@plaineliciajane | Instagram & Facebook
withloveelli.substack.com | Newsletter

PLEASE LEAVE A REVIEW

Please leave a review for *Endling*. Reviews go a long way in helping the authors you love get noticed by other readers. So if you enjoyed *Endling* please leave a review on Amazon and recommend it to friends and family. YOU are our greatest asset for spreading the word about EPIC stories!

If you want to be one of the first to know about new releases and updates, sign up for Descendant Publishing's mailing list by visiting www.descendantpublishing.com. Scroll to the bottom of the page and fill out the form with your name and email.

Continue your **EPIC** journey
with more great reads…

9 781965 948118